Clara Wu

and the

Final Battle

by Vincent Yee

This is a Vincent Yee book

www.clarawubooks.com

ISBN 978-0-9859320-6-0

Library of Congress Control Number: 2022914659

First Edition

DEDICATION

Dedicated to all my amazing Asian friends who were involved in their own way in making this ambitious book series a reality:

Ashley, Rob, Alex, Seraphina, Amy, Emma, Kayden, Rebecca, Tess, Kelly, Korina, Cindy, Jacob, Cindy, Ben, Bella, Linda, Julie, Maggie, Thuy, Natsuki, Soo

CHAPTERS

ONE

Clara's eyes trained on the page of the Portal Book as she brushed out the last stroke for the Chinese character for *earthquake*. She had first successfully manifested the character earlier that day and couldn't wait to see it blaze out of the page again.

She let out a breath, and her eyes glowed as the embers in the black strokes started to rise. She pulled back and held her breath as the beautiful fiery character lifted off the page and floated in front of her. She gazed at it until it finally floated toward her and seeped into her chest.

"So cool!" said Clara before thinking to herself, *So that makes ten?*

Clara sat at her desk barefoot in a pair of jeans and a T-shirt with a cute Asian cartoon on the front. She set down her brush and leaned back in her chair. She massaged her right wrist with her left hand: She'd spent hours manifesting, attempting to discover new Qi elements. Her eyes looked down at the page. Despite having brushed out almost one hundred characters for *earthquake*, only ten had successfully manifested. She pondered why this character was so hard to manifest.

As she continued massaging her right wrist, her eye caught the green jade bracelet on her left wrist. An expression of wonder came over her as she examined it, turning her hand palm up, palm down, then palm up again.

"Hmmm," Clara murmured as she reached for her brush. She leaned over and flipped to a new page. With her left hand, she carefully lathered black ink onto the brush. She was very deliberate, since she'd never attempted to brush out Chinese calligraphy with her left hand. But slowly, she brushed out the strokes for *wall*, and leaned back to see her brush strokes. Her laugh of embarrassment bounced off her bedroom walls.

"Oh my god!" Clara exclaimed. "That is so ugly!"

Clara leaned over the Portal Book and fiddled with the brush. She tried to find a position where she could lay her hand on the page of the Portal Book. She attempted many more practice strokes, but her subsequent characters looked even worse than the first. Frustration set in, but she didn't let it hold her back. She wasn't expecting any of her ugly brushed characters to manifest, but after her fiftieth attempt, a decent-looking character for *wall* manifested.

Her eyes reflected the fiery character before it seeped in her chest. She looked at her left hand and turned it over again. *I wonder*, she thought.

Clara went back to brushing out characters for *wall*. Some were growing uglier with each attempt, but two more manifested. Before she had realized it, three hours had passed. She finally leaned back into her chair with a grin of satisfaction. She massaged her left wrist and stared at the wall.

With a smile, both of her hands shot forward. As she uttered the Cantonese word for *wall*, "*ten-bing*," she traced out the character in the air with both of her hands. Her eyes were frozen in anticipation. But nothing happened.

"Hmph," said Clara. "I'll need to see if it'll work in Azen."

Clara turned her head to the slight knock at her door and she heard her father say gently *come to dinner* in Cantonese. "*Sik fan*."

She smiled and replied, "I'll be right there!"

Leaning forward, her eyes quickly gazed with dismay at her less-than-elegant left-handed calligraphy. She was surprised that any of them had manifested. But she grinned, closed the Portal Book, and pushed away from her desk. She stood up, spun around while glancing over at her stuffed panda, Bo Bo. With a raging appetite, she left her room for dinner on that Monday night.

* * *

Emboldened despite her limited success, she continued manifesting the following days. There weren't that many days left until Friday, which was the day the Portal Book usually summoned her. The last battle was looming, and she had to make sure she manifested enough Qi elements. She was certain that Sung, Yuka, and Daniel were doing the same.

She wondered whether or not Yuka was still mad at Daniel. Then again, she wondered whether or not Daniel was ready to sincerely apologize to Yuka. Only then should Yuka forgive him. Then her mind wandered to Sung, and she smiled at the thought of him. She didn't know why, but she often wondered whether or not he was playing StarCraft, even though it seemed he'd started to help his father more with this Tae Kwan Do classes. Between him and Daniel, they'd both used up many of their Qi elements in the last battle, she thought.

For hours a day, she 'd been manifesting multiple Qi elements and spending an additional hour or two practicing with her left hand. Despite the additional practice, she was only able to manifest a few more Qi elements for *wall* and *split* with her left hand. She imagined that invoking two walls at the same time would be very cool.

By the time Friday afternoon rolled around, Clara found herself pacing in her bedroom. Her hair was tied back that day, and she wore a pair of jeans, a cropped sweater top, and crew socks. She was alternating stretching exercises between her hands as she prepared for the looming battle. Her eyes glanced back at the opened Portal Book for the eventual Chinese character for *return*, but it was like watching a kettle come to a boil.

She exhaled and pensively looked at her bedroom door when something shimmered out of the corner of her eye. She spun toward the Portal Book. It was glowing. She rushed over to it and saw the character for *return* pulsating with a fiery glow.

She didn't know why, but unlike the other times, when she was excited to see the Portal Book glow with the Chinese character for *return*, this time she felt nervous. She straightened up and turned toward her bed, where she saw her stuffed panda. She quickly crossed the room and upon reaching her bed, she gently picked it up. His black shiny eyes stared soulfully back at her as she smiled.

"I'll be back soon, Bo-Bo. Guardian Panda and all the other pandas need me right now," Clara said reassuringly as she hugged him. She gently placed Bo Bo back onto her pillow when her eye caught her mobile phone. There was a glimmer in her eye as she quickly picked it up. As she did, the time of 4:43 PM appeared. She presumed she'd be back just in time for dinner. She smirked and slipped her phone into her back pocket, then crossed back to her desk and exhaled. As she stood over her desk, with a trembling hand, she brushed out her name and closed her eyes. The characters of her name, *Wu Chu Hua*, blazed as the bright light emanating from the Portal Book engulfed the room.

As the light began to fade away, her phone slipped out from the receding ball of light and onto the edge of the chair, ricocheting off as it bounced onto the wooden floor, landing face up. The time on the phone's display was 4:44 PM.

TWO

The bright warming light glowed yellowish-pink against Clara's closed eyelids as she allowed the Portal Book to whisk her to Azen. Soon, she felt a slight thud as the light started to wane. Before she could open her eyes, she heard someone in the distance, uttering enthusiastically, "Yes!" multiple times.

She opened her eyes and was greeted by the black eye patches of the Guardian Panda, who smiled at her.

"Welcome back, Empress Warrior Wu," he said.

"Guardian Panda! It's so…" but before Clara could finish, she turned her head to see Sung who was gleefully shouting into the air, "Yes!"

"Emperor Warrior Kim is very happy that he is the first to arrive this time," said the Guardian Panda as Clara turned to him.

Clara smiled. Sung's whimsical gloating was actually cute.

"I should go say hi to him…" said Clara, but before she could finish, the Guardian Panda caught her attention.

As she turned, a panda attendant came up with a pair of shoes on a large pillow.

"Your shoes, Empress Warrior Wu," said the Guardian Panda.

Clara squinted in delight and nodded to the panda attendant. She reached out for the soft shoes and slipped them on before turning toward Sung.

"Hi, Sung," said Clara as she quickly nodded in mid-stride to the Guardian Tiger, Buffalo, and Crane, who were by their Portal Books. In their usual stately manner, they nodded back.

"Hi, Clara!" exclaimed Sung as he bounced toward her. "I'm first this time! You can't give me a hard time for being last."

Clara laughed as she watched Sung's black hair bounce up and down. His shoulders seemed broader than before under his long-sleeved black athletic shirt. He was wearing navy blue jogging pants along with his Azen shoes.

As they stopped in front of each other, Clara couldn't help noticing that Sung seemed a bit taller as she looked up at him. Suddenly, she felt her cheeks blush slightly.

"Were you working out?" asked Clara.

Sung looked down at his athleticwear and ran his fingers through his hair, which showed off his boyish good looks. "Ah, yes, I was working out just before."

Clara smiled, but before she could respond, a bright light emanated from the Portal Book by the Guardian Crane. Both Clara and Sung shielded their eyes with their hands. When the light vanished, Yuka appeared.

Yuka was dressed in a navy skirt and a matching jacket over a white blouse. She was wearing socks that reached midway up her calves. Clara and Sung could see her bowing to the Guardian Crane, who returned the bow. She then turned with a smile as she saw Clara and Sung. Before she could skip over, a crane attendant extended to her a pair of shoes, which she quickly slipped on.

"Clara! Sung!" exclaimed Yuka happily as she approached them with a wave.

Clara took a couple of steps toward Yuka and tenderly reached out with her fingertips as Yuka joined them with her own. "Hi Yuka!" responded Clara joyfully.

Yuka gently pulled her right hand away and smiled as she waved at Sung.

"Hi Yuka! Guess what? I was the first to appear this time!" said Sung proudly.

Yuka looked at Clara and asked with a smile, "Sung was really first?"

Clara smiled and nodded as Yuka asked Sung, "You really stopped playing that game?"

"Yep," said Sung confidently. "I've been training more these days, with my *abeoji*. He's really impressed that I've picked up so much. I have to hold back, you know. Because I can't let on that I already know everything about Tae Kwan Do, but it's been really great to get to do things with my *abeoji*. And my *eomma* says my appetite has grown too, and she has to cook more now!"

"I'm very happy to hear…" responded Yuka before she was interrupted by a bright light emanating at the Portal Book by the Guardian Buffalo.

"It's Daniel!" shouted Sung. "I'm going to surprise him! I'll be back!"

As Sung sauntered slowly toward the blinding light with his hand over his eyes, Clara and Yuka also had to shield their eyes until the light began to fade. Clara glanced over as she saw Sung waiting patiently and quietly behind the apparated Daniel, whose back was turned. She turned back to Yuka.

"So… can you still see your Qi?" Clara asked curiously.

Yuka furtively glanced left and right and saw that everyone was looking in Daniel's direction. With a grin, she responded with a quick "mmm." She then closed her eyes and focused as Clara watched. Soon a faint, bluish, cobweb-like pattern appeared beneath the skin of Yuka's cheeks.

Clara was spellbound. As the bluish pattern faded away, Yuka opened her eyes.

"So cool!" said Clara. "Did you find out what you could do with it?"

Yuka shook her head, "No. I don't know if I have any additional powers, but I can will my Qi to appear anywhere on my body or see it all at once." With a self-deprecating giggle, she continued, "I scared myself one night while I was alone in the dark and I glowed."

Clara's eyes widened as she imagined Yuka glowing in the dark. "Oh my god, that is so funny!"

"It was!" said Yuka. "I can't figure out if there is more to it, but I'm much more connected to my Qi. I just feel much healthier."

"Oh!" exclaimed Clara as she reached toward her back pocket and twisted her waist in bewilderment.

"What's wrong, Clara?"

"My phone," said Clara as she turned back toward Yuka.

"Your phone?"

"Yes," said Clara as she looked puzzled. "It was right here in my back pocket…"

Yuka laughed as she teased Clara, "Don't be silly. How would a big phone fit into your back pocket?"

Clara laughed. She was able to tuck the large-screen cell phone into her back pocket, but it was a tight squeeze sometimes. *It must have slipped out before the Portal Book brought her back to Azen,* she thought. "You're probably right."

Yuka gave a furtive glance toward Clara and whispered, "Oh, the guys are coming. Don't tell, okay?"

Clara nodded as a jovial Sung and Daniel approached.

"Looks like he's the last one this time," said Sung as Daniel was a step behind him, wearing blue jeans and a black hoodie.

Daniel shook his head as he looked at Clara and Yuka. "Hey Clara, hey Yuka," he said as he gazed at Yuka.

"Hey Daniel," said Clara as Yuka gave Daniel a halfhearted wave before turning away.

Daniel nodded at Yuka's tepid response. He surmised that Yuka still held some ill feelings toward him since their last experience. But he knew that he had not found a way to apologize to her yet.

Before they could catch up, the Guardian Panda walked toward them along with the other guardians.

"Empress and emperor warriors," he said soothingly. "Again, welcome back to Azen. We have food waiting for you. Is anyone hungry?"

"You bet!" said Sung enthusiastically as everyone smiled and laughed.

"Our warriors are growing," said the Guardian Tiger as he gave Sung a once over. The Guardian Panda responded, "Very well then, please gather up your weapons and let's head to the meal table."

The Guardian Crane bent down near Yuka and asked, "Empress Warrior Satoh, would you like to ride with me?"

Yuka looked up with a smile but quickly slid her arm into Clara's right arm and responded, "Would you mind if I walk with Clara? I have so much I want to tell her."

The Guardian Crane's beady eye blinked as she nodded, "But of course, Empress Warrior Satoh. I will meet you at the meal table, then."

As the Guardian Crane gently flapped her wings and rose upward, Yuka waved when a crane attendant approached her with the Moon Star *shuriken* nestled in a pillow. She stared at it for a moment as if a part of her was being given back to her. She slipped her arm out of Clara's just as a panda attendant presented Clara with the Bow of Destiny. With both hands, Yuka gently picked up the Moon Star and smiled at it. She looked up at the crane attendant and smiled as the crane nodded back. After slipping the Moon Star *shuriken* into her outer jacket pocket, she turned to Clara and chuckled as Clara slipped the Bow of Destiny over her cropped sweater top. She jaunted next to Clara and slipped her arm back into Clara's as they proceeded to follow the rest of the guardians and warriors.

* * *

It certainly wasn't a light meal, the panda and tiger attendants served up ample dishes of *baos*, *kimchi* pancakes, tradition *soba* noodles, vegetable spring rolls, and other assorted delicacies. In the kitchen prep area, attendants from all the kingdoms were working on more delicious dishes.

Clara didn't know why, but she found herself to be hungrier than expected and was surprised at how much she was able to eat. She noticed that her fellow warriors were also feasting away. It made her smile that everyone was enjoying the food. There was definitely something about the food on Azen that was more delicious than what they were used to back home. Her attention was diverted as she watched the Guardian Crane slurp up a single long rice noodle, and she chuckled.

"Empress and emperor warriors," stated the Guardian Panda as he looked down at everyone from his dark eyes nestled within the black eye patches. "The kitchen attendants wanted to present all the cuisines of your heritage upon your return to Azen. I hope everyone is enjoying the variety of food this evening."

The warriors nodded with contentment as Daniel spoke up, "The food here on Azen is so delicious, Guardian Panda. A big thank you to all the kitchen attendants who worked on all the dishes."

"I'll be certain to tell them, Emperor Warrior Nguyen," said the Guardian Panda. "Before we settle in for the night to allow you to get some rest, has anyone mastered any additional Qi elemental powers?"

All the guardians turned their heads to their respective warriors, and they too felt all the guardians' eyes on them.

"I mastered *steam, jeung-gi* and *ice, bing,"* said Sung.

"You've mastered ice in its raw form then," said the Guardian Tiger approvingly as Sung nodded.

"I think I got *ignite, đốt cháy*," said Daniel. "I tried to ask my *mẹ* for help, but she wondered why I was so interested in Vietnamese words for fire and explosions."

The entire table laughed, and Daniel laughed sheepishly as he added, "So I had to stop because I didn't want my mom to think I was going to burn down the house."

"That was wise of you," said the Guardian Buffalo. "*đốt cháy* is a very useful Qi element. We can practice it tomorrow morning."

"I was able to manifest *taifū, typhoon*," said Yuka confidently.

The Guardian Crane looked down at her and blinked. "That is a very powerful Qi element, but it must be paired with water to have the greatest effect. If you are able to invoke that properly, even the cranes and the powerful eagles would not be able to escape those torrential winds. You will need to hone that Qi element carefully."

Yuka could sense the Guardian Crane's concern and nodded respectfully, but she was even more curious now about invoking the typhoon Qi element.

"I got *tunnel, sui dao,*" said Clara. "I think it'll allow me to create tunnels. Is that right, Guardian Panda?"

"Yes, if you are able to invoke tunnel, you'll be able to tunnel through the earth," said the Guardian Panda. "Anything else?"

Clara looked up at the Guardian Panda and simply said *earthquake* in Cantonese. "*Tei-cheng*."

The Guardian Panda's eyes widened as he looked at the other guardians' surprised expressions. The other warriors noticed their guardians' astonishment as the Guardian Panda spoke. "That is a very powerful Qi element. The more powerful the Qi element, the harder it is to manifest. We will need to carefully practice that in the next few days. We wouldn't want you to split Azen apart."

"Whoa," said Clara as she realized that her yet-invoked earthquake Qi element could be disastrous. As she pondered that possibility, Sung spoke up.

"Guardian Tiger, since this is the last battle, is there anything we should know?"

The Guardian Panda looked into the eyes of the Guardian Tiger, who responded, "Emperor and empress warriors, we can discuss more tomorrow before your final training with us. For now, finish your food and rest well. You'll be flown back to your respective kingdoms tonight as our leaders would like to greet you. We'll meet back at the Portal Circle tomorrow morning. There is much to do."

The warriors nodded and finished off their last bites of food. A squadron of cranes and a pair of eagles soon flew in, and Clara was delighted to see Shiori the crane again. With the weight of the food making them weary, they said their goodbyes before being flown off to their kingdoms for the night.

THREE

The next morning, Clara felt the eastern rays warming her cheeks. She'd tied her hair into a ponytail with her ribbon bamboo hair accessory as two strands of green ribbon dangled down from it. The wind ruffled the feathers along Shiori's neck as they flew toward the Portal Circle. After a restful night's sleep in her room at Bamboo Tower, she felt removed from her earthly concerns and could feel the responsibility of being Empress Warrior Wu.

She looked over to her right and ahead of her. She smiled as she eyed the furry white-and- black backside of the Guardian Panda, also on a graceful crane. She wondered how his family was doing and what new puzzle games his cubs were now playing. She saw the Guardian Panda looking back at her and pointing downward. Looking down, she could see the Portal Circle. She looked back up at him and nodded as they started their descent.

She held on tighter as Shiori swooped down and landed delicately on the stone Portal Circle. Her hands quickly unfastened her harness clip as Shiori folded her wings inward. Carefully, Clara slid from Shiori's back. She straightened up and quickly adjusted her bow and quiver. She came around to Shiori with a big smile. As she looked down at her with her left beady eye, Clara said, "*Xie xie.*"

Shiori blinked and nodded her feathery head. "It's always a pleasure serving the Empress Warrior Wu."

With that, she took a few steps forward, unfurled her great wings, and flew upward, followed quickly by the crane that had carried the Guardian Panda. He soon waddled toward Clara as she took in a deep breath. Her eyes met his calm gaze, but before she could see anything, a large shadow loomed over the Portal Circle, causing Clara to look up. She could see the belly of a crane with a majestic wingspan as it spiraled down into the Portal Circle. It was the Guardian Crane, who landed gracefully.

Yuka waved from the atop the Guardian Crane and Clara waved back. The Guardian Crane gently lowered herself as Yuka carefully slid off and landed on both feet. Like Clara, she was dressed in bamboo-colored training attire. She adjusted the edge of the outer flap as the white jade of the Moon Star along her waist glistened in the sunlight.

"*Ohayo gozaimasu*!" exclaimed Yuka in Japanese for *good morning*.

Clara smiled and responded, "*Jo sun*," for *good morning* in Cantonese.

Yuka stopped in front of Clara, who noticed how healthy Yuka seemed to be, considering her ordeal during their last time on Azen.

Clara quickly looked past Yuka and saw the Guardian Panda had walked toward the Guardian Crane and was exchanging a few words with her. She looked back at Yuka and asked, "I wonder where the guys are?"

"Oh, I saw them over there when I flew in. They're with the Guardian Tiger and Buffalo. They seem to be practicing," said Yuka as she turned in their direction before turning back toward her.

"Already?" responded Clara before she said nonchalantly. "They must have gotten here early."

"They must have," said Yuka. "I don't know about you, but I can feel the fourth battle ahead of us."

"Is that what this feeling is?" asked Clara as she pondered the strange heavy feeling that had been lingering in her mind. So much depended on the fourth battle. It would also mean, once they had won, it would be the last time that she'd be on Azen with her friends.

But Clara shook off her momentary distraction and looked back at Yuka. "Hey, are you still mad at Daniel?" she asked softly.

Yuka shifted her feet and replied, "Not really, but I'm not ready to talk to him."

Clara nodded. "You know, it's important that you two talk it out. We have a battle ahead of us."

Yuka nodded, but added, "But he needs to say he's sorry first."

"I know," said Clara reassuringly. "But if it makes you feel any better, I know he feels awful about what happened."

"Then he needs to tell me," said Yuka firmly. "You don't ask for forgiveness; you have to earn it."

Clara nodded as she glanced at Sung and Daniel entering the Portal Circle with their guardians behind them.

"Empress and emperor warriors," the Guardian Panda bellowed out. "Please stand by your Portal Books."

Yuka nodded at Clara as she ran to her Portal Book as the other warriors did the same.

As Daniel got to his Portal Book, he leaned the Horn of *Kting voar* along its side before straightening up and turned around. As he shuffled, he glanced over at Yuka, who simply stared at the Guardian Panda, who was at the center of the circle. He sighed before shifting his own gaze at the Guardian Panda.

"Empress and emperor warriors," said the Guardian Panda solemnly. "You must know that your presence here, for the fourth time, signifies your final battle with the Warlock's army. If we prevail, and we are certain we will, Azen will be at peace once more before the next lunar alignment. If you are feeling some unknown weight on you, this is what you are feeling."

"But along with the other guardians, we are confident you have the skills and the experience now to defeat the last Warlock army. Yes, Empress Warrior Wu?" asked the Guardian Panda as he noted Clara's raised hand.

"Do we know what the next creature will be?" she asked.

The Guardian Panda exhaled and then whipped his paws toward Clara's Portal Book to summon fiery streams, which rushed toward him. With a few gestures of his paws, he shaped a large creature from the fiery pulsating streams. It had the massive shape of a *Hou Dou* demon dog but was muscular like the massive buffalo. Menacing horns protruded from its head and its claws were massive. But its face was similar to that of a lion. A thick furry mane ran down its back, ending in a strong tail.

Everyone looked at the creature in awe as the Guardian Panda's arms came to rest at his sides. "This is the *Nian*."

"I thought the *Nian* was only a myth?" said Clara incredulously.

"In your world," said the Guardian Panda. "But not in ours."

"How do we know that it is the *Nian* this time?" asked Sung. "I thought you only knew what the creature would be after the lunar eclipse."

"It is always the *Nian*," said the Guardian Panda gravely. "*Nians* are always among the Warlock's creatures."

Clara simply nodded along with the others, feeling small in the *Nian's* fiery presence.

"The Warlock has crafted this destructive creature over the centuries. It is more massive than our battle buffalos. Its teeth are as sharp as the dreaded *Huo Dou* demon dogs. Its claws slash just like tigers. Its mane is as tough as our own panda fur. It is a formidable creature to do battle with."

Silence descended upon the Portal Circle as the Guardian Panda waved away the fiery image of the fearsome *Nian* and exited the circle.

The Guardian Crane then entered the center of the Portal Circle and wove the terrain of the southern battlefront from Yuka's Portal Book. It was a long a narrow peninsula that extended beyond the southern coast. Standing upright were seemingly thousands of tall stone pillars. At its southernmost point was a bulge where the terrain was somewhat flattish and rocky. Moving north, many of the tall stone pillars served as natural obstacles that didn't allow for any straight path through. But midway up the peninsula, past the stretch of pillars, was a swath of land free of stone pillars but strewn with large rocky boulders that finally connected with the southern cliffs of Azen.

"These are the Sky Pillars," said the Guardian Crane.

Clara recognized them. She remembered seeing the long peninsula with its sky-reaching stone pillars when they were flying to the Healing Pool to save Yuka.

"When we are not engaged in battle, these pillars are a natural obstacle course for our cranes to navigate through to hone their flying skills. It is an amazing natural wonder to see with your own eyes," reminisced the Guardian Crane. But her tone changed solemnly as she continued, "But when in battle, our armies will defend the mouth of the peninsula. The sky pillars provide a natural defense to slow down the hordes of *Nians* as they rumble through them. We must stop as many of them as possible before they enter this open land and not allow them to reach the southern cliffs, which we call The Sheers."

The Guardian Crane walked about, looking into the eyes of each of the warriors before continuing. "Because we know that the last battle will be there, we have already deployed our armies to the location. This creature will test all of our capabilities."

The Guardian Crane looked eastward into the sky and said, "In a few days, the fourth lunar eclipse will occur, but we will be ready, with you, our warriors, at our side. It's important that over the next few days, you hone your Qi elemental powers, go through your training in its entirety, and prepare yourselves for this last battle."

As the Guardian Crane concluded her grave instructions, the Guardian Tiger looked over at the Guardian Panda, who met his gaze. The Guardian Panda soon broke his gaze from the Guardian Tiger as his brown eyes fell silently onto the back of Clara's head.

FOUR

The Guardian Buffalo was the next to enter the Portal Circle. He spun slowly around, giving each warrior a good once-over with his reddish eyes. In his low voice, he bellowed out, "As this is your last battle, we are going to review all your Qi elemental powers. Emperor and empress warriors, please follow your guardians as we head down to the Gauntlet."

The Guardian Buffalo focused on Daniel and gave him a nod of his snout. Daniel nodded back, picked up his club horn, and followed the Guardian Buffalo toward the Gauntlet. The rest of the warriors also followed their guardians.

When they reached the Gauntlet, each pair stood evenly spaced out from each other. The Guardian Buffalo was on the right, followed by the Guardian Panda, the Guardian Crane, and lastly, the Guardian Tiger on his left. The Guardian Panda turned toward Clara and simply said the Cantonese word for *wall*, "Show me *teng-bing*"

Clara nodded. She felt like starting with the basics all over again. She looked down the Gauntlet and without any effort, she said firmly, "*Teng-bing*!" as she quickly traced out the character in the air. The conjured Chinese character glowed blue at her fingertips as she cast it out. It flew into the earth and sent up a dirt wall some twenty feet high and fifty feet long. The Guardian Panda nodded.

The Guardian Crane turned toward Yuka and asked her to invoke an air wall. Yuka looked down the Gauntlet. With authority, she said "*kabe!*" as she traced the Japanese character for *wall* into the air. The glowing character leapt from her fingertips and ran parallel to the dirt wall that Clara had created, leaving an air wall in its wake.

Without hesitation, the Guardian Tiger commanded Sung to do the same. Sung nodded and took a step forward. He brushed out the Korean word for *wall*, shouting, "*dahm*!" The bluish Korean word appeared at his fingertips and flew through the air, leaving a glistening ice wall behind it. Sung nodded at its near-perfect match in height and length to the dirt wall.

Finally, the Guardian Buffalo looked at Daniel and asked him to do the same. With authority, Daniel looked down the Gauntlet. He took a step forward and thrust out his right arm while brushing out the Vietnamese word for *wall* and shouting "*tường!*" As the bluish Vietnamese word appeared in his hand, he pulled his arm back. The Vietnamese word for *wall* tingled along the top of his fingertips, and with a swift motion, flung out his hand, casting the Vietnamese Qi element down the Gauntlet as a wall of fire trailed it.

Everyone gazed down the Gauntlet at the walls of hard ice, glistening air, sturdy dirt, and flaming fire. The guardians nodded and then asked the warriors to take down their walls.

Once the Gauntlet was cleared, the guardians worked with each of their warriors, conjuring and invoking their next set of Qi elements within their arsenals. The earth was split and recombined, gusts of wind whipped down the Gauntlet, and ice bridges spanned its length as fireballs flew down it.

By the time all the warriors executed all the Qi elemental powers that they had previously used, they went through a review. At lunchtime, they all marched toward the meal table and ate a plentiful meal prepared by the pandas. Bamboo *baos*, dumplings, and noodles were served, and Clara ate the bamboo dumplings fondly.

After lunch and a light rest, the warriors and guardians marched back down toward the Gauntlet and resumed their places.

The Guardian Buffalo spoke up, "Emperor and empress warriors, that was a good review of your proven Qi elemental powers. Now we'll try to invoke your newest and untested Qi elements. Emperor Warrior Nguyen, I believe you mentioned you successfully manifested *đốt cháy*, *ignite*?"

Daniel nodded. But for a moment, he wasn't sure how to use the new Qi element. With a snort, two buffalo soldiers appeared from behind bamboo screens down the Gauntlet. Each held a large melon in his hooves and placed it on the ground some fifty feet away. They quickly slipped out of sight behind the bamboo screen.

"With *đốt cháy*, you can ignite the water or air within an object," explained the Guardian Buffalo. "Be sure to cast the Qi element at the object. Show me now, Emperor Warrior Nguyen."

Daniel nodded and stepped forward, eying the massive melons down the Gauntlet. He conjured ignite and drew his hand towards himself, admiring the bluish glowing Qi element. Shifting his focus down toward the Gauntlet, he thrust his arm and fingers forward, casting the Qi element into the melon. The melon shattered into pieces, and without hesitation, he invoked another Qi element and sent it into the second melon, which too shattered.

"Well done, Emperor Warrior Nguyen," said the Guardian Buffalo.

Going in reverse order, the Guardian Tiger shifted his attention to Sung and asked what new Qi element he would like to try.

Sung looked up at the Guardian Tiger and responded, "*jeung-gi,"* for *steam.*

"Very well, Emperor Warrior Kim," said the Guardian Tiger. "Show me

jeung-gi."

Sung stepped forward and conjured up the element as he yelled out, "*jeung-gi!*" Without hesitation, he cast the Qi element down the Gauntlet, where steam suddenly bellowed out in large puffs until almost half of the Gauntlet was engulfed in heavy white steam.

"Excellent, Emperor Warrior Kim," said the Guardian Tiger. "Steam is a good means of obscurement, and you can raise its temperature to scald living skin. Now, please dissipate it."

Sung nodded and invoked the evaporate Qi element.

The Guardian Crane looked at Yuka and asked, "Empress Warrior Satoh, if I heard correctly, you successfully manifested *taifū*, for *typhoon*?"

Yuka nodded in anticipation.

The Guardian Crane saw her eagerness, but warned, "Empress Warrior Satoh, *taifū*, is a very powerful Qi element. Please cast it out further down the Gauntlet and be prepared to stop it when I ask you to. But before we do that, Emperor Warrior Kim, would you mind creating some water?"

Sung took a few steps forward and turned toward Yuka. She leaned back and smiled at him. Without hesitation, he invoked water, and a large pool appeared further down the Gauntlet.

All eyes were suddenly on Yuka. She pursed her lips and stepped forward, imagining where over the water she would be casting out the Qi element for typhoon. Without further hesitation, she conjured the element into the cup of her hand and softly said, "*Taifū*." With her forearm held straight in front of her chest, she looked at the bluish Japanese character in her hand. She admired its iridescent beauty before flinging it out from her fingertips. The Qi element floated toward the water before it soared into the air, disappearing into the sky.

Nothing happened. The sky was still calm.

Clara, Sung, and Daniel stared in bewilderment as the guardians gazed at the sky. But something soon changed, and the sky started to darken. Ominous gray clouds started to rumble at the far end of the Gauntlet as a whipping wind gathered strength. The wind seemed to reach into the water that Sung had created, whipping it up and sucking streams of water into air. The water raced back down in slicing sheets of rain.

The warriors stepped back in awe. "Empress Warrior Satoh, please stop it now," the Guardian Crane asked.

While still spellbound by the torrential gusts of rain coming towards them, Yuka nodded and quickly invoked the Qi element to stop the typhoon. As the Qi element soared through the sheeting rain and into the dark clouds, the typhoon dissipated, and the clear skies appeared once more.

"Well done, Empress Warrior Satoh," said the Guardian Crane. *Taifū* is a very powerful Qi element and if not stopped, it will wreak havoc before it dissipates on its own. Please be careful when you invoke this Qi element."

Yuka nodded in understanding.

The Guardian Panda turned to Clara and asked, "Empress Warrior Wu, I believe you manifested earthquake?"

Clara nodded. She could anticipate what the Guardian Panda was about to tell her. "The Qi element for earthquake is also very powerful. It is invoked differently, since you will need to push the Qi element into the ground. It will literally shake the very ground that we stand upon. The strength of the earthquake will be proportional to your clenched fist, so use a light touch on your first attempt. Also, once you invoke it, please be prepared to stop it."

Clara nodded and exhaled. She looked left and right and saw that all eyes were on her. She looked at Daniel as he teasingly mouthed her superhero name, "Quake."

Clara smiled and stepped forward. She exhaled and conjured up the *earthquake* Qi element as she shouted out, "*Tei-cheng*!" The bluish character for earthquake appeared in her hand as she drew her hand close to admire it before she gracefully arced her hand outward and toward the ground as the Guardian Panda screamed out, "NO!"

But it was too late. The ground shifted suddenly, and everyone struggled to balance themselves as the earth shook again, causing everyone to wobble. Clara looked up with wide eyes as the Guardian Panda's eyes bulged along with his open jaw.

The Guardian Panda shouted at Clara, "Empress Warrior Wu, stop it now!"

Clara nodded furiously, but before she could invoke the reverse Qi element, the ground beneath her shook again, sending her to the ground. The Guardian Panda plopped onto the ground in a heap of white-and-black fur. The Guardian Crane flew safely upward. Before Yuka could do the same, she fell onto her side but was able to quickly invoke the fly Qi element and soar above the shifting ground. The Guardian Tiger was flat on his belly, with his limbs splayed out, as was Sung. The Guardian Buffalo tipped over onto his side, but Daniel was able to muster the thrust Qi element and hover in the air, looking panicked.

Clara was on her back and felt the earth beneath her shift a few inches to her right. As the ground settled for a moment, Clara invoked the reverse Qi element. The Chinese character appeared at her fingertips, and she smacked it down into the earth as hard as she could, stinging the palm of her hand.

The ground shook no more. Everyone got their bearings and got back on their feet.

"What did I do wrong?" asked Clara, bewildered.

The Guardian Panda looked around, reassured that his fellow guardians and the warriors were fine. "Empress Warrior Wu, I forgot to mention that any additional motion of your hand before sending the earthquake Qi element into the earth will also increase its intensity."

"Oh," said Clara with guilt. "I didn't know. I'm sorry."

"You were able to stop it in time," said the Guardian Panda. "Why don't we take a break and head back to the tent compound?"

"I agree with you, old friend," hollered out the Guardian Tiger as he vigorously shook his fur.

"Wow!" exclaimed Daniel as he looked over at Clara. "That was intense, Quake!"

The warriors paired up with their guardians as they walked back to the tent quarters with Clara and the Guardian Panda in the lead. As the tent compound came into view, a couple of panda attendants came rushing to meet the Guardian Panda, who asked everyone to stay back as he went to meet them. Clara could see some hushed words being exchanged as the Guardian Panda let out a heavy sigh. The pandas bowed to each other as the two pandas turned away.

When the Guardian Panda returned, he looked disappointed. "I'm afraid we cannot go back to the tent compound. The earthquake seemed to have shifted everything, so everything needs to be reset."

"I'm so sorry," said Clara as she looked downcast. "I didn't mean to cause so much trouble."

"Empress Warrior Wu," said the Guardian Panda reassuringly. "It's nothing that we can't fix. Besides, this isn't the first time that we've dealt with the unexpected effects of the earthquake Qi element."

"It isn't?" asked Clara.

"No, it is not, Empress Warrior Wu," said the Guardian Panda. "You are not the first earth Wu warrior who may have shaken Azen up a little bit."

"I see," said a still remorseful Clara. "So, what now?"

"The attendants will need the remaining part of the day to inspect the compound and stabilize anything that may have been shaken out of place," said the Guardian Panda matter-of-factly. "But that means you'll spend the rest of your day in your kingdom."

FIVE

Several moons hung high overhead that night, like luminescent pearls in the navy-brushed night. Their moonbeams glanced off the calm waters of the caldera that surrounded Crane Castle. Yuka was sitting outside in a section of Crane Castle called The Perch. A cool whisper of air gently brushed past her, and she pulled her thick Japanese robe with its magnetically sealed front edging tighter. It was white, but what gave her a smile each time she looked at it was the black embroidered crane's head over her upper left chest.

Yuka reached for the warm cup of green tea that she was so fond of. The teacup rested gingerly in her hands as she could feel the warmth easing the soreness of her fingers from a full day of manifesting. She needed to make sure her arsenal was full for the looming battle.

Her attention turned upward, where she heard the soft flap of wings as a crane slowly rose before her.

Yuka grinned and whispered, "Guardian Crane."

The Guardian Crane blinked a few times and hovered before moving forward and tiptoeing onto The Perch. She walked a few steps and gracefully pivoted and folded her wings before sitting down next to Yuka.

"Empress Warrior Satoh," greeted the Guardian Crane. "I was told you were up here all by yourself. Taking in the quiet of the night?"

"I am," said Yuka. "It's relaxing."

"I see. Empress Warrior Satoh," the Guardian Crane replied. "May I ask you something?"

Yuka lowered her teacup and looked up at the Guardian Crane with a grin and a nod.

"Have you recovered from your ordeal? When you were—" the Guardian Crane paused before she continued, "—held captive by the Warlock?"

Yuka placed the teacup into her lap and looked down into the tea at her reflection. She knew in her heart and mind that she was fine, despite the torture that the Warlock had imposed on her. And whatever the Longevity Tree had done, it made her better than before. She could not only feel it, but she could also see it. Yet she was hesitant to tell the Guardian Crane about her new gift, a gift whose capabilities were unknown, if there were any at all. Up until that point, she could not determine the purpose of her shimmering Qi.

She turned to the Guardian Crane with a reassuring smile and simply said, "I'm all right. The Longevity Tree fixed me. I can feel that I'm better. Thank you for rescuing me."

The Guardian Crane bowed her head slightly as she gently closed her beady eye before it opened up to look at Yuka.

"I'm glad to hear that, Empress Warrior Satoh."

"Guardian Crane?" asked Yuka.

"Yes?"

"Will this be the last time I will see you? After we conquer the last Warlock army?"

The Guardian Crane paused and looked fondly at Yuka before answering, "Yes, this may very well be the last time I will get to serve with you."

Yuka looked down into the teacup as thoughts swirled in her mind. Despite her tortuous near-death experience, she loved Azen. She enjoyed being the Empress Warrior for the Red Crown Crane Kingdom. She also adored her superhero name, Airess. She cherished her friendships with Clara, Sung, and Daniel. She held all the guardians in high regard, but she was most fond of her Guardian Crane. But what she loved most was the simple freedom of being able to fly through the air untethered. She was going to miss Azen once her duties were finished.

Yuka sighed and looked back up at the Guardian Crane. "We've been training and battling for most of our time here on Azen, and there is so much that I haven't seen. Show me more of Crane Kingdom."

The Guardian Crane stared down at her empress warrior and contemplated. She looked up and pointed with her left wing.

"Well over there is *tō* sentinel number 5. It was where I was first stationed as I entered the service..." The Guardian Crane paused as she felt Yuka's hand on the feathers of her right wing. She looked down and into Yuka's beseeching eyes.

"No," pleaded Yuka. "Show me."

The Guardian Crane's eyes glistened and then she smiled. She gently rose, craned her head toward Yuka and simply said, "Then hop on, Empress Warrior Satoh."

Yuka gleefully sprung up. Shedding her robe, she quickly folded it into a neat square, placed it onto the floor of The Perch, and weighted it with the half-filled teacup. She spun around as the Guardian Crane lowered herself. Yuka climbed atop the Guardian Crane, securing her harness with its metal fastener.

"Ready!" exclaimed Yuka.

"*Jōshō suru*!" the Guardian Crane said in Japanese for *ascend* as she flapped into the night sky.

The Guardian Crane flew toward the rim of the caldera, where there was a stir of cranes from the closest *tō* sentinels. Upon recognizing the Guardian Crane, they settled back into their sentry duties.

"Empress Warrior Satoh," said the Guardian Crane.

"Hmmm?"

"That is *tō* sentinel number 5. It was my first military assignment many years ago before I joined the Top Talon team. As I fly around the rim of the caldera, you'll see that there are seven of these *tō* sentinels. The lower three floors are their living and sleeping quarters. The next two floors are open hangars that our rapid response and intercept teams fly out of. The next two upper floors are the armament floors, where each floor has two repeating crossbows. Yes, we cranes do operate weapons as well to repel any intruders. The topmost floor is the sentinel floor, which is monitored by a pair of cranes all day and night."

"That spire on top is so tall!" Yuka observed.

As the Guardian Crane was gracefully completing a full circle around the caldera, she remarked, "The spires themselves are special. Within each spire is an illumination jade. A twist of the spire would not only cast a bright light to indicate a nighttime intrusion, but would signal to all cranes within Red Crown Crane Kingdom that Crane Castle was under attack."

"Has Crane Castle ever been under attack?" asked Yuka as the Guardian Crane flew away from the caldera in a southerly direction.

"No, it has not, but we are always prepared," said the Guardian Crane as she flew toward several structures that were wider and lower but also in a Japanese architectural style. "The island that is home to Crane Castle is more heavily guarded, and there are several squadrons of cranes and eagles nested within a fortified hangar at each of the cardinal points. Where I'm taking you now is the southern hangar, where the Top Talon team is based."

"How long did you train before you became the leader of the Top Talon team?" asked Yuka as she spied the multi-hangar complex below. Even if no one had told her that it was a hangar, she would have admired its beautiful Japanese architecture lit up by soft illumination jades. Each of the three floors were open, allowing the cranes to enter and exit freely.

"About a year, Empress Warrior Satoh," said the Guardian Crane fondly. "But those were the best days of my life, as I realized my flight talent before becoming the leader of the Top Talon squadron. The hangar closest to the base of the volcano is the Top Talon hangar."

Yuka nodded in admiration as the Guardian Crane continued to fly southward. Soon, they flew past the shoreline of Crane Castle Island and were over the water. The sound of lapping waves tickled Yuka's ears.

"Where are we going now?" asked Yuka.

"It's a surprise, Empress Warrior Satoh," said the Guardian Crane cryptically.

Yuka smiled and exclaimed, "I love surprises!"

They continued to fly over the dark ocean waters, passing other large islands on either side. The Guardian Crane explained that each island was its own crane city, filled with either cranes, eagles, or both. As they flew past the islands, the silence was pierced every now and then by the pulsating waves below. Soon, Yuka's eyes perked up when off into the distance, she saw another island. It was large, dark and strangely shaped, and it glistened.

"What is that?" asked Yuka curiously.

"That, Empress Warrior Satoh, is one of the most beautiful wonders in all of Crane Kingdom's purview. Thousands of years ago, before there was ever a Crane Kingdom, these volcanic islands were still forming. But that island before you, was once a violent volcano. We can only imagine that during a moment of a violent eruption, a large tsunami was triggered. As the volcanic island shot streams of oozing lava into the air, a large tsunami came crashing down on the island, beautifully hardening the lava all at once. Welcome to The Lava Blossom."

Yuka could see The Lava Blossom ahead and gazed in awe at the frozen arcs of lava that sprung out from its center, creating a dome-like shape in the middle of the ocean. "Wow," she said before she asked, "Why are we headed toward it?"

"Because, Empress Warrior Satoh, these amazing lava arcs form the obstacle course that each aspiring Top Talon crane needs to successfully navigate in order to become a Top Talon. So, are you ready?"

"Ready for what?" asked Yuka nervously.

"To see what it's like to fly through all these lava structures," said the Guardian Crane.

Yuka's eyes perked up. "Really?"

"Yes, Empress Warrior Satoh," said the Guardian Crane. "Please take a wide grip of the harness and press your body into my back as tightly as you can."

A mixed sense of nervousness and excitement welled up within Yuka as she tightened her grip, pressing her body into the Guardian Crane's feathers. She peered over the Guardian Crane's right shoulder, where she could see the silhouettes of large lava arcs curving high above and into the water. Her heart pounded. "All set."

The Guardian Crane's eyes blinked as she exclaimed, "Hold on!"

Before Yuka could inhale, they plunged downward. Her stomach smacked into her heart as the Guardian Crane dove fast toward the arches of The Lava Blossom. The wind raced through her hair, and she struggled to peer over the Guardian Crane's shoulder.

The Guardian Crane flapped furiously toward the first lava arch, passing it without ruffling a feather. She then veered right and flew through another, smaller, lava arch. Her streamlined body took a hard left turn and flew through a series of slender lava arches. The next turn led them into a volcanic chasm whose walls seemed to press closer as the Guardian Crane raced ahead in the moonlit darkness. She pulled in her wings, and Yuka hung on desperately before they exited the chasm, flying effortlessly over and under several lava arches. Yuka could feel the fear and excitement all at once when the Guardian Crane yelled out, "Hold on!"

Yuka gulped and pressed herself hard against the Guardian Crane's nape as she looked ahead. Frozen in midair were large, hardened sheets of lava slit open with narrow cracks. The Guardian Crane easily flew through the first one. She turned a bit to navigate the second one, and Yuka almost felt the scrape of the crackling edges against her back. But ahead of her, she saw one final lava sheet with a crack that seemed dangerously narrow. Yuka's eyes widened as she screamed out, "It's too narrow!"

The Guardian Crane exhaled hard, pulling in her wings as tightly as she could as her body straightened out like a missile on approach to the narrow crack. Even the tufts of her regal red feathers atop her head seemed to fold themselves downward. Yuka screamed as she buried her face and body into the Guardian Crane's feathers. In an instant, they disappeared into the narrow crack with a swoosh.

As they exited the other side, the Guardian Crane unfurled her massive wings as Yuka thrust her hands into the night sky and screamed out gleefully, "Amazing!"

SIX

The looming shadows cast by the large firepit at the center of the Warrior's Soul were eerie. But the chamber beneath Claw House, carved into the soul of the mountain itself, also felt sacred. The firepit was fed with a blend of bamboo and dark coal chunks. Their embers glowed red, and every now and then, they would crackle. Sung had learned that the firepit had been burning nonstop for hundreds of years.

Sung walked slowly around the firepit, dressed in comfortable attire with a thick blue robe draped over his shoulders. The white edging on the front was open, and over the left side of his chest, was the emblem of a white tiger. The Claw Staff was magnetically held in place across his back.

He stopped in front of a stone pedestal holding an imposing stone statue made entirely of Clawdium. Its details were impressive—the intricate chest plate, the gauntlets on the statue's forearm, and the boots and the helmet, which looked as if they could be separated from the statue itself. Even the Claw Staff looked like it could have been lifted out of the statue's hands.

But it was the faces of these teenaged Korean warriors that moved Sung the most. He couldn't believe that there were so many of them, teenaged Korean boys and girls like himself who came before him and fought for Azen to keep Earth safe.

He looked up at the teenage warrior and clearly saw the features of his people. The clear cheekbones and the stern stare of the eyes were so familiar. *They could have been brothers*, he thought.

He looked down at the Clawdium nameplate and noted the name of the warrior, Kwon Yul. He brought up a sheet of paper folded in quarters and a writing instrument that functioned very much like a fountain pen. He wrote down the warrior's name. His eyes went back up to meet those of Kwon Yul as he bowed and said *thank you* in Korean. "*Gam-sa-ham-ni-da.*"

"Emperor Warrior Kwon, I am Emperor Warrior Kim, also a Tiger Warrior for Claw House. I am from Los Angeles, California. In America. Something tells me you were probably in Korea before the Portal Book brought you here. I wish we could have known each other. Thank you for sharing with me all your experience and giving me the courage to fight for Azen, *gam-sa-ham-ni-da.*"

Sung looked about him and saw the many other sculpted Clawdium warriors to whom he had still yet to pay his respects. Soon, he was in front of another statue, an empress warrior, and he couldn't help admiring her beauty. He felt a little embarrassed for thinking about it, but despite her magnificent battle armor, which was tailored for a girl's body, he noticed her softer features and the way her hair flowed behind her shoulders. But he could tell from her stern eyes that she must have been a formidable Tiger Empress Warrior. His eyes traveled down to her nameplate, which read, Choi Jin-joo. He smiled as he looked up into her eyes. But as he did, her stare was somewhere else. He then wrote down her name. With a step back, he bowed to her and said *thank you* in Korean, "*gam-sa-ham-ni-da.*"

"Empress Warrior Choi, I am Emperor Warrior Kim, also a Tiger Warrior for Claw House. I am from Los Angeles, California. I'm sure you're also from Korea. Korea is doing very well now. We make some of the best mobile phones and we have some of the best music and shows these days. It would have been an honor to have met you. Thank you for giving me your experience so that I too may fight for Azen, *gam-sa-ham-ni-da.*"

As Sung lowered his head to bow, he heard the familiar voice of the Guardian Tiger. He had stealthily walked down the arched tunnel and meandered around the Clawdium warrior statues without giving up his presence. "Good evening, Emperor Warrior Kim."

Sung looked up and smiled, coming face-to-face with the large white-and-black striped tiger. His coat of fur draped magnificently over his streamlined, muscular feline body. But it was his steely blue eyes that always caught Sung off guard. There was such depth behind those eyes, that upon looking at them one could sense soulful courage.

"Good evening, Guardian Tiger," said Sung as he relaxed. He lowered the paper and pen.

The Guardian Tiger's fluffy head craned up at the statue as he mouthed, "Empress Warrior Choi. She was indeed an impressive Tiger Warrior."

His head turned back and faced Sung as he continued, "I am told, she was gifted with resonance. She was able to wield the Claw Staff masterfully and exploit its resonance power in battle."

"So, you didn't fight with her?" asked Sung.

The Guardian Tiger chuckled, "No, she was before my time. The inner circle are the oldest warriors, and each outer circle represents the more recent warriors."

"Will one be made of me?" asked Sung.

The Guardian Tiger nodded and smiled, "But of course, you will be honored for all time. Would you like to see where your statue will be?"

Sung's eyes lit up as he grinned sheepishly, "Yes, that would be great."

The Guardian Tiger swung his massive body around and led Sung westward to the third concentric circle. Only two other statues were there. Several empty stone pedestals ringed the circle at regular intervals, and the Guardian Tiger stopped at one.

"I don't know exactly where your statue will be placed, but it would be one of these," said the Guardian Tiger as he looked around the open pedestals.

Sung looked down and his eyes fixed on the stone pedestal closest to him. He imagined a Clawdium warrior statue of himself, looking confident and strong, in full battle armor while holding the Claw Staff. He smiled at his own vision of himself.

Sung broke out of his reverie as the Guardian Tiger began to walk to the closest statue and Sung followed. They stopped in front of another empress warrior for the Tiger Kingdom, and Sung admired her as well. Her hair was pulled neatly back into a beautiful bun. Despite her delicate build, her battle armor accentuated her warrior-like demeanor. Sung eyed her features and noted how young she looked. But her eyes were furrowed, and they too seemed focused on something far away.

"This is Empress Warrior Lee Min-ji," said the Guardian Tiger. "I had the pleasure of fighting with her."

Sung's eyes lit up as he took a step back to admire Empress Warrior Lee better. His eyes gazed upon her before returning to the Guardian Tiger. He envisioned them together, fighting the battles that he was fighting now.

"Whoa," exclaimed Sung. "This is amazing! Was she the Tiger Warrior before me?"

The Guardian Tiger's head nodded a few times. "She was master of her ice Qi elemental powers. Very similar to you, Emperor Warrior Kim."

Sung nodded in awe as he came face-to-face with his immediate past warrior. He took a step toward her statue and bowed deeply as he said *thank you* in Korean, "*gam-sa-ham-ni-da.*"

He looked back up and continued, "Empress Warrior Lee, I am Emperor Warrior Kim. I am honored to meet the warrior that came before me. I too will fight hard for White Tiger Kingdom and all of Azen, *gam-sa-ham-ni-da.*"

"She would appreciate that," said the Guardian Tiger as Sung quickly scribbled down her name. He placed the piece of paper and pen back into his inner robe pocket.

"What was she like?" asked Sung.

"She was shy at first," began the Guardian Tiger. "Surprised that she had traveled to Azen and then asked to defend it or Earth would fall to the Warlock. But she took up the duty immediately, and like you, worked very hard as her powers came quickly to her. When she mastered her skills, she wielded them confidently. She fought bravely and courageously alongside the other warriors, the other guardians, and myself. She was well honored. White Tiger Kingdom was indebted to her."

Sung's eyes perked up as he asked, "How long ago was this?"

The Guardian Tiger turned his head toward Sung and answered, "That would be almost forty Azen years."

Sung realized he didn't know what that may be in Earth years, but he had the suspicion that maybe Lee Min-Ji could be alive back home. He became excited and quickly jotted down something.

"What are you thinking, Emperor Warrior Kim?" asked the Guardian Tiger curiously.

"I'm going to try to find her back on Earth! She may still be alive! Assuming that forty Azen years are similar to forty of our years," said Sung excitedly.

"I see," the Guardian Tiger uttered. "Will you have to travel far and wide to find her?"

"Oh no, we have the Internet for that," said Sung excitedly.

"The inter… net?" asked the Guardian Tiger.

Sung paused and he realized he didn't know how to explain Earth technology to him. He flubbed trying to find the words but instead, all he could say was, "It's a fast way for people back on my world to communicate with each other."

There was a pause until the Guardian Tiger answered simply, "I see. Like when our scout birds tweet to each other along the chain?"

Sung smirked and stifled a chuckle before he answered simply, "Kinda." He then glanced up before looking back at the Guardian Tiger and asked, "Will this battle be the last time we see each other?"

The Guardian Tiger looked soulfully at his young Tiger Warrior and said, "Yes, this battle will be the last time that we will see each other. Once we are victorious, you will take one last trip through the Portal Book back to your home world."

Sung nodded sadly as that realization set in. He looked back up at the Guardian Tiger, whom he had come to admire, and said, "Then I will make it count as we defeat the Warlock."

"Very good, Emperor Warrior Kim," said the Guardian Tiger solemnly. "I'm confident you will."

"Is there anything that I need to know before the last battle?" asked Sung.

"The most important thing is that you warriors need to stay together, work together, and harness your collective strengths to overcome the Warlock army. No one warrior can defeat the Warlock's armies alone. Do you understand, Emperor Warrior Kim?" asked the Guardian Tiger.

Sung nodded and replied, "I do."

"The Warlock will take every advantage to break apart the alliance of the warriors. Sometimes, it isn't even his own doing. Like prior to the first battle, when Empress Warrior Wu was almost taken by the *Huo Dou* demon dogs. The most devastating incident was when Empress Warrior Satoh was taken hostage by the Warlock, and she too almost fell to him. And lastly, you almost fell to the deadly ways of the *gumiho*."

Sung looked sullen as he reflected on how he had foolishly almost allowed the *gumiho* to seduce him and siphon off his Qi.

"Emperor Warrior Kim," admonished the Guardian Tiger. "There is no need to fret on the experience with the *gumiho*. They are designed to seduce young men with their irresistible beauty."

Sung nodded and mouthed under his breath, "Yah, she was hot."

"Hot?" asked the Guardian Tiger. "I do not understand."

"Oh," said Sung embarrassingly. "Never mind. Could we see the other statues?"

The Guardian Tiger nodded. He spun around and walked toward the other recent statues as Sung followed. The Guardian Tiger introduced him to all the remaining Tiger Emperor and Empress Warriors for the remainder of the evening.

SEVEN

"Oh, he's so adorable!" exclaimed Clara as she struggled to keep the curious panda cub from climbing all over her.

"They are usually a paw full," said the panda attendant, who was sitting by Clara's side in the panda playpen of the nursery. This particular nursery was home to panda cubs recovering from health issues. To ensure that they did not feel lonely, the cubs were often entertained by a panda attendant outside of visiting hours. But that night, Clara wanted to visit the nursery to play with a panda cub.

Clara let out a laugh as the panda cub, Zhen Zhen, tried to climb onto her chest and nuzzle her nose against her own. Though the panda's claws were tiny, they still poked into the white bamboo-silk gown that she wore to protect her underlying clothing. Clara gently supported the panda cub under her armpits and pushed her back so that she could stare into the cub's adorable white-and-black furry face.

Instinctively, she cooed at the panda cub, and it chuckled, which made Clara's heart melt even more as she pulled the panda cub to her chest.

"Oh, why are you so cute?" asked Clara.

As Clara continued to affectionately hug the panda cub, another panda attendant quietly appeared from atop the raised bamboo decking that separated the individual panda playpens. "Empress Warrior Wu."

Clara looked up just as the panda attendant rose from her bow. She was also draped in a white gown, which was mandatory for anyone coming into the nursery. "Yes?" answered Clara as the panda cub gently pawed at her cheeks.

"Empress Warrior Wu," said the panda attendant cautiously. "I do not mean to disturb you, but Emperor Warrior Nguyen is here to see you."

Clara's eyes perked up and nodded. *That's odd*, she thought. *Why was Daniel here to see her?* The panda attendant anticipated Clara's needs as she got up and started to walk over to take the cub. Clara extended her arms as she tried to tame the panda cub's playfulness by cooing at her.

"Okay, Zhen Zhen," Clara said playfully. "I have to go now, but it was so nice playing with you. Be a nice panda."

The panda cub's eyes joyfully squinted and let out a chuckle as Clara carefully handed her over to the panda attendant. The panda cub turned toward Clara and reached out with her paw but soon, her attention was directed toward the panda attendant. With a smile, Clara got up and stepped up onto the pair of bamboo steps that led up onto the bamboo deck. Another panda attendant opened the bamboo gate. As Clara stepped onto the deck, another panda attendant appeared as the other gently closed the gate. With gestures from the panda attendants, Clara stretched out her arms in front of her as the two panda attendants carefully removed her white gown. Clara pressed down on her casual evening attire, a bamboo-silken Mandarin-styled collared top. It was fastened at the shoulder with cloth knob buttons with an embroidered panda head along the edge.

Clara bowed to the panda attendants and offered a *thank you* in Mandarin, "*Xie xie*." She liked to switch up the Chinese languages amongst the pandas and enjoyed speaking with them because when would she ever get the chance to speak Mandarin or Cantonese with a panda? She gently spun around, picked up her quiver, and slung it over her back. She then reached out for the Bow of Destiny, which she gently held in her left hand as she nodded to the panda attendant.

The panda attendant nodded as they traversed the bamboo deck and Clara passed several playpens. Most were empty, but a few were occupied by the more playful panda cubs who didn't want to go to sleep. Each one made her smile as she passed by and stole glimpses of them. As they neared the end, the panda attendant carefully slid the door open as Clara passed through.

Daniel was waiting off to the side and upon seeing Clara stepping through, he straightened up. "Hey, Clara."

Clara looked up with a smile and responded cheerfully, "Hey Daniel, what's up?"

Before Daniel could answer, the panda attendant gently slid the nursery door shut, bowed slightly, and waddled off in the other direction.

"Hey," said Daniel casually. "I didn't mean to come unannounced, but I was wondering if there is a place where I can chat with you? It's about Yuka."

Clara looked up at him and could feel that something was weighing on him. Though his face was serious, she could detect a sense of helplessness. Her eyes lit up as she said, "I know the perfect place. Follow me."

Clara jaunted past him as he followed along the inner Bamboo Tower corridor, which was gently lit from above by illumination jades. They hopped into an ascending bamboo lift and rode it all the way to the top.

As they stepped off, they entered a tight corridor. Daniel looked to the left and saw that the corridor curved further down a passage while on the right side were steps leading toward the topmost segment of Bamboo Tower.

"Come on," said Clara eagerly as she walked up the steps hewn into the thick bamboo walls of Bamboo Tower. Daniel followed, and after what seemed like tens of steps, they emerged into the tranquil night sky. Clara stepped up onto the bamboo decking and pivoted to face Daniel just as he stepped up onto the bamboo decking. Then his ears caught the sound of water. He looked to his left and his eyes widened as he let out a "Whoa!"

As his eyes adjusted to the night, he became amazed by the sight in front of him. He was looking at a pool of water that covered the entire top of Bamboo Tower. At each quarter of the perimeter was a bamboo structure whose windows were gently lit. Panda guards were standing tall at the bamboo structure closest to him and on the one opposite side of the pool. The pool itself was surrounded by a wide waist-high bamboo wall. A path was carved between it and the outer wall, which was about chest high, allowing a full view of Bamboo City below. Along regular intervals, inset into the inside of the outer wall at waist level, were illumination jades that ringed the top segment of Bamboo Tower.

"What is this place? And why is there a pond on top of Bamboo Tower?" asked Daniel as he glanced at the dark still pond reflecting the night sky above.

Clara giggled and walked a little closer to the pond as Daniel followed.

"This is the reservoir that collects rainwater. The top segment of the Bamboo Tower's stalk is left open. As the rainwater is collected, it seeps into the next segment of the bamboo that has been filled with charcoal to filter the water. Then that water seeps into the third segment, and that is how clean water is made available to all the residents of Bamboo Tower. Amazing, right?" Clara explained proudly.

"Way cool!" echoed Daniel as he tried to envision how the water collection and filtration system worked. "So it's like a big Brita?"

Clara laughed and nodded. "Follow me," said Clara, leading Daniel along the outer wall away from the guard structure.

Clara stopped and leaned up against the outer bamboo wall. She rested her elbows comfortably along the rim of the wall and Daniel did the same. She looked up at him and quickly pointed her finger and looked outward.

Daniel followed her gaze in awe. The tops of all the bamboo stalks, which were the homes and businesses to all the inhabitants of Bamboo City, were also filled with water. As he looked out, he saw The Meridian, the primary path of Bamboo City. He admired the neatly laid-out bamboo stalks along the concentric circles. From his vantage point atop Bamboo Tower, the scene looked like he was looking down at several teacups filled with water reflecting the starry night sky and its moons.

"Calming, right?" asked Clara.

"Amazing is more like it," said Daniel. "The Buffalo Kingdom is so different. We have cities atop tall limestone outcroppings. In order to get from one limestone city to another, you need to take a boat from dock to dock. Luckily, I have my escort crane or I could fly, but it's not as easy to get from one city to another."

"We should visit!" said Clara. "I haven't seen Buffalo Kingdom yet."

"Totally," said Daniel. "We've been so busy training and fighting."

"And eating!" exclaimed Clara as the wind gently swept her hair back as she closed her eyes against it. When she opened them, she saw the seriousness in Daniel's eyes and asked, "So what's up?"

Daniel shifted in his feet, leaned up against the wall. He looked at Clara, exhaled and simply said, "I don't know how to apologize to Yuka."

Clara paused and simply said, "I'm sorry?"

"Yah, easier said than done. I need to like distract her so I brought these from home." Daniel reached into this pant pocket and pulled out a slender package.

"What's that?" asked Clara as Daniel held the package in front of her eyes.

"Sparklers!" said Daniel excitedly. "I thought maybe after dinner, I could light these and you know, it'll make her happy. Then I'll slip in the 'I'm sorry,' and with her being in a good mood, she'll accept my apology and forgive me."

Clara scrunched her face. "That's the dumbest thing I've ever heard!"

Daniel's smile faded. He looked down at his toes as the sparklers fell to his side. "I don't know what to do! I'm not really good at saying I'm sorry, especially when I'm the one to blame. The guilt has been unbearable. What happens if saying sorry isn't enough?"

"It's not that hard, Daniel," said Clara with a hint of annoyance.

"Come on," Daniel said firmly. "Haven't you ever felt so much guilt or shame that it made it hard to say I'm sorry because you felt the person would not accept it?"

Clara was about to interject when suddenly, she remembered how she was scared to apologize to her mother for simply spilling soy sauce on her old calligraphy book. And right there and then, she was talking to Daniel, who almost got Yuka killed. The annoyance she felt at Daniel subsided, and she realized how much his inner turmoil was weighing on him.

In a soothing voice Clara responded, "I get it now."

With a hint of frustration, Daniel let out, "What should I do? I was hoping I can think of something by tonight after talking with you. My crane can't wait for me forever."

For a moment, Clara didn't have an answer. Then her eyes lit up. She moved toward Daniel and grabbed his left hand in both of hers. Caught off guard, Daniel flinched for a moment as Clara asked him, "How's your *origami* skills?"

EIGHT

The next morning, as Shiori touched down by the meal area, Clara smiled as she unharnessed herself. She'd flown solo that morning as the Guardian Panda had flown on ahead of her. She carefully slid down Shiori's feathers and walked around to face her. The crane fluttered her feathers and looked down at Clara with her beady eyes. Clara smiled, bowed slightly and said *thank you* in Mandarin, "*Xie xie.*"

"You are more than welcome, Empress Warrior Wu," said Shiori as she nodded and closed her eyes briefly.

Clara turned around as Shiori unfurled her wings and flew off to meet up with the two other escort cranes circling above. They soon flew off in a V formation.

Her hands gently wrapped around the Bamboo Jade of her bow. She could feel the warmth of its soft glow and felt a more personal connection to it. It gave her strength and reminded her of the eerie panda monks who deemed her to be true. It reinforced her confidence that she was indeed the Panda Warrior of Azen.

As she neared the prep meal area, she saw that her fellow warriors had already arrived and were chatting at the meal table. The Guardian Buffalo was by the prep area along with several buffalo attendants. *Vietnamese food,* she thought as her eager appetite started to awaken. Near the entrance of the food prep area, she could see that the Guardian Tiger and Crane chatting. But she could not see her Guardian Panda anywhere. Just then her stomach growled, and she smiled as she quickened her pace.

"*Ohayo gozaimasu!*" said Yuka in Japanese for *good morning* as she rose and gently waved at Clara.

Both Sung and Daniel turned as Sung hollered out *good morning* in Korean, "*Joh-eun achim,*" as Daniel did the same in Vietnamese, "*Buổi sáng tốt lành!*"

Clara smiled and blurted out, "*Jo sun*!" in Cantonese for *good morning.* As she rounded the other side, her eyes trailed cheerfully, as she said, "And in Mandarin, it's *zao shang hao!*"

As Clara unslung her bow and quiver, Yuka asked, "Guardian Panda isn't with you?"

Clara sat herself down and responded, "No, he flew on ahead this morning. No one's seen him?"

Sung and Daniel shook their heads as Yuka suddenly exclaimed as she pointed past Sung and Daniel, "Oh, there he is now."

Clara looked up and she could see her Guardian Panda lumbering toward her. Upon seeing him, the Guardian Tiger and Crane also moved toward the meal table.

As the graceful Guardian Crane moved around, she nodded at Clara as she said, "Empress Warrior Wu, *ohayo gozaimasu.*"

Clara nodded and responded, "*Domo arigato.*"

The muscular and agile Guardian Tiger glided onto his seat as he nodded at Clara as he uttered, "*Joh-eun achim.*"

Clara nodded at him and replied, "*Gam-sa-ham-ni-da.*"

The Guardian Panda arrived at the head of the table closest to Clara looking relieved. He looked toward Clara and nodded as he said, "*Zao shang hao*, Empress Warrior Wu."

"You too," said Clara with a smile as the Guardian Panda gave everyone a quick look. Sounding relieved, he said, "You'll be happy to know that the attendants and soldiers were able to inspect all the tent quarters yesterday, and all issues have been resolved."

With a guilty conscience, Clara muttered softly, "I'm sorry."

The Guardian Panda looked reassuringly as his furry black ears flickered. "Empress Warrior Wu, please do not feel bad about what happened yesterday with the earthquake Qi element. As mentioned, you are not the first to shake the earth."

"I see," said Clara curiously. "But I didn't cause the most, I hope?"

"Oh no," said the Guardian Panda, "In Azen's history, a few Panda Warriors also successfully manifested and invoked the earthquake Qi element. We'll work on honing its massive power."

"Speaking of massive," said the Guardian Buffalo as he passed behind Sung and Daniel. "Who here has a massive appetite? Empress Warrior Wu, *buổi sáng tốt lành*."

"You too," said Clara as she nodded to the Guardian Buffalo. "I'm hungry!"

At that moment, several buffalo attendants moved in and placed bowls of soup with a rich broth. It was brimming with rice noodles, sliced onions, and tofu. On top was a thin egg crepe folded in half.

Daniel looked up at the buffalo attendants and hollered out *thank you* in Vietnamese, "*Cảm ơn bạn!*"

The buffalo attendants nodded as Clara, Sung, and Yuka echoed in their best Vietnamese, "*Cảm ơn bạn.*"

Everyone picked up their chopsticks and gently dove into the Vietnamese noodle dish as the Guardian Crane carefully picked at it with her beak in a larger bowl that was provided for her ease.

"Always delicious," said Daniel as his wide eyes looked into the bowl as he shoved a large portion of rice noodles into his mouth. As he enjoyed the rice noodles as glistening broth dripped down them, he put down his chopsticks as he massaged his hands, especially around the fingertips. Clara took notice and smiled as her eyes went back to the thin egg crepe that she began to break apart.

While Clara was gentle with her egg crepe, the Guardian Panda picked up his entire crepe with his chopsticks and stuffed it into his mouth with a wanting appetite. He chewed a few times and swallowed it all. He looked out at the table and asked, "Before we continue our training and building up your Qi elemental arsenal over the next few days, is there anything else that you have learned and what to share?"

Sung, Yuka, and Daniel looked up at each other with blank faces and Clara raised her hand.

The Guardian Panda looked down at Clara curiously, "Empress Warrior Wu, what other Qi elements have you manifested?"

Clara put down her chopsticks and responded, "Well not a new Qi element, but I was able to manifest *teng-bing*, for *wall* with my left hand."

The Guardian Panda's brown eyes widened against his black furry eye patches. "Empress Warrior Wu, you were able to manifest the wall Qi element with your left hand?"

"Yes," said Clara. "But not really well. My right hand was really tired after manifesting one day, so for fun, I was just trying to write the word for wall with my left hand. I don't remember how many times I tried to write it, but finally one did manifest. It was very cool!"

"Wow," said Sung. "You were able to write with your left hand?"

"Yep," said Clara confidently as she turned back to the Guardian Panda. "But what does this mean?"

"It means, Empress Warrior Wu," said the Guardian Panda. "That you'll be able to invoke two Qi elements at the same time. You would have full capabilities of both hands."

"Oh cool!" said an excited Clara. "So, I can invoke any of my manifested Qi elements in battle?"

"Well, not exactly," said the Guardian Panda. "Your left hand can only invoke those Qi elements you've already manifested successfully with your left hand. Your Qi elements are not transferrable from one hand to the other."

"Oh," said Clara with disappointment.

"But it's still a worthy skill," said the Guardian Panda. "You are not the first warrior who exhibited the ability to invoke Qi elements with both hands. However, most of our warriors only had one dominant hand, and therefore we didn't spend much time training their other hand."

"I see," said Clara. "But even though I have a small number of *ten-bings*, I can still invoke *them* with my left hand?"

"Yes," said the Guardian Panda.

"It would be so much faster if I could invoke two icicles at the same time," exclaimed Sung.

"Or two fireballs!" said Daniel enthusiastically.

"Oh Guardian Crane!" beseeched Yuka. "Can we spend a little time this morning trying to write with our left hands?"

The Guardian Crane looked over at the Guardian Panda, who nodded. "I guess it would not hurt if we spent the morning trying, Empress Warrior Satoh," she said. "But you'll need to spend the rest of the afternoon using your right hand to build up your Qi elements."

Yuka gently brought her hands together and smiled, "*Domo arigato!*"

"Well, it looks like we are finished with our delicious breakfast," said the Guardian Panda. "Let's all head to the Portal Circle and see if we can train your non-dominant hand to manifest Qi elements."

* * *

At the Portal Circle, with each of the warriors and their guardians at their Portal Books, Sung, Yuka, and Daniel laughed at their horrible brushing for wall in their respective languages. Only Clara, who had already been practicing, was able to manifest the wall Qi element—but just once. As the bluish Chinese character for wall floated off the page and seeped into her chest, the other warriors became jealous and tried harder. Even their guardians started to gently mock their horrible brushing to the laughter of the other warriors. Daniel put down the brush often and rubbed his hands together between attempts.

As the warriors practiced, Yuka gave off a squeal of happiness at finally manifesting *kabe,* the wall Qi element in Japanese. The red glow of the character reflected in her eyes as it floated toward her and seeped into her chest. She spun around and hopped a few times as if she was reliving the first time she manifested a Qi element.

"Emperor and empress warriors," bellowed out the Guardian Buffalo. "Why don't we take a rest and have lunch? I can see your hands are tired."

Daniel rubbed his hands and nodded. "I agree. My hands can use a rest."

NINE

Daniel brushed off the baguette crumbs from the tasty *banh mi* sandwiches from his lunch. Never did he expect that grilled tofu could be so good in a warm baguette with pickled radishes and carrots. He walked alongside Sung as they followed the Guardian Buffalo and Tiger toward the Gauntlet.

Clara and Yuka, strolling arm in arm, were cheerily following the teenaged boys. Yuka playfully brushed into the air with her left hand and giggled at the earlier moment when she manifested the Qi element for wall, *kabe*: Just the one.

Clara looked at Yuka and asked, "Will that be your secret? Your left-handed *kabe*?"

Yuka gave her a devious stare and said uncharacteristically, "Yes! It will be my one secret weapon."

Yuka and Clara then erupted into laughter as Yuka brought her hand gently to her mouth.

The Guardian Panda and Crane took up the rear, speaking in hushed tones. As they descended toward the Gauntlet, the Guardian Tiger and Buffalo gestured to the warriors to the left. The Guardian Panda and Crane stopped at the center of the Gauntlet's beginning as the Guardian Crane walked behind the Guardian Panda.

"Empress Warrior Wu, please stand by my side," asked the Guardian Panda.

Clara glanced at her fellow warriors, Yuka at her left and Sung and Daniel to her right. She placed her hand on her bow and walked toward the Guardian Panda, who stared back her with his calm brown eyes.

The Guardian Panda turned his gaze down the Gauntlet, pivoted his entire body to face it, and pointed both of his furry paws down the Gauntlet. "Empress Warrior Wu, give me two walls going straight down."

Clara nodded slightly and took a few cautious steps forward, leaving the Guardian Panda behind her to the right. A light wind blew strands of hair across her face, but she gently brushed them back, leaving her hair to wave behind her. She looked down the open dirt path with splotches of grass and weeds and steadied her breath for the double invocation.

In a fluid motion, she brought her hands to her ears and paused. She then extended her hands, brushing into the air and loudly reciting Cantonese for *wall*, "*Ten-bing*!"

In an instant, two Chinese characters for wall appeared at her fingertips, and the sight of them mesmerized Clara. She quickly composed herself and cast both forward and into the ground. The ground rumbled as a wall of dirt rose ten feet in height and fifty feet in length to her right. But the wall on her left sputtered upward a mere two feet and ten feet in length. Clara stared at her unequal creations, which she had envisioned quite differently, and suddenly let out a laugh that rippled through her body as she doubled over and heard her friends also laughing. The Guardian Tiger pointed to the stunted wall as the Guardian Buffalo snorted a few times.

Clara turned up at the Guardian Panda, who smiled down at her. There was even a smile on the Guardian Crane's beak as her beady eyes glistened.

Clara straightened up and exclaimed, "Well, that did not go as planned."

The Guardian Panda walked toward Clara as she turned towards him. He gently placed his right paw on Clara's shoulder and said with a smirk, "Certainly not, Empress Warrior Wu."

With a slight motion of his paw, Clara turned toward everyone as the Guardian Panda began to speak reassuringly. "Empress and emperor warriors, as you can see from Empress Warrior Wu's demonstration, commanding the Qi element with your left hand will also take practice. But if time permitted, practice would have allowed Empress Warrior Wu to invoke two walls with one command. It is not an easy task, but to prepare for the next battle, please focus on manifesting with your primary hand to build up your arsenal. Is that clear?"

Clara turned and looked up at her Guardian Panda and said, "Yes, Guardian Panda."

The other warriors also nodded.

* * *

For the rest of the day, the guardians put their young emperor and empress warriors through their paces. The Gauntlet saw heaving walls of dirt rumble upward and collapse as ice walls took their place. Ice walls dripped with water as walls of fire sprung up next to them before flaring up as the air walls fed them. The ground split as ice bridges sailed over them. Gusts of wind barreled along and blew past solid ice bridges as fireballs of all sizes flew past. Sinkholes formed and filled with water. Tornados touched down as streams of fire fed into them.

At the end the of the day, Clara rose on a column of dirt as she watched Yuka and Daniel racing each other through the air. Yuka could always outfly Daniel. As Clara sighed, disappointed that she couldn't fly like her friends, Sung abruptly appeared in front of her, surfing on the tip of his ice bridge.

Clara smiled as he said, "Hop on, I'll take us back to the beginning."

Clara smiled at the offer as he took her hand and gently pulled her onto the tip of the ice bridge. She clumsily pressed her back into Sung's body as he slid his left arm around her waist, which she held with both arms. He invoked the Korean word for bridge, which appeared in a blue glow in his right hand. It was the first time that Clara could see a Korean Qi element up close and soon, with a flick of Sung's hand, the Korean bridge Qi element descended as ice reformed at the tip. They soon spanned the Gauntlet back toward the base.

As the wind sailed through Clara's hair, she didn't notice the ends of her hair slapping Sung in the face. But he didn't let on as Yuka appeared on his left and Daniel on his right. They grinned and focused on landing at the beginning of the Gauntlet, where their guardians were waiting.

The ice bridge descended and slowed. Clara pursed her lips and just as she was a foot off the ground, she could feel Sung loosen his arm from her waist. She pushed off her back foot as she leapt off, taking a couple of steps before coming to a complete stop. Sung also stopped to her right near Daniel. Yuka settled ever so gracefully to Clara's left.

"Well done," said the Guardian Panda as he looked at his fellow guardians. They also nodded in agreement. "You have all invoked all your known battle Qi elements effortlessly, except for the most powerful ones, earthquake, and typhoon. Yes, Empress Warrior Satoh?"

"When can Clara and I try out typhoon and earthquake?"

The Guardian Panda looked at Yuka and said slyly, "As soon as all four of you reverse all your Qi elements in the Gauntlet."

Yuka's eyes widened as she and her fellow warriors stared at the Gauntlet. Down its entire length were ice bridges and walls, dirt columns and walls, and a stationary tornado with a stream of fire spiraling within it. Everyone chuckled as they undid all their Qi elemental creations.

But Clara and Yuka did not invoke earthquakes or typhoons afterwards. Instead, they decided dinner was more appealing.

The next morning, the warriors were busy at their Portal Books, continually manifesting away their arsenal of Qi elements. Everyone's hands were sore, and Daniel found he had to stop often to massage his hands.

After a hearty lunch of *baos* and egg noodles with vegetables, the warriors were back at the Gauntlet, working on their Qi elemental pairing exercises. Paired pillars of dirt sprung up simultaneously as Sung spanned each pair with a slab of ice. Clara then invoked a Qi element to flatten them, causing the large slabs of ice to crash down dramatically. Yuka cocooned fireballs invoked by Daniel. Then with a gust of air, she sent the fiery cocoons against the Gauntlet wall, where their fiery payloads exploded on impact. It was a new trick that Yuka had devised, and Daniel smiled at how well it worked. Yuka looked at Daniel and invoked a tornado behind him. Instinctively, he fed it with a stream of fire, a deadly pairing.

A strange rumbling came from the ground, and Yuka and Daniel flew up as a hole appeared beneath them. It wasn't a sinkhole, but the end of a tunnel. Yuka and Daniel looked at Clara and Sung, who were still at the beginning of the Gauntlet. Yuka gestured to Daniel, who smiled as he invoked the stream Qi element, releasing a stream of fire from his hand into the tunnel with intense ferocity.

"Whoa," said Sung. "Can you hear that?"

Clara nodded as she heard the rumbling of something moving towards them from within the tunnel. Sung, knowing what Daniel had invoked, invoked the water Qi element and sent a torrent of water into the entrance of the tunnel. In seconds, they heard the muffled but unmistakable crash of fire and water. Sprays of water splashed from the hole, but Sung kept at it until water no longer splashed back. The dark, muddy water in the hole sloshed gently back and forth as Yuka and Daniel flew back and touched down near Clara and Sung.

"Clara," said Daniel as she looked up. "What do you think we can use that for?"

"A trap, maybe? Lure in the enemy and when they are in, you can scorch them?" said Clara as she then turned to Sung. "Or you can drown them?"

"Smart," said Sung.

"Emperor Warrior Kim is correct," exclaimed the Guardian Tiger. "Sometimes, your Qi elemental pairings can be accidental."

"Emperor Warrior Nguyen," said the Guardian Buffalo. "Is your hand sore?"

Daniel suddenly felt all eyes on him as he unconsciously massaged his hands. "Oh, it's nothing. Just a lot manifesting."

"Very well," said the Guardian Buffalo. "You have all exceeded the goals for the day, I believe we can feast on an early dinner. Guardian Panda, what is on the Chinese menu tonight?"

"*Da bin lo*," said the Guardian Panda calmly.

Clara's eyes lit up as she exclaimed, "*Da bin lo*? We're having hot pot?"

The Guardian Panda nodded with a smile.

At dinner that night, Clara was eating joyously and found she had to show Daniel how to enjoy hot pot. The meal table was filled with assorted veggies, everything from cabbage, leafy greens, and taro root. There were varied types of tofu from firm slices, fried tofu skin and puffed tofu. As the steamed broth filled the evening air, the warriors and guardians happily indulged in all the delicious foods of an Azen hot pot.

By the next afternoon, after a morning of manifesting that was beginning to tire everyone's hands, the Gauntlet was filled with crushed melons that had been shot down with arrows or struck with moon stars. Countless boulders of varying sizes had been pulverized with the club horn or shattered with the Claw Staff.

For their last exercise, the warriors were put through the Gauntlet individually. After Daniel burst apart the large bamboo attack dummies with his fireballs, evaded flying arrows, smashed through rock barriers, and finally sent fireballs into the chests of the buffalos from the Rammers, Daniel was the first to cross over the white line.

Yuka also quickly flew through her course as her powerful gusts pushed the attack dummies back against the Gauntlet walls. She trapped flying arrows in air walls and encased archers in cocoons of air. Finally, she easily flew around the agile Prowler tigers, kicking them away before gracefully crossing over the white line.

Sung barreled through the Gauntlet, trapping his attack dummies behind ice walls. He shattered incoming arrows with icicles and encased panda spearmen in ice. He parried members of the Prowlers with his Tae Kwon Do prowess until they were about to get the best of him. But he soon felled each of them with an icicle to their chest armor as he confidently stepped over the white line.

Finally, Clara stepped through. Before the attack dummies could get near her, she used her dual Qi elemental skill and split the earth beneath them, causing them to tumble in. She raced toward the archers, and after quickly averting the first volley of arrows, she raised two dirt walls to block their line of sight. As panda spearmen came toward her, she invoked twin walls that pushed them back and pinned them against the Gauntlet wall. She placed three arrows into her bow and collapsed the dirt wall on her right. She sent three glowing green jade-tipped arrows squarely into the chest armor of each archer, then did the same to the three archers on her left. She raced into the last section to confront the lumbering members of the Pandemonium Squad. She dispatched the closest two with arrows to the chest and pushed the third back against the Gauntlet wall with a dirt wall. She flipped over the Head of the Pandemonium Squad, Xi Peng, as he attempted to charge at her. When she landed, she delivered a firm sidekick to his chest. But this only pushed him back a couple of steps before he charged at her with his spear. In an instant, she sent up a column of dirt underneath his feet, sending him ten feet into the air. As he tried to find his footing, the column of dirt collapsed beneath him, sending him to the ground with a thud. As his daze cleared, Clara's face appeared above him with her arrow pulled taut in the Bow of Destiny aimed at his forehead. The Head of the Pandemonium Squad blinked and uttered, "I yield."

Clara smiled and slid the arrow back into her quiver as she slung the bow across her chest. She pivoted to the side of Xi Peng and with both hands, grabbed his furry paw and helped him up onto his two padded feet. Though beaten, he straightened up and bowed to Clara and she did the same.

Clara gleefully turned away and crossed over the white line as she let her hands relax at her sides.

"Finished!" said Clara confidently as her fellow warriors clapped and the guardians nodded in approval.

"Indeed, Empress Warrior Wu," said the Guardian Panda. "Your dual Qi elemental prowess is getting much better."

"It's so much more efficient," said Clara. "What's next, Guardian Panda?"

The Guardian Panda turned to the Guardian Buffalo and Crane and then to his left at the Guardian Tiger. He looked back at Clara and said, "Empress Warrior Wu, the four of you have sped through your review and training. You are ahead of schedule, as the next lunar eclipse will not be upon us for a few more days. We can rehearse any training that anyone of you may like."

There was silence from the warriors until Clara asked, "Guardian Panda and guardians, I have a favor to ask."

The Guardian Panda's right eye rose as he responded. "A favor, Empress Warrior Wu?"

"Yes," said Clara respectfully. "As this may be the last time we may be in Azen, could we visit each other's kingdoms? There is so much I want to show everyone at Bamboo City."

Yuka turned toward the guardians and pleaded with her palms together, "Oh, please let us, Guardian Crane!"

"It'll be like a field trip!" exclaimed Sung.

"Field trip? Who calls it a field trip?" teased Daniel. "A day trip. I have yet to have anyone visit the palace. Could I have them over, Guardian Buffalo?"

The sudden teenage pleadings overwhelmed the Guardian Panda, but he quickly composed himself and said, "Empress and emperor warriors, I believe that we can accommodate that. I think seeing each other's kingdoms would be beneficial for all of you as well. Tomorrow morning then, a… day trip, as Emperor Warrior Nguyen had called it."

The warriors cheered. And for a moment, they were not warriors but simply curious Asian American teenagers.

TEN

Clara's green robe flowed over her as she squinted against the chilly headwind. As she shifted her thighs atop Shiori, she was grateful for the magnetically sealed front edging of the robe that warded off the cold. She was flying solo that morning as the guardians were preparing their kingdoms for their visits.

She left Bamboo Tower earlier than usual to fly toward Crane Castle. She was looking forward to the tour.

Her ears perked up as Shiori squawked and pointed ahead. Clara nodded, glancing over Shiori's left shoulder. Her eyes took in the chain of dormant volcanic islands, but she knew which one they were headed for: It was the largest of them all, an island with black-ridged terrain encircled by sandy black beaches. But at its base and around the entire dormant volcano were lush green treetops. Interspersed among the trees were the spires of large *tō* towers. From her higher vantage point before the descent, she saw in the center of the collapsed volcano the magnificent and majestic Crane Castle, which glistened for a fleeting moment in the morning sun.

Clara felt Shiori descending, and she gripped the harness tighter and pushed forward into her nape. They leveled out as they flew above the waters, aiming for the treetops ashore. They passed over the black sandy beaches as Shiori's belly seemed to skim across the treetops. A few squawks were exchanged between Shiori and the cranes stationed within the slender *tō* towers. They whizzed by the outermost *tō* towers unimpeded.

Clara looked ahead as the green treetops started to become sparse. They headed toward the barren side of the volcano, where she could feel Shiori ascending. With a few graceful flaps, they flew up along the side of the volcano before they crested the rocky rim of the caldera. A few more squawks were exchanged with cranes in the sentinel *tō* towers before Shiori quickly dove downward.

By the time Clara's stomach fell back into place and she'd exhaled in relief, she saw it: Crane Castle. It was as beautiful as it was large. It had no equal back in Japan as far as she could tell. How the cranes built such a magnificent structure, she had no idea. Its multi-floor construction was unparalleled, covered in what appeared to be rice paper partitions. It was just catching the morning sun that crept over the caldera and the tall, topmost, red-lacquered spire glistened. Being nestled in the calming waters of the caldera provided an added touch of Zen.

Shiori calmly aimed for the hangar opening. Clara stared ahead with a grin as Crane Castle loomed ahead. In an instant, Shiori flew in, and she could hear the change in the air going from outdoors to indoors. With a few flaps of the crane's wings, she landed onto the bamboo deck.

Shiori twisted her head around as her beady eye looked at Clara. "Empress Warrior Wu, we have arrived."

Clara smiled as she started to unfasten the clip from the harness as she replied cheerily in Japanese for *thank you*, "*Domo arigato*."

Clara carefully slid off the crane and landed on both feet when she heard, "*Ohayo gozaimasu*!"

Clara turned to see Yuka approaching her with a grin. Yuka stopped a few feet away from Clara and she bowed with her hands clasped at her waist. Clara responded in the best Japanese she could muster for *good morning*, "*Ohayo gozaimasu*."

Yuka looked up with an approving smile. "Your Japanese is getting really good!"

Clara grinned and approached Yuka and asked, "And the others?"

Yuka pointed over her left shoulder, and Clara saw Sung toward the back of the hangar. He was admiring the shiny and sharp *katana* wings hanging from the ceiling. A pair could slide out on each side along metal tracks hung above. They were positioned so that a crane could walk between them to have them clipped onto its outer wings. Once so armed, they could fly out to protect Crane Castle.

"There are fifty *katana* wings on each side of the arming section per channel. From this hangar alone, two hundred *katana*-winged cranes can fly out at a moment's notice. Amazing, right?" asked Yuka proudly.

Clara nodded when her attention was diverted to the front of the hangar as another crane flew in. It landed gracefully and settled onto the bamboo deck. As the crane tipped its head, Daniel's head popped up.

Yuka took a step past Clara, and as the representative for the Red Crown Crane Kingdom, she bowed respectfully as she greeted Daniel. "*Ohayo gozaimasu*!"

Once Daniel slid off the crane, he responded with a smile and bowed back to Yuka. As he came toward them in his red robe, he parted the front white edging, where the white embroidered buffalo's head ruffled slightly.

"Hey guys," said Sung as he walked toward Clara and Yuka, who turned towards him. "You need to check out the *katana* wings, they are awesome!"

"They are," said Yuka proudly. "They're forged from Clawdium too."

"That's what the crane told me as well," said Sung.

"I'm so glad you're all here!" said Yuka gleefully as she brought her hands together. "There is so much I want you to see!"

"Empress Warrior Satoh," said the Guardian Crane as she gracefully came upon the warriors.

All eyes fell on the Guardian Crane as they nodded toward her. Then in clumsy unison, they said, "*Ohayo gozaimasu*!"

The Guardian Crane smiled and echoed their greeting. "Before we begin our tour of Red Crown Crane Kingdom, a delightful breakfast is waiting for you. Please hop onto your designated cranes, and we'll fly up to the meal hall. Also, out of respect for Crane Castle, please do not invoke your Qi elemental powers."

Everyone nodded as they went back to their feathered escorts and followed the Guardian Crane with Yuka atop of her. The cranes flapped and flew toward the back of the hangar. Daniel was enthralled by the throngs of *katana* wings. A pair of partition doors slid open, and they flew gently past them into another room. At the center of that room was a large circular opening in the floor and ceiling. A crane swooshed from above and through the opening below. The Guardian Crane flew around the circle as the other cranes spiraled behind her. The Guardian Crane quickly peered up and down and seeing that there were no oncoming cranes, flew upward through the circular opening. They flew past a few floors, and the Guardian Crane flew onto a floor and landed.

Several crane attendants were waiting. As the warriors slid off their cranes, a crane attendant came up behind them.

"Empress Warrior Wu and Emperor Warriors Kim and Nguyen," the crane attendant said. "You'll no longer need your robes. Please remove your weapons from them, and a crane attendant will take them.

Clara nodded and unslung her bow as a crane attendant gently took it in its beak. Another crane took her quiver. A voice from behind asked her, "Empress Warrior Wu, please sweep your hair away from the back of your neck." Clara nodded as she gathered her hair and pulled it forward over her left shoulder. She felt an upward nudge as the third crane attendant grabbed the back of her robe by its beak. Clara placed her hands off to the sides and with a swift up-and-down tug, the attendant crane peeled off the robe. Clara looked up and couldn't help grinning at the sight of the robe in the crane's beak. A fourth crane came into view and asked her to follow. Clara was surprised by all the attention but started to follow the fourth crane, who was draped in a silk robe with a cute *obi* on her back. The cranes followed her, carrying all her items in their beaks.

Walking ahead of Clara was Yuka, who had gone through a similar experience of de-robing, and was now following the Guardian Crane. A crane attendant followed holding Yuka's robe.

Behind Clara was Sung, who followed the crane attendants carrying his Claw Staff and his blue robe in their beaks. Daniel took up the rear with a similar formation of cranes.

As they approached a rice-paper-partitioned wall, it slid back to reveal a large expansive room. The far wall was open as the sun was just rising over the rim of the caldera. In the middle was a large white table with a red circle in the middle. Five bamboo chairs ringed the large circular table. The Guardian Crane turned around and asked, "Empress warriors to your right and emperor warriors, to your left. Breakfast will be served."

"Follow me, Clara!" said Yuka excitedly.

The Guardian Crane flew over the table and took the seat directly opposite the entrance. Yuka sat to the Guardian Crane's left, followed by Clara, then Sung and Daniel.

As they sat, the crane attendants placed their weapons in a cylindrical bamboo container and draped their robes over a bamboo rack that had been set up behind each chair.

Clara looked to her right. Yuka was some twenty feet away. She felt awkwardly small at the large table and chuckled when Yuka waved at her. Her eyes shifted left and she saw Sung and wondered if he felt the same as he waved. Sung then turned to his left and fist bumped Daniel from afar. He returned the gesture, and Clara had to laugh as he was at least twenty feet away.

Clara's eyes then fell onto the red circle in the middle of the table when she said, "It's like the Japanese flag!"

Yuka chuckled as she shook her head playfully.

"What's so funny?" asked Clara.

"I thought so too," said Yuka. "But it's not. It's the red crown on the cranes head!"

Clara looked back at the red circle and then at the red feathers and crown atop the Guardian Crane's head and her eyes widened in realization, "Oh!"

But soon, Clara was distracted as a multitude of cranes flew in. From strings held in their beaks, one gently plopped down a beautifully decorated box with a lid. Another crane placed a tray to her left, and on it were an empty teacup and a small metal tea kettle.

"It's a bento box!" hollered Yuka to everyone.

As the cranes flew away, Clara pulled the tray toward her. She lifted off the lid and was astonished to see the beautiful assortment of food. There were slices of *tamago*, rice balls, maki rolls, and a fruit that looked like an orange.

The Guardian Crane shifted her head as the warriors took delight in their breakfast bento box. She then spoke, "Empress and emperor warriors, please enjoy this simple breakfast before we enjoy a morning of touring Red Crown Crane Kingdom. As we eat, Empress Warrior Satoh, please think of the places that you'd like your fellow warriors to see."

Yuka responded excitedly as she clicked the chopsticks in her hand. "There is so much to see! I would like for my friends to see the hatchery, The Nest, the jade's smith, the silkworms, the Top Talon hangar, the Eagle's hangar, The Lava Blossom, The Ascending of course, the…"

But before Yuka could continue with her never-ending list, the Guardian Crane gently interrupted her. "Empress Warrior Satoh, I'm so touched that there are so many places in Red Crown Crane Kingdom that you want to show to your fellow warriors, but we won't have the time. We'll need to fly toward Claw Mountain for lunch. I'm afraid you'll have to choose only three places to visit."

Yuka frowned and sighed. She realized that all the places that she wanted to go could have very well been an entire day. She thought for a moment then looked up at the Guardian Crane. "Guardian Crane, if I can only choose three, then I'd like to show them the hatchery, the silkworms, and The Lava Blossom."

The Guardian Crane nodded and replied, "Empress Warrior Satoh, that we can do. Everyone, please enjoy your breakfast."

With that, Clara eagerly picked up her chopsticks and picked up a rice ball that she was eyeing. She bit into it and her face melted as the blended flavors of fresh mushrooms, bamboo, and something crunchy burst with flavor. The rest of the warriors also took in the delicate flavors within their bento box.

After their breakfast, Clara quickly tied back her hair with the bamboo hair accessory that she had tucked into the robe's inner pocket. A crane helped her back into her robe before she swung the quiver and the bow across her body. Yuka walked alongside Clara and slid her right arm into Clara's left arm. Clara smiled as Yuka said, "Let's go!"

Clara and Yuka quickened their pace as Sung and Daniel followed, adjusting their weapons along their backs. The Guardian Crane gently flew over them and through the entrance. There, Clara could see their waiting cranes.

Yuka let go of Clara and remarked, "I have a favor to ask of the Guardian Crane, but I'll see you at the first destination. Clara nodded with a smile as Yuka dashed off.

Yuka reached the Guardian Crane and asked, "Guardian Crane, before we visit the hatchery, could we fly through The Ascending?"

The Guardian Crane looked down at Yuka, then looked at everyone else mounting their cranes. She looked back down at Yuka and asked, "Just a fly-by?"

Yuka nodded and clasped her hands in front of her, pleading. The Guardian Crane would do anything for her Crane Warrior, so she assented.

"*Domo arigato!*" said Yuka appreciatively as she bowed. Without any hesitation, she mounted the Guardian Crane and secured herself with the harness.

The Guardian Crane turned on her talons and faced everyone else, "Empress and emperor warriors, before we visit the hatchery, we are going to fly through The Ascending, which is a sacred place where we honor all of our past Crane Warriors. But before we do that, please ensure you are securely harnessed in."

Everyone nodded. But Clara suddenly had a sinking feeling. Clara fidgeted with a magnetic strap around the rim of her quiver to lock in her arrows and pulled the Bow of Destiny tight against her chest. She was confirming the clasp was firmly fastened when she heard Sung and Daniel saying from behind, "Ready, Guardian Crane."

Clara looked up as Yuka stared back at her with a mischievous smile. She didn't want to, but felt compelled to ask, "Where are we going?"

Yuka replied simply, "Down."

The Guardian Crane shot upward and swiftly dove while Yuka turned ahead. Clara felt Shiori jolt upward before shooting toward the circular opening in the floor. In an instant, they were diving straight down, and Clara pressed herself into the feathers of her crane. She could feel the rush of the wind whipping past her face as they passed one floor after another. Clara's eyes widened as she watched the Guardian Crane and Yuka diving toward a solid floor. But before what seemed like an inevitable crash, curved metal blades spiraled away, revealing a dark abyss.

Shiori dove through, with Sung and Daniel following on their cranes. It was dark, but as her crane leveled out, Clara let out a sigh as she saw that her crane was following the Guardian Crane into a large dark cavern. Clara looked about the rocky walls lit by illumination jades. As Clara looked up and saw what looked like a tiny hole through which they had dived from, she suddenly realized where she was: inside the dormant volcano!

Suddenly, her queasiness was replaced by awe as they continued to spiral downward and outward following the Guardian Crane. Clara looked right, where she could see many openings in the rocky walls. Soon, the Guardian Crane flew directly toward one of the openings. Clara herself would not have chosen to fly through it, but the Guardian Crane did just that as Clara gripped the harness tighter and gulped as they entered the tunnel. Despite her fear, she also felt a sense of excitement as Shiori gracefully flew through the tunnel, and just when she asked herself when the tunnel would end, they flew into a large rocky chamber.

Shiori gently swooped right and followed the Guardian Crane with Sung and Daniel following on their cranes in single file. As Clara looked around to take in the giant chamber, she realized to her astonishment that she was inside a large magma pocket. Along the wall was a continuous ledge that must have been carved into the rocky chamber at some point. Clara heard her name and looked up to see Yuka looking at her. Yuka pointed upward and Clara looked up.

Clara's jaw dropped at the sight of a large collection of pearl shaped illumination jades that resembled a bunch of grapes dangling from the apex of the magma pocket. But that wasn't what really surprised her. Rather, it was the figures floating in mid-air. Dangling from the top of the magma pocket from chains were several concentric metal rings. From these hung figures dangling from metal cords.

The Guardian Crane gently rose as the gentle wind from her wings brushed up against the human figures. As Clara got a better look at them, she realized to her astonishment that they were not solid statues as light peeped through their joints. On the pass of a second figure, she could see that each part of the metal body was delicately and elaborately crafted. As she passed the third figure, she finally saw how the figures were created: they were assembled with metallic *origami* pieces!

She could see that they were teenage boys and girls in different flight poses: the Japanese Crane Warriors past. As they swayed gently, the light from the illumination jades revealed their facial features. Their faces were shaped from a single piece of metal, giving them a smooth complexion. She saw their young faces looking back at her. There was something majestic and serene about seeing them all suspended in their natural airy environment.

The Guardian Crane was approaching the top when she passed the last Japanese Crane Warrior and gently started to descend toward the tunnel entrance. Soon, the cranes flew through the tunnel and back into the dimly lit dormant volcano. In single file, they all few up through the hole into Crane Castle.

As Clara kept her eye on Yuka in front of her, she could feel the weight of gravity pulling her downward and gripped the harness even tighter, while pressing her thighs harder into her crane. As they flew past several floors, the Guardian Crane flew into a floor and Clara's crane followed suit. As Clara was enjoying feeling level again, she saw that they were on the hangar deck and were flying straight through as they exited into the warm sky. Clara looked behind her and she could see Sung and Daniel with excited grins.

Clara faced forward and inhaled the fresh air as she leveled her sights on Yuka's back. They flew out of the caldera, swooped down the volcano's side, and flew over a large patch of thick trees. In a clearing, she saw a wide Japanese structure only a few floors tall. The Guardian Crane gently swooped in and landed on the dirt ground in front of the main entrance. As soon as everyone landed and dismounted their cranes, the warriors gathered, and Yuka came to meet them.

"Did you see them?" asked Yuka.

"Were those the warriors that came before you?" asked Sung excitedly.

Yuka nodded. "I wish I could have introduced each of them to you, but we didn't have time. But wasn't it amazing how they were flying?"

"Were the figures all *origami*?!" asked Clara excitedly.

"Yes!" said Yuka proudly! "Each Crane Warrior was created using lots of *origami* pieces using Clawdium sheets. They were attached to a frame that matched their pose. Except for the face of course. They carefully shaped the faces using a Clawdium sheet but everything else was Clawdium *origami*!"

"That was tight!" said Daniel.

"Tight?" asked Yuka.

"You know," said Daniel. "Like how all the pieces were fitted so carefully together, tight!"

"Ah, tight," said Yuka. "Yes, tight they were!"

"That's tight!" echoed Clara. "What's next?"

Yuka squinted her eyes in glee as she said, "The cutest thing. The Hatchery!"

Yuka grabbed Clara by the arm and led her to the front entrance of The Hatchery. It was a long, wide three-level building of classic Japanese design. Both Clara and Yuka hopped onto the bamboo flooring followed by the others. The Guardian Crane was already present, and she was wiping her feet on a mat. Two crane attendants, who also had a *kimono* fabric draped over their backs with an *obi*, bowed and slid open the tall, wide doors.

As the Guardian Crane entered, Clara was wide eyed as she entered the room. It was laid out like a checkerboard, and each square held meticulously arranged nesting material. Several crane attendants were walking about. They bowed as they saw the Guardian Crane, who reciprocated. Bamboo pathways connected the hatching squares. But what caught Clara's attention were the large white eggs nestled ever so carefully in the middle of the nesting material. Some of the hatching squares had one egg, some had two, while others had three. In a few of the hatching squares were pairs of doting cranes.

Yuka ran to a hatching square and beckoned for everyone to follow quietly. They leaned against a rail by the square, where they saw two large white eggs. At the top of each egg was a Japanese name. The Guardian Crane came up to the left of Yuka.

As Sung's eyes fell onto the two large white eggs, he asked incredulously, "Are those what I think they are?"

Yuka nodded and said, "This is The Hatchery. It's where all expectant cranes lay their eggs and are cared for. They are kept warm until they hatch. So cute, right?"

"Oh my god, so cute!" exclaimed Clara. "And the Japanese on the eggs?"

"Oh, that's the family name," said Yuka. "Beautiful, isn't it?"

"Very," said Daniel, looking astounded. "So there are like baby cranes?"

"There are!" said Yuka. "Guardian Crane has a young son. He and I played *go* a number of times!"

"No way!" said Sung as his mouth dropped open as he tried to imagine Yuka playing the game of *go* with a young crane.

"I stayed here one day for a few hours until one of the eggs hatched," said Yuka. "It was so cute! But you have to be really patient, so I don't think we'll see one hatching today."

"Yes, Empress Warrior Satoh," said the Guardian Crane. "We should prepare to go to our next destination."

"Silkworms?" asked Yuka.

"Yes," said the Guardian Crane. "I think your fellow warriors will enjoy seeing where our Azen silk comes from."

After another trip to a smaller island, the warriors soon found themselves inside a large glass enclosure. It was warm and filled with bamboo stalks that yielded larger-than-usual bamboo leaves.

"These guys are huge!" said Sung as he struggled to hold in his hands a squirming white silkworm that was about a foot long. Its head was writhing, and its many feet were wiggling in place as Clara stood behind a giggling Yuka in fear and admiration. The sound of munching was all around them as hundreds, if not thousands, of large silkworms were voraciously eating bamboo leaves. Daniel spun around and held a bamboo leaf that was larger than his entire torso.

"I can't get over the size of these leaves!" said Daniel incredulously. "No wonder these silkworms are so big!"

"Emperor Warrior Kim and Nguyen," admonished gently the Guardian Crane. "Let's put the silkworm back down, and let's not play with its food."

"Oh yes," said Sung with embarrassment. "Let me put this guy back."

"Will do, Guardian Crane," said Daniel awkwardly as he extended the large bamboo leaf to the silkworm that Sung had just placed back onto the ground. It took it without hesitation and started to munch along its length.

"Please follow me," said the Guardian Crane as she walked down the length of the glass enclosure and into the next section. Clara's eyes panned upward at the large bamboo lattice that was about thirty feet tall. She looked left and right and the bamboo lattice extended all the way down and there were at least a hundred rows of them. But from each lattice, hung on each side, were hundreds of white cocoons that were evenly spaced out.

"Whoa!" said Clara.

"Amazing, right?" asked Yuka.

"I have a bad feeling about this," said Daniel.

"Why?" asked Sung as his eyes wandered all about.

"Have you ever seen the movie *Alien*?" asked Daniel.

Sung's eyes widened as his eyes came to level with Daniel's, "Oh!"

"When the silkworms cocoon themselves amongst the bamboo stalks," the Guardian Crane explained. "The cranes take them here. They are gently hung onto this bamboo lattice. The most recent ones are toward the back and the more mature ones are rotated to the front. Please follow me."

The Guardian Crane walked along the bamboo-decked path as the warriors continued to look in awe at the thousands of hanging white silken cocoons. Soon, they heard a buzzing noise. It was intermittent, and a cold shiver shot down Daniel's spine. He rushed up alongside Sung, and he heard the buzzing noise again. As Daniel spun around, he saw two large eyes flying at him and he let out a shriek and cowered away, pulling Sung along with him. The large moth buzzed them and flew harmlessly away.

"What was that?!" asked Daniel as he cautiously rose with his right forearm covering his head.

Sung laughed as he rose, as Yuka and Clara giggled as well, even though Clara looked pensively about.

"That, Emperor Warrior Nguyen," said the Guardian Crane, "is a mature silkworm moth. They usually fly through the openings at the top of this structure. Once they wiggle out of their cocoons, our cranes harvest the cocoons and bring them to the next section."

The Guardian Crane walked ahead as the warriors followed briskly.

In the next section of the very long glass enclosure were hundreds of empty cocoons stacked neatly in square bins. Several cranes were working in the area. Some were inspecting the newly harvested cocoons. Others fed the cocoons into contraptions that unwound the silken thread onto spools. And at the end, there were stacks of spun Azen silk, which were stronger than anything on Earth.

"Things like your robes were all spun from these silkworms," said the Guardian Crane. "When we want the pliability of silk but the strength of the mesh body armor, they are interwoven with Clawdium threads that our fellow battle tigers wear along with our crane aviators."

"This is like the best day trip ever!" exclaimed Daniel.

"It is the best, isn't it?" asked Yuka. "But you haven't seen the best yet! We have one more place to go."

"Where's that?" asked Daniel curiously.

"The Lava Blossom," Yuka said mysteriously.

* * *

Shiori raced through the air and was about five crane lengths behind the Guardian Crane and Yuka. Clara's green robe ruffled in the wind. She turned and saw Sung immediately behind her and Daniel in the last position.

A squawk made Clara turn her head forward as Shiori said, "Empress Warrior Wu, The Lava Blossom is straight ahead."

Clara looked past the feathery neck of her crane. Out in the water, she saw a dark volcanic island with fantastic dark arches sprouting from the center and over the sides of the island. Unlike the previous volcanic islands of Red Crown Crane Kingdom, no beaches surrounded it. Instead, there were cliffs. They were sheer and jagged, but sprouting from them were sheets of lava, frozen in time.

As Shiori spread her wings to descend toward the island, she spoke. "Empress Warrior Wu. Welcome to The Lava Blossom. Long ago, before Crane Kingdom came to be, this violent volcano thrust upward from the seabed, sending lava everywhere. Streams of lava oozed into the ocean. We believe the violent rise of this volcano also triggered a massive tsunami that washed over the volcano and solidified all the lava in an instant, leaving these amazing lava arches. From the top, it looks like a blossoming flower."

Clara's eyes lit up. "All those arches were lava flowing into the ocean and the tsunami froze them?"

Shiori's beady eyes rolled backwards for a moment before gazing back out as she began to descend. "Yes, all these structures were once molten lava, but the tsunami froze its young life in time. Do you see the sheets of lava flowing over the edge at the center?"

"Yes," said Clara.

"Those were once sheets of lava that flowed into the ocean. What was left were all these beautiful structures with crevices and openings. The Top Talon team uses them as a training course for their Top Talon candidates."

Clara's eyes widened as she asked alarmingly, "We're not going to fly through them, are we?"

"No, Empress Warrior Wu," said Shiori. "I'm a junior Top Talon candidate on escort duties."

Clara let out a sigh of relief as she replied, "You're still a very good flier."

"*Domo arigato.* But to complete your tour," said the crane. "We will fly through the larger arches. Hold on!"

Before Clara could answer, she felt her crane dive and immediately gripped onto her harness. She pressed the side of her face into the right side of the crane's neck and could see Yuka staring back with a mischievous grin. *What was she up to?* thought Clara.

As Clara's crane flew low, barely ten feet above the water, she could feel the ocean mist beneath her and hear the sound of lapping water everywhere. As they neared the island, she could see the dark, sheer cliffs. Clara looked up against the bright blue sky, in awe of the colossal lava arches that once flowed from the cliffs and into the ocean. Waves crashed loudly into the lava arch that dove into the water. As they flew out from underneath the first lava arch, Clara could see a series of lava arches of varying shapes and sizes.

The crane veered right under a small lava arch, then veered left and under another larger lava arch. The sounds of the water crashing against the lava arches and the cliffs was deafening. A double lava arch loomed ahead, the closest being the smaller of the two. Shiori rose sharply upward as Clara gripped the harness as tightly as she could. They flew over the arch and suddenly dove downward beneath the second arch. As they lurched back up, Clara could feel her breakfast bouncing around in her stomach. But Shiori finally leveled out and followed the Guardian Crane as she gently soared upward.

Clara looked down, admiring the other lava arches as they soared around The Lava Blossom. It was as beautiful as it was treacherous. She looked ahead and saw Yuka waving back at her as she pointed past her. Clara turned around and saw that Sung was all smiles while Daniel, bent over to his right, was facing away from them. Shiori's squawk brought Clara's attention forward as the Guardian Crane flew away from The Lava Blossom toward White Tiger Kingdom.

ELEVEN

Clara felt a crispness in the air as they ascended. She was certain that she was flying higher than she had ever been as wisps of clouds passed by. The chill against her face felt like miniature icicles, prompting her to pull her robe tighter to keep the warmth within. She had only visited Claw House once, when Sung was recuperating from his encounter with the *gumiho.*

Shiori opened her wings to slow their descent as Clara looked ahead. The wispy white clouds were starting to dissipate when she finally saw Claw House with its triple-tiered, navy-grayish-metallic sloping roof. Atop the flattened mountaintop was the massive four-sided stone fortress with an imposing stone staircase that led up to the main entrance. Like all the buildings in Azen, it was large and impressive.

Clara smiled at the thought of the Korean food that must be awaiting them, since it was a bit past noon. She wondered what places Sung was going to show them during the tour and then she got to wondering, *what would she show her friends?* It was fortunate that the tour of Bamboo City would be last. She couldn't decide among the many places.

Clara gripped her harness and kept her eyes on the Guardian Crane on final approach as Shiori opened her wings and lowered her legs. They were approaching the expansive stone terrace that was laid in front of the main entrance of Claw House. Standing in front of Claw House was the Guardian Tiger.

The Guardian Crane flapped her wings one final time, gracefully landing on the stone surface in front of the main entrance. Her talons clicked a few times on the stone, and soon the other three cranes landed behind her. As Clara relaxed her grip, she looked down the stone steps behind her and was glad that she didn't need to climb them. As she fumbled with her harness clip, she was distracted by the pattering of feet on her left as Sung briskly walked by.

Sung looked up at her with a big grin and said, "Come on, Clara!"

Clara smiled as he walked ahead, watching his hair bounce up and down a bit. She looked right and saw that Daniel had just slid off his crane and wobbled a bit as he landed. Looking ahead, she saw Yuka eagerly running after Sung. She finally unfastened herself and carefully slid off Shiori, who she thanked.

Clara stepped onto the stone landing, skipped a short distance, and soon caught up with Yuka, who was standing in front of the Guardian Tiger and Sung. Daniel soon reached Yuka's right side.

"Welcome, emperor and empress warriors, to Claw House," the Guardian Tiger greeted. "I hope your flight here from Crane Castle was a pleasant one."

The Guardian Tiger shifted his steely blue eyes onto Daniel and asked, "Emperor Warrior Nguyen, are you all right?"

Clara and Yuka turned to Daniel who had just wiped his sleeve along his mouth. There was a pause as he muttered, "I threw up."

Both Clara and Yuka looked over at Daniel with curious expressions as he looked embarrassed.

"Well, Emperor Warrior Nguyen," said the Guardian Tiger. "We'll get you cleaned up just in time for the wonderful lunch that we have prepared. But before we head on in, Emperor Warrior Kim, have you decided where you'd like to take your fellow Azen warriors today?"

"I sure have, Guardian Tiger," said Sung eagerly. "I'd like for them to see The Anvil, the Cub's Den, and Soohorang Square."

"Very well, Emperor Warrior Kim," said the Guardian Tiger. "Please follow me to our meal hall, and Emperor Warrior Nguyen, one of the tiger attendants will show you where you may wash up."

"Thank you," said Daniel sheepishly as everyone followed the Guardian Tiger and Sung toward the entrance of Claw House.

As they approached the meal hall, tiger attendants took their robes and weapons, except for Yuka's Moon Star. A tiger attendant led Daniel away as the Guardian Tiger led Sung, Clara, Yuka, and the Guardian Crane through a large doorway where there was a large square table.

Clara stepped into the brightly lit room, where she waited to the left of Sung with Yuka on his right. The Guardian Tiger's white-and-black tail wagged as he slowly turned around and licked his lips for a moment.

"Emperor Warrior Kim," stated the Guardian Tiger. Please take the far seat on the right and empress warriors, please take the two seats to my left."

The warriors nodded as Clara tried to walk past Sung, who unintentionally obstructed her. She smirked and moved to her right as he did the same. They awkwardly blocked each other's paths before Sung stopped and sighed. He kindly looked at Clara and gestured with his hands for her to pass.

Clara smiled sheepishly and walked past Sung, glancing up at him with a smile. He smiled back before confidently striding off to his seat. As Clara reached her seat, Daniel eagerly walked in, and the Guardian Tiger directed him to his seat. Moments later, the Guardian Crane stepped into the room. She motioned her red-crown-feathered head slightly at the Guardian Tiger, who directed her to the seat behind him. He then managed to slide his large body past Clara and Yuka. He rounded the corner and sat in his seat, opposite of the Guardian Crane.

Clara smiled at the ornate slender metal chopsticks and long spoon before her. She eagerly rubbed her palms together in anticipation of the meal when seemingly out of nowhere, stealthy tiger attendants appeared behind everyone. Clara looked up to her left as a fastidious tiger attendant glanced at her. He expertly laid out several small dishes containing a multitude of *ban chans.* Clara's eyes lit up at the sight of the cubed kimchi radish laid down on the table. Clara looked across the way from her to see Daniel, who must have been starving, since he couldn't keep his breakfast down. She looked diagonally and could see that Sung had already picked up his chopsticks in anticipation of the food that he so enjoyed.

As the first tiger departed, Clara turned and said in her best Korean for *thank you*, "*Gam-sa-ham-ni-da.*" Just then, a second tiger appeared on her right. That tiger attendant placed a dark, heavy stone bowl in front of her. Clara could still feel the heat emanating from it. When she looked down into it, she realized that it was *bi bim bap.* Her eyes lit up as her tastebuds salivated as she said "*gam-sa-ham-ni-da,*" once again when another tiger attendant came upon her left. The last tiger attendant placed in front of her some small dishes with assorted red sauces, and a teacup filled with hot tea. Clara nodded and thanked the last tiger.

The Guardian Tiger looked about as he saw a large bowl of the Guardian Crane's favorite Korean dish, long rice cakes, which she enjoyed slurping up. With that, he addressed everyone, "Emperor and empress warriors, please enjoy your lunch."

Sung and Clara both leaned forward with a nod, and both said, "*Gam-sa-ham-ni-da!*" Yuka and Daniel followed suit and also said *thank you* in their best Korean.

Sung's eyes widened and his tongue seemed to almost fall out of his mouth as he looked at the beautifully arranged *bi bim bap*. Pickled carrots, bean sprouts, sliced cucumbers, tofu, and an egg sat on a bed of rice. When he looked over at Daniel, he saw that he was picking at the individual ingredients of the *bi bim bap*. He coughed lightly to get Daniel's attention, and he looked up curiously. Sung reached over for the small dish of *gochujang* and invited Daniel to mimic him as he poured it into the *bi bim bap*. With the spoon and the chopsticks, he mixed up the rice and ingredients of the *bi bim bap* thoroughly. Daniel smiled and did the same.

Yuka tried each of the *ban chans*, and each made her smile. Clara looked to her left as the Guardian Crane eyed the bowl of rice cakes that was made specifically for her. Without hesitation, she dove her beak into them, threw her feathery head back as she slurped up a long strand of rice cake. Clara chuckled as she panned the room as she saw everyone enjoying their food. Her eyes settled on the cubed *kimchi* radish and plucked one out with her chopsticks and placed it into her mouth. Her eyes squinted as she savored the freshness of the crunchy radish and the spice that accentuated it. After picking at a few more *ban chans*, her eyes fixated on the *bi bim bap* and like the others, she thoroughly mixed it, being careful not to spill any of it over the side of the stone bowl. Once mixed, she sank the chopsticks into it and started to enjoy it as she let out a loud, "Mmmmm."

* * *

After their lunch, the warriors were gathered in a circle, facing each other, at the front entrance of Claw House. They donned their robes with all their weapons fastened firmly in place as they chuckled amongst each other.

"You're going to really like seeing The Anvil, or *molu* in Korean," exclaimed Sung.

"*Mo-lu*? What's in there," asked Daniel as the wind caught a bit of his wispy dark brown bangs.

Sung took a half step forward and looked at everyone as he said, "It's where all the Clawdium is forged into weapons!"

Everyone's eyes lit up as Daniel responded, "Really?"

"Not only weapons, Emperor Warrior Nguyen," said the Guardian Tiger as he sauntered up behind them. Everyone turned to him as he settled onto his haunches, his front paws in front of him as he straightened up giving himself a very regal stature.

"Clawdium only exists in Claw Mountain. Deep beneath the mountain, it is mined, processed, refined, and then melted down into its pure form, which makes its way into several of our products," explained the Guardian Tiger. "We won't be going into the mine as it's too dangerous, but we'll see where the Clawdium is forged into many things, such as staffs, spearheads, harpoons…"

"Weapons!" said Sung proudly as the Guardian Tiger gave him a look.

"Guardian Tiger," said Sung respectfully.

"Yes, weapons, but the chopsticks and spoons you used today were also forged from Clawdium. The mesh battle suits that you've seen the tigers wear in battle are made from a blend of Clawdium threads and Azen silk," the Guardian Tiger added. "Follow me and we can descend into The Anvil."

The Guardian Tiger got onto all four paws and walked past the warriors as they followed closely and excitedly down the steps.

They passed over the terrace and came to a section along the front where there were several large dark shafts. Thick metal poles rose up on each side held together by a crossbar at the top that supported a pulley system. Two Clawdium lines ascended from the shafts into the housing that hid the pulley system. The handful of tiger attendants supervising the shafts nodded as they approached. As they waited, Clara looked to her left and right and saw several tiger guards standing stoically as they held Clawdium staffs vertically in front of them.

Soon, two sturdily constructed bamboo lifts emerged from the shafts. They were cylindrical, with four upright metal rails on the outside with metallic wheels attached. These ran along the inner rails set into the walls of the shafts. The top of the bamboo lift was topped off with a Clawdium cap and lit from below with illumination jades.

"One lift should hold the four of you," said the Guardian Tiger. "Emperor Warrior Kim, please get off at The Anvil."

"Yes, Guardian Tiger," said Sung as the Guardian Tiger entered the lift.

With a nod, the lift carrying the Guardian Tiger descended into the shaft as air swooshed loudly upward. Sung gestured to everyone to step into the second lift, which was quite spacious. Everyone grabbed the middle pole as Clara looked up to see the illumination jades. Soon the sky started to fade away as the lift descended and the Clawdium cap eventually blocked the light of the sky.

The illumination jades provided a glowing light from which Clara could see the smooth walls of the shaft. She wondered how the tigers had clawed their way through the mountain to create this space. As they descended, she could see many floors whizzing by, similarly to Bamboo Tower, but what each floor was, she could not tell.

"The tigers carved out chambers into the mountain itself. Claw Mountain is the ultimate protection should they need it," said Sung. "Okay, here's The Anvil. This is going to be so cool, follow me!"

The lift slowed down as an entrance came into view. Beyond it was a chamber where Clara could hear a lot of clanging. As she and everyone stepped off, she spun around to see the lift continue to descend. The low growl of the Guardian Tiger caused her to turn back around as he greeted everyone.

"Emperor and empress warriors," said the Guardian Tiger. "Please follow me."

The Guardian Tiger spun around as his tail swayed. The warriors followed him with Sung and Daniel in the lead as Clara and Yuka followed.

Clara looked up at the high ceiling chamber that was somehow hollowed out of the mountain itself. To her left were stacks of Clawdium cubes, each measuring one foot on all sides. Clara and Yuka rushed up to one of the stacks, which were about five feet high and ten feet wide on each side. Looking around, Clara saw rows of the Clawdium stacks that filled the long rectangular chamber. Further down, she could see rows of seemingly tall blast furnaces and many tiger forgers.

Yuka tugged on Clara's sleeve, getting her attention. Yuka's fingers pointed to the imprint on the side of the Clawdium cube. It was in the shape of a tiger's paw.

Yuka turned to Clara and flashed her open palm at Clara, which made Clara laugh.

"It's the final seal," said Sung. "It means that it has passed all inspections for purity, weight, and strength."

"Emperor Warrior Kim is correct," said the Guardian Tiger as he moved alongside Clara. "Clawdium has special properties aside from its strength. You already know its special magnetic properties. But it's also very light, yet stronger than other metals. Empress Warrior Wu, why don't you lift off the corner cube?"

Clara's look of surprise pleased the Guardian Tiger as he nodded in encouragement. Clara carefully placed her hands on the corner cube and expected to pull hard, but she was shocked at how easily she pulled it off the stack. What should have weighed ten to twenty pounds seemed to weigh only a pound at most.

"It's so light!" exclaimed Clara.

"Can I hold it?" asked Yuka and before she was ready, Clara playfully tossed it to Yuka.

Expecting to struggle catching it, the Clawdium cube landed softly in Yuka's hands as she admired its lightness. Daniel stepped in with his open hands and Yuka tossed it to him. As he caught it in his hands, he too was astonished by how light it was.

"Amazing, right?" asked Sung.

"It is," said Daniel as he placed it back into the corner of the stack.

"Now that you have seen the refined Clawdium," began the Guardian Tiger as he started to walk down toward the blast furnaces, "we'll walk past the blast furnaces. Please mind your robes and keep away from the embers."

The Guardian Tiger turned and briskly walked toward the blast furnaces as the clanging grew louder. Each clang rang in Clara's ears. She looked curiously as she saw tigers in what were presumably Clawdium body suits that prevented their fur from being singed. Clara suddenly felt the intense heat emanating from the ten blast furnaces, which seemed to come at her like steady waves on both sides. The tiger forgers were feeding Clawdium cubes into the furnaces. The Azen warriors moved briskly past the hot blast furnaces as molten Clawdium splashed into staff molds. Red-hot Clawdium was also extracted and given to other forgers, who banged away on their pieces on large anvils. The clanging and pounding of the forging tools roared rhythmically throughout the chamber as tigers in protective outfits were busily forming spearheads, harpoon heads, and *katana* wings.

As they passed the last of the blast furnaces, they came into a section of the chamber where tigers were sharpening or polishing the Clawdium items. Yuka pulled on Clara's sleeve as she pointed with pride at the newly minted Clawdium *katana* wings that would adorn her cranes' wings. Clara's eyes were drawn to several stacks of large, inverted cylindrical-cone-tipped Clawdium objects with fins around them.

"What are those?" asked Clara of the Guardian Tiger.

The Guardian Tiger turned his steely blue eyes toward the seemingly hundreds of the inverted cones, neatly packed and stacked in a bamboo-framed container. He turned his gaze back on Clara and said, "*Nian* piercers."

The warriors' eyes all lit up as the Guardian Tiger continued. "The hide of the *Nian* is the toughest, and these gravity-assisted Clawdium piercers will be released from the top of the Sky Pillars to stop them."

Clara glanced over at a *Nian* piercer as its sharp point glinted. They were so large, she shuddered to imagine how massive the *Nian* would be in battle.

For a moment, Clara thought that maybe Sung was right that everything being made were weapons when she heard a smattering of growls from a team of hard-working tigers to her right. A smile eked across her face when she saw them working on smaller items, including chopsticks, long spoons, and rice bowls with lids.

As they neared the end, they were in the section where final products were stored and organized. There were crates of Clawdium staffs, spear and harpoon heads, *Nian* piercers, rice bowls, and chopsticks, along with several smaller items. That's when Yuka walked over to a crate and picked up a spool.

"Guardian Tiger," asked Yuka, "What is this?"

The Guardian Tiger looked at the spool that she was holding and smiled. "You should take great interest in that. That is a spool of Clawdium thread to be woven with silk from your kingdom. They can also be woven into bamboo thread in the Panda Kingdom."

Yuka's eyes lit up as she asked, "May I have one?"

"Certainly," said the Guardian Tiger. "It would be an honor for you to have something from Tiger Kingdom. Empress Warrior Wu and Emperor Warrior Nguyen, you may take one as well."

Clara eagerly walked over to the open crate and picked up one of the spools of Clawdium thread along with Daniel.

"I've already got a couple," said Sung proudly.

"Emperor and empress warriors," said the Guardian Tiger. "Any questions before we move to the next destination?"

Clara raised her hand and spoke, "Guardian Tiger, what are those big doors behind you?"

The Guardian Tiger's eyebrows rose as he slowly spun halfway around to face the large, dark, double arched metal doors behind him. His ear fluttered as he turned back around and he responded. "Oh, those doors lead to the outside. There is a mountain ledge beyond it. This is how the eagles of the Crane Kingdom enter to pick up items to fly to the other kingdoms."

Sung leaned into Clara and whispered, "It like FedEx."

Clara looked up amused and giggled coyly at Sung's humor.

Yuka raised her hand, which the Guardian Tiger acknowledged before she asked. "Does all Clawdium resonate?"

"Emperor Warrior Kim, would you like to answer that?" asked the Guardian Tiger.

"Sure thing," said Sung as he fetched the Claw Staff from his back. "Actually no. Only my Claw Staff resonates, and that's because of the blue jade that gives it that power."

Yuka nodded as she said, "I see."

"If there are no additional questions," said the Guardian Tiger before he concluded, "We shall visit the Cub's Den.

* * *

"Purr, purr, purr," was all Clara heard from the relaxed white-and-black striped tiger cub that she held delicately in her lap as she gazed fondly. As she gently stroked the cub, it elicited a low purr.

"This is too cute!" said Clara to Yuka, who was sitting next to her.

Yuka was feeding her tiger cub, who was eagerly sucking on a bamboo milk bottle. She focused intently on the furry white-and-black tiger cub who rested in her lap, savoring each stream of milk that flowed from the bottle with each gulp. The tiger cub's eyes squinted ever so slightly with each sweet sip as it attempted to hold the bottle with its fluffy paws.

An excited yip made Clara turn away as she saw Sung and Daniel playing with two other tiger cubs, who were running around their legs. The two tiger cubs playfully lunged at Sung's and Daniel's calves with their baby claws.

They had been doting and playing with the tiger cubs for a better part of an hour in the Cub's Den, a large stone building with a distinctive sloped Korean roof. Once they entered, they were entirely captivated by the tiger cubs, who were vying for attention in the private playpen.

The door to the playpen slid open, and Clara turned toward it as the Guardian Tiger walked in. The inner border of the playpen was surrounded by bamboo decking on all four sides and the playpen itself was sunk about a foot below the floor. Four additional tiger attendants came in and silently walked about the bamboo decking.

"Emperor and empress warriors," said the Guardian Tiger. "It's time that the tiger cubs return to their parents."

"Another fifteen minutes? Please?" pleaded Yuka.

"That's what you said fifteen minutes ago," the Guardian Tiger replied with a smile.

Yuka's face fell as she gently pulled away the milk bottle. The tiger cub looked up at Yuka with half-opened eyes as it licked its lips. She tickled its fluffy white chest fur as a tiger attendant looked down and nodded. Yuka sighed as she gently held the cub, who yipped, toward the tiger attendant. The tiger attendant leaned over and gently took the back of the tiger cub's neck with its mouth. The tiger cub's eyes went catatonic, and its tail curled upward as the tiger attendant carried it out of the playpen.

Clara too reluctantly returned her sleeping cub. Sung and Daniel had to catch their tiger cubs and lift them toward the gentle mouths of the tiger attendants. As the four tiger attendants exited, the warriors brushed stray straw from their robes as they collected their weapons.

The Guardian Tiger turned and said to Sung, "Emperor Warrior Kim, Soohorang Square is next."

Sung perked up and looked at his friends, "You're going to love this!"

Clara, Yuka, and Daniel followed Sung, who stepped up onto the bamboo decking as he followed the Guardian Tiger out of the Cub's Den.

As they passed into the lobby of the Cub's Den, several tigers bowed to the warriors. Sung brought his two feet together and bowed as he exclaimed, "*gam-sa-ham-ni-da*."

This prompted Clara, Yuka and Daniel to also do the same as they expressed in their best Korean for *thank you*, "*gam-sa-ham-ni-da.*"

As they exited, throngs of tigers were walking about. Some sauntered on all fours, while others strode upright. The warriors' presence prompted many subtle stares and quick nods from all the white tigers. Yuka walked arm in arm with Clara as they smiled and nodded to every tiger who acknowledged them.

"Is it like this each time you walk through White Tiger Kingdom?" asked Daniel, as he likewise greeted the tigers.

"Yep, each time, but you know, it's not every day you get to bow to a white tiger," Sung said with a smile.

Daniel nodded in agreement as Sung said, "We're almost there."

Daniel looked ahead past the agile muscular body of the Guardian Tiger and saw that something tall and large loomed ahead.

"What is that?" asked Yuka as she pointed to the same object.

Clara looked up and responded, "It looks like a statue, of a tiger. A really tall one."

The Guardian Tiger walked out of the path and into a large, bustling square. Large stone rectangular slabs formed the square, which four stone roads, including the one that the warriors were just on, fed into.

Sung quickly broke away from his friends to walk alongside the Guardian Tiger. As they walked to the front of the tiger statue on a massive stone pedestal, Clara's eyes moved upward to take it in—a tall, regal tiger that had to be about fifty feet tall. The tiger was on its haunches, sitting straight up as its two front paws rested on the pedestal in front of him. His muscular body was imposing and seemed to convey strength and agility. The huge tiger looked straight ahead; its eyes focusing on something far away as its whiskers flared from his snout. From its color, it was apparent that the entire statue was made of Clawdium.

The Guardian Tiger turned around, with Sung at his side as they faced the other warriors, who were still looking up in awe at the statue. The Guardian Tiger grunted to catch the attention of the other warriors, who then leveled their gaze at his steely blue eyes.

"This is Soohorang," said the Guardian Tiger in a tone of reverence. "The greatest of all Guardian Tigers."

A collective "whoa" came from Clara, Yuka, and Daniel as they quickly glanced back up the imposing Soohorang.

"There have been many great Guardian Tigers," said the Guardian Tiger. "But Soohorang is the greatest."

"Tell them what you told me," urged Sung.

The Guardian Tiger gave Sung a glance as his eyes narrowed. "It is said that long ago, when the Korean people were in great need, Soohorang heard them. Somehow, Soohorang knew this and was able to travel to your world to protect them."

"How?" asked Clara incredulously.

The Guardian Tiger's eyes narrowed onto Clara and responded, "With the Portal Book."

There was an incredulous silence from the warriors as Clara asked, "Soohorang wrote his name in Korean, and it transported him to Korea?"

The Guardian Tiger snickered and said, "It is only legend. No one can confirm this as it has been lost to history, but it's the legend that makes Soohorang so revered in our kingdom. Each time any white tiger passes in front of this regal statue of Soohorang, they bow."

Clara, Yuka, and Daniel furtively looked around and saw that indeed, every tiger that passed in front of the statue looked up, bowed, and then continued on their way.

"Amazing, right?" asked Sung. "All this time, I've only read about Soohorang, and here he is!"

"That is so cool!" said Clara. "So it's not really a myth. Soohorang actually did use the Portal Book to travel to Korea."

"Legend," said the Guardian Tiger cautiously. "But as the greatest Guardian Tiger in our history, there is nothing that I would put past him. I only hope to be half as great."

Just then, several crane shadows appeared on the square causing everyone to look up. Clara could see that it was the Guardian Crane and four cranes. They were gracefully descending into the square. They landed behind the warriors as the Guardian Crane landed near the Guardian Tiger.

The Guardian Crane folded in her white-and-black feathery wings and shook her head. It looked up at the grand statue of Soohorang, and along with the other cranes, gave a quick respectful bow.

"Guardian Crane," said the Guardian Tiger.

"Guardian Tiger," said the Guardian Crane. "Are we ready to head to Buffalo Kingdom?"

The Guardian Tiger nodded, and the Guardian Crane turned on her talons. "Empress and emperor warriors, please mount up. Empress Warrior Satoh, you're with me to our next destination, the Palace of Divine Horns."

TWELVE

The sea breeze wafted through Clara's nose. She knew she was nearing the northern oceans of the Buffalo Kingdom, the one kingdom that she had not yet visited during her time in Azen. She was bristling with anticipation. She looked to her right and could see Daniel on his crane in the second position, followed by Sung on his crane. She turned and saw the Guardian Tiger behind her. He nodded as they made eye contact before she turned forward again. As usual, the Guardian Crane and Yuka were always in the lead position, forming the iconic V-shaped flying formation.

Shiori extended her wings as they started to descend, and Clara could see that they were headed toward a beach covered with inviting white sand secluded inside a cove. She thought it was odd, as it was not how she envisioned the Palace of Divine Horns to be. But one thing that she learned while on Azen, things were not always as they seemed.

As they flew closer, Clara could make out a dock with two schooners on each side. They were like the ones that she had seen in the previous battle when they were trying to harpoon the great sea serpents. But what caught her attention was the tall grayish limestone outcropping with its sloping top covered in dark green vegetation. It was beautiful.

As the cranes made their final descent, she gripped her harness a bit tighter and soon enough, the cranes landed as their talons dug into the white sand.

"Empress Warrior Wu," said Shiori. "We have arrived."

Clara smiled and for a moment, she didn't know how she wanted to say thank you, whether it'd be in Mandarin or Cantonese. Before she realized it, she simply blurted out, "Thank you."

Clara slid down the crane and her feet landed in the soft white sand, sending up small puffs around the soles of her boots. She straightened up and walked around Shiori and looked out into the cove. Water lapped gently against the white beach. Beyond it, she could see the crack that split the rock formation surrounding the cove.

"Follow me!" hollered Daniel as he started to walk briskly toward the dock. Sung and Yuka were close behind as the Guardian Tiger snuck up along Clara.

"Empress Warrior Wu," he said in his low but calming tone. "Shall we?"

Clara nodded and walked side-by-side with the Guardian Tiger. As they walked, she asked him, "Guardian Tiger, this isn't the Palace of Divine Horns, is it?"

The Guardian Tiger looked up at Clara for a moment and returned his forward gaze as he responded, "No, it is not, Empress Warrior Wu, but those schooners will take us there."

Clara looked up to see an eager Daniel facing his friends from the dock as Sung and Yuka, in their blue and white robes, clamored up the wooden ramp, each footfall making a thud. Clara reached the wooden ramp and briskly walked up followed by the silent footfalls of the Guardian Tiger.

"Come!" said Daniel as he waved everyone forward and walked toward the wide wooden plank that spanned the dock's edge to the schooner. As Clara followed her friends, she could see several buffalos working on the schooner's deck, preparing it to sail.

As they climbed aboard the boat, the Guardian Tiger gently hopped onto the deck and landed silently. The Guardian Buffalo walked towards them.

"Emperor and empress warriors," said the Guardian Buffalo proudly. "Welcome to Horned Bay."

The warriors smiled and bowed slightly to the Guardian Buffalo, who did the same. As Clara turned back toward the rhythmic sound of the lapping waves, she remarked, "It's beautiful."

"You haven't seen the half of it," said Daniel excitedly.

"Patience, Emperor Warrior Nguyen," admonished the Guardian Buffalo.

Daniel nodded respectfully and uttered, "Sorry. I'm just so excited."

The Guardian Buffalo nodded, pleased by Daniel's excitement. "Where would you like to take your fellow warriors?"

"Well, for starters, a ride through the limestones," said Daniel as he counted on his fingers. "Then the Palace, the Throne of Horns, and finally, The Cave of Horns."

The Guardian Buffalo looked at Daniel guardedly and said, "Well, if we are to make The Cave of Horns, we'll need to get started before high tide sets in. Emperor and empress warriors, and Guardian Tiger, please follow me to the aft."

As the Guardian Buffalo turned his massive body away from everyone, Daniel followed but quickly turned to his friends and said, "*Aft* means the back of the boat."

As everyone settled in, the buffalo captain nodded. He rose to his hind legs as his chest puffed out and rested his front hooves on the steering wheel as he shouted commands to the other scurrying buffalos on deck. They untethered the heavy mooring ropes and tossed them back into the hooves of buffalo dock hands while others began to unfurl the sails. As the sails unfurled, they bellowed and pulled taut the ropes as creaks from the schooner rocked the air. Soon, the schooner sailed away from the dock.

As a strong gust of wind caught the main sail, the schooner lurched forward, causing Clara to grip the railing.

"Hang on, guys!" yelled Daniel as the wind caught his dark brown hair, flaring it past his forehead. "You haven't seen anything yet!"

With that warning, the warriors held tight to the railing as their anticipation grew. The schooner was soon on its way, as it sailed from the dock and headed toward the crack in the rocky formation that shielded the cove.

As they neared it, Clara could hear the waves crashing against the bow of the schooner, which effortlessly slipped through them and picked up speed. The sea buffalos were working in unison, anticipating the wind and adjusting the rigging as necessary. The buffalo captain was calm as the Guardian Buffalo stood to his right. Daniel was to his left along with Sung on the far side of the left rail. Clara and Yuka held onto the right rail as the Guardian Tiger settled onto his belly, wagging his furry tail calmly as he surveyed his bobbing surroundings.

Clara's eyes fixed on the crack in the rock formation. It was similar to the crack at Jagged Pass, with water falling from overhead. As the schooner closed in on the narrow-jagged opening, the sound of clashing waves and water flowing from above and hitting the deck was deafening. But the schooner pierced the sheet of water as large wayward watery drops splattered onto the deck as its hull scraped by the opening.

The deafening sound abated as Clara focused on the sight before her: several limestone outcroppings of varying sizes, each covered in lush green vegetation. She watched in amazement as the schooner navigated between the limestones, and she admired how large they were. But something caught her attention. She couldn't believe it. She leaned up against the side rail, so that Yuka, who was behind her, could see them. Clara pointed and exclaimed, "They're moving!"

Yuka's eyes widened. She felt her feet wobble a bit as she steadied her footing, but her eyes were also fixed on the moving limestone outcropping. She gripped the side rail with both of her hands and found that she was breathily heavily.

Sung hollered out as he asked Daniel, "Why is the rock moving?"

Daniel smiled as he said, "Turtles! Big ones!"

The buffalo captain looked at the Guardian Buffalo, who both smirked at each other, and he continued steering.

"Turtles?" asked Sung incredulously.

"Yep!" said Daniel excitedly. "And we're going to sail right in!"

Sung's eyes opened wide as he looked at the moving limestone outcropping that was moving toward the stationary one. He turned back to Daniel with a shocked expression, "We're going to do what?"

Daniel smiled to him as he said, "Just hold on!"

Sung suddenly steadied his stance and gripped the wooden railing as Clara and Yuka heard Daniel's claim. They clung tightly as the schooner raced furiously ahead and the massive limestone outcropping was closing the gap toward the stationary one.

"Time it perfectly, captain," said the steady Guardian Buffalo to the buffalo captain, who nodded confidently.

With a stern command, the buffalo captain bellowed to his crew, who let loose another set of sails, which caught the wind. As the moving limestone outcropping moved away, the schooner lurched into the void formed by the receding outcropping. As the schooner entered the watery void, Clara, Yuka, and Sung stared all around them as they passed by the soaring grayish limestone outcropping covered in green vegetation. They suddenly felt the schooner push upward as the moving limestone outcropping started to move towards them. As it pushed more water towards them, the water swelled upward and coupled with the wind caught in the sails, the schooner shot out of the watery swell as water crashed and roared against the back of the schooner.

The schooner took a sudden dip back into calmer waters as Daniel spun around yelling, "Awesome!"

Sung's and Clara's jaws dropped in disbelief, but Yuka's cheeks puffed outward. She frantically brought her hand to her mouth, looked right, bounded down the steps, and slammed into the side of the ship as she vomited overboard.

"Yuka!" Daniel yelled as he quickly crossed the aft deck and bounded after Yuka, placing his hand on her right shoulder as she straightened up. "Are you okay?"

She wiped her mouth and looked embarrassed. "I guess I need to clean up now too."

Daniel looked down at her and in a reassuring tone, "It'll be smooth sailing from here on, I promise."

* * *

The warriors stood about the aft deck as the schooner sailed smoothly between the limestone outcroppings. The warriors marveled in awe as they passed each one, admiring their beauty and immense presence. But it was the ones that moved rhythmically and mysteriously that captivated them. They sailed past the limestone islands with wooden docks, and Daniel explained that the buffalos lived atop the larger limestone islands.

The sails shifted, and a few were lowered as the schooner made its way into a crescent- shaped limestone formation. The warriors looked before them and could see a massive limestone tower. Other sailing vessels were moored in the water, but it was the two larger sea vessels that caught the warriors' eyes. They were the same ones that formed the blockade in the previous sea battle with the sea serpents. Massive harpoon bows stood sentry along their decks, and their ornate hulls were heavily armored. They were protector ships. Soon they sailed past these mighty ships as they moved slowly towards the dock and moored alongside it.

"Emperor and empress warriors," stated the Guardian Buffalo as everyone looked at him. "Please follow me."

As his thick tail swayed from side to side, the warriors and the Guardian Tiger followed. They walked over the wooden plank, each step making a hollow thud as they walked on it. As they stepped onto the deck, they followed the Guardian Buffalo onto a large wooden platform with wooden railings. Each corner had a thick rope that ran upward toward the center where they connected to another thick rope that reached skyward.

As the Guardian Tiger stepped silently aboard and settled down onto all fours, the warriors felt a jolt as the platform started to rise upward. Daniel watched as his friends caught their balance, but their eyes soon turned at the view before them. They were in awe of the gentle blue waters inside the crescent limestone formation. As they neared the top, they turned to see the edge of the limestone tower come into view. There was a stately path lined with massive rectangular stone slabs. On each side were silent buffalo guards draped in red robes.

There was a winching sound as the wooden cantilever that held onto the platform started to slowly swivel. A couple of buffalo workers on the other end were steadily swinging the wooden beam until the platform swung over the stone slabs. It landed with a thud, and the Guardian Buffalo stepped onto the stone slab, followed by the eager warriors with the Guardian Tiger behind them.

They walked up the stone slab path as Daniel walked tall and proud behind the Guardian Buffalo. Clara pointed past Daniel as Sung's and Yuka's eyes followed. They were approaching a formidable structure with a stately red swooping roof. It sat atop a lower stone structure that was surrounded by a moat. A broad stone bridge spanned the moat and soon, they crossed it and transitioned onto a thick red carpet.

They followed the red carpet until they reached the palace's entrance, when the Guardian Buffalo slowly turned to face everyone. A couple of buffalo attendants silently appeared at each side of the grand entrance.

"Emperor and empress warriors," said the Guardian Buffalo. "Welcome to the Palace of Divine Horns. We have midafternoon snacks for you. Empress Warrior Satoh, I believe you need to wash up? One of the buffalo attendants will take you to get cleaned up. For the rest of you… Yes, Emperor Warrior Nguyen?"

Daniel put his hand down and asked, "Guardian Buffalo, I need to go to my room. I'll meet you back along the front balcony. I know the way."

The Guardian Buffalo nodded and replied, "Certainly, Emperor Warrior Nguyen. Please be mindful of the time as high tide will begin in about an hour."

Daniel nodded as he responded, "Thank you, Guardian Buffalo. I'll see you guys soon."

Before Clara and Sung could say anything, Daniel turned and raced up the stone steps, his red robe flowing behind him. One of the buffalo attendants beckoned for Yuka to follow her. Yuka gently waved to everyone as she followed the buffalo attendant beyond the entrance. The Guardian Buffalo then snorted at Clara, Sung, and the Guardian Tiger as he led them past the grand entrance into the Palace of Divine Horns.

* * *

Clara and Sung were debating the assortment of spring rolls that were neatly stacked on the table before them. To the side were also an assortment of fruit. Clara picked off a red bumpy round fruit and looked at it. Holding it in her chopsticks, she turned to Sung. "It looks like a lychee!"

Sung smiled and turned toward Clara with a red hairy fruit snared between his chopsticks. "What's this?"

"That looks like a rambutan!" said Clara with a smile. "You peel them like a lychee and eat the fruit inside. They're sweet!"

Sung's eyes widened as he looked at the red hairy fruit. "There's always a first time for everything."

"I can't believe you're going to be eating a rambutan on Azen for the first time instead of Earth," teased Clara.

"There's a lot of firsts on Azen!" said Sung with a laugh.

Clara playfully chuckled as she reached for a spring roll with her chopsticks when Sung's chopsticks unintentionally blocked hers. Clara looked up with embarrassment as Sung gave her a similar look. He smiled with his eyes and pulled his chopsticks away and said, "You first."

Clara smiled, her cheeks blushing as she turned away from him. As she averted her eyes and delicately picked up the spring roll, she heard footsteps behind Sung and saw Yuka walking toward them.

"Hey Yuka!" exclaimed Clara as Yuka approached them. "How do you feel?"

Yuka smiled and gave a carefree shrug. "I'm fine, but I'm really hungry. Oh! What is that?"

Sung moved his dish toward Yuka's curious finger. He smiled and looked at Clara and said, "It's a rambutan. I guess I'm not the only one trying it for the first time."

Clara, Yuka, and Sung quickly sat down around a square wooden table ornately draped with a red tablecloth with golden embroidery along the edges. The Guardian Buffalo and Tiger were talking amongst themselves at another similarly decorated square table. With the front of their robes thrown over their shoulders dangling like capes, they were about to enjoy their food when Daniel appeared behind Clara.

"Hey guys," said Daniel as everyone looked up. He came up to the open seat that faced Sung and with Yuka and Clara to his left and right respectively. In his hands was a red cloth bag cinched shut by white twisted tassels. He gently placed the bag on the table as the mysterious object inside made a slight thud.

Everyone looked at the bag as Sung asked, "What's in the bag?"

Daniel sighed and dropped his shoulders as he started to untie the white tassels. Clara's eyes lit up as she clasped her hands in anticipation. Daniel reached into the bag and slowly pulled out a glass jar. A thick white ribbon was tied around the top of the jar as its two ends dangled beneath the black lid. One end of the ribbon was the Vietnamese phrase for *I'm sorry*, "*Tôi xin lỗi*," while the other end simply said, "I'm sorry." The objects within were small and of a multitude of colors. He gently placed the jar in front of Yuka as he quickly took back the red bag and folded it.

Yuka looked at it when her eyes glinted in recognition of the contents of the jar. She looked up at Daniel and asked incredulously, "*Origami* cranes?"

"Not only *origami* cranes," said Daniel solemnly. "But one thousand cranes."

Yuka's lips parted as she reached out for the glass jar. As her wide eyes neared the glass jar, she could see the small *origami* cranes inside. A multitude of paper squares were used to fold them. She looked up at Daniel, as the Japanese word for *beautiful* tumbled from her lips, "*Utsukushī.*"

Daniel's hands trembled as he placed them into each other and he uttered, "I know that I needed to say I'm sorry for what happened before. I just didn't know how. I know you went through a lot, and it was my fault. I didn't know if a simple apology would ever be enough. So I offer you a thousand cranes as my apology to you. I'm sorry Yuka for putting you in danger."

Daniel then bowed deeply to Yuka and when he straightened up, he kept his gaze downcast.

Yuka paused when she gently placed the glass jar down on the table. She rose and placed her hands together as she said politely *thank you* in Japanese while bowing, "*Arigato gozaimasu.*"

Daniel felt his heart pounding. He knew the guilt wouldn't leave him. Yet he hoped his atonement with the presentation of one thousand cranes was a worthy first step.

Yuka looked up and saw that Daniel was still looking penitent and smiled. She saw Clara looking at her with happiness in her eyes. She placed her hand on the glass jar. "I will treasure this, Daniel."

"You will?" said Daniel as he looked up cautiously at Yuka.

Yuka smiled as she said comfortingly, "I will. Now please go get something to eat."

Daniel smiled and let out a relieved sigh as he thrust his hands out in front of him. "My hands are so sore from folding the cranes, I don't know if I can peel a rambutan."

Clara laughed and picked up a half-peeled rambutan from her plate and placed it on the table in front of him. Daniel looked down at it and as he looked up relieved, causing everyone to laugh.

"But I can definitely pick up a couple of spring rolls," said Daniel as he passed behind Yuka toward the food. As he approached the balcony, he couldn't help but admire the beautiful watery view of Crescent Horn.

The Guardian Buffalo soon walked up to the smiling and talkative warriors as they snacked. He stopped behind Daniel, who was swallowing his last bite of his food, before turning around to face the Guardian Buffalo.

"Emperor and empress warriors," said the Guardian Buffalo. "Please finish up your food so that we may visit the Throne of Horns and The Cave of Horns."

"Yes, Guardian Buffalo," Daniel replied.

When the warriors enjoyed the last of their delicious snacks, the plates were taken away by attentive buffalo attendants. Daniel swung around behind his rectangular chair and removed the Horn of *Kting voar*, which had a convenient wooden ring designed to hold horns. Sung used it to hold his Claw Staff while Clara hung her bow and quiver from it.

Daniel smoothly slid his club horn through the slit in the back of his robe as Sung slapped his staff diagonally across his back. Clara slung her bow and quiver around her. They were ready to leave.

The Guardian Buffalo led them up the wide stone stairs to the top floor, which opened up into an open hallway that allowed the sea breeze to enter and fill the room with the soothing aroma of seawater. The Guardian Buffalo soon turned right and stopped as everyone fell in behind him.

It was a solemn and expansive room. Down its middle was a rich, red carpet that divided the room in half. The ceiling had to be at least thirty feet in height, and massive red columns ran along the length of the room. Along the far walls were stoic buffalo guards in red robes, and at the far end of the red carpet was a stone throne. But the most striking part of the throne were the many curved objects lining its sides. The Guardian Buffalo started to walk respectfully toward the throne.

Clara could only surmise that this was the Throne of Horns. A sense of calm started to fall upon them as the ambiance of the room enveloped them.

As they reached the end, the Guardian Buffalo stopped, and Clara could see the throne more clearly. Jutting from each side of the stone throne were several buffalo horns, curving upward and giving the entire throne an imposing feel. But embedded in the backside of the throne were two vertical slots. The left slot held a slightly curved horn while the right was empty. The Guardian Buffalo slowly turned toward the visitors with a serious expression.

"Welcome to the Throne of Horns," said the Guardian Buffalo. "Behind me is the throne that only our Horned Protectoress may sit in. She sits here for all ceremonial events in addition to all kingdom affairs that require an audience. Emperor Warrior Nguyen, why don't you explain what makes this throne so important to the Buffalo Kingdom?"

Daniel nodded and turned toward his friends. "As you can see, the Throne of Horns is just that. Each side is lined with pair of horns from a Horned Protector from long ago. But as you can also see, there are two slots at the top of the throne. Before the red jade was discovered, both were filled with horns from the mystical *Kting voar*. But when the red jade was discovered, one of the *Kting voar's* horns was needed to create a weapon that only the Buffalo Warrior could wield to carry the mighty spirit of the buffalos."

Daniel reached over his back and slid out the Horn of *Kting voar*. He held it respectfully, with its tapered end in his right hand and the club end with its embedded red jade resting in the other. "And I have the other horn of the *Kting voar*, to protect the Buffalo Kingdom.

"Whoa," said Sung. "That's pretty cool."

Clara noticed how Daniel straightened as he held the Horn of the *Kting voar*. She sensed the weight of responsibility that Daniel felt—the same that she believed she, Yuka, and Sung felt as well—responsibility to protect the kingdoms they have come to love and adore.

"The *Kting voar* was a mystical creature," the Guardian Buffalo said. "No one in our kingdom knows exactly how it looked. Before the *Kting voar's* horns were part of the Throne of Horns, the pair of horns were found in a cave here in the crescent. They were used for ceremonies. We believe that we are direct descendants of this mystical horned creature, so we protect its legacy."

A thick, heavy silence fell upon the warriors as they hung onto the Guardian Buffalo's every word. He slowly turned around and walked behind Daniel, his gaze falling onto the Throne of Horns as he bowed his head reverently and whispered something in Vietnamese under his breath. He then turned to face Daniel. "If we are to make The Cave of Horns before high tide, we should go now."

Daniel slipped the Horn of *Kting voar* into the back of his robe. He nodded and turned to face his friends. "Next, The Cave of Horns!" he said excitedly.

The Guardian Buffalo, followed by Daniel, briskly led everyone out of the throne room and Palace of Divine Horns, over the stone bridge, down the stone slab path, and back to the cantilevered platform. They were lowered quickly and briskly to the wooden deck. They ambled onto the schooner as Yuka embraced her jar of *origami* cranes with a smile.

When the schooner unmoored, several sea buffalos went into action on the deck. With little wind within the confines of the crescent, they lowered long oars into the water, locked them into metal deck riggings, and started to row around the limestone tower. Everyone was on the aft deck, as the walls of the limestone island bore out on the right and the jagged slope of the crescent formation was a way off on their left. The schooner soon broke away from the crescent and headed toward a cave entrance. Each side of the cave entrance was protected by a large, anchored battle vessel.

The sea buffalos rowed steadily and rhythmically. The warriors watched as they got closer to the triangular cave entrance. Clara pressed against the railing and kept her eyes focused on the dark entrance. As her eyes panned the crescent rock formation, she noticed a difference in color between the lower and upper portions of the crescent wall. The lower portion, ringing the entire crescent, was darker.

The schooner bobbed, and Clara leaned over and looked left. Daniel was staring ahead into the cave, and Clara wondered what he wanted to show them. The sea buffalos' rowing slowed. As the cave entrance loomed closer, Clara noticed that the top of the mast was perhaps only a few feet away from the top of the cave entrance.

"Steady as she goes," warned the Guardian Buffalo as the buffalo captain grunted. "Emperor and empress warriors, please hold on as we slip into The Cave of Horns."

Clara held on tighter, but she noticed that Yuka was not holding onto the rail. Instead, she was grinning as she still held the jar. Clara glanced at Yuka's feet and she saw that Yuka was floating about an inch above the wooden deck. Clara smiled. *Of course the Airess can float on a bobbing boat to avoid getting seasick!*

The schooner slipped in as the sound from the crescent's water was replaced by the echoey sound of the cave. The cave was dark, but illumination jades were positioned along the entire length of the cave walls. Clara could see a light at the distant end of the tunnel. As the schooner continued to move through the cave tunnel, she saw ledges perfectly hewn from the cave walls on each side. Empty square stone pedestals along the ledges faced each other across the tunnel. Each was lit by an illumination jade.

As they traveled deeper into the tunnel, the sounds of the lapping waves were amplified, but the sea buffalos continued to row forward. Clara looked up and saw the sea mast bobbing a few feet away from the roof of the cave tunnel.

"Look," Yuka said.

Clara focused on the ledges and she saw them. Statues started to appear out of the darkness on each side of the tunnel: figures of teenaged boys and girls in regal poses. They were proud and emboldened. Clara was looking at the Vietnamese emperor and empress warriors that had protected the Buffalo Kingdom before Daniel.

"Awesome, right?" asked Daniel as his voice echoed off the tunnel walls before trailing off into each end of the tunnel.

"Welcome to The Cave of Horns, emperor and empress warriors," said the Guardian Buffalo reverently.

The warriors gazed curiously as they slowly floated down the tunnel. The sea buffalos soon reversed their rowing, bringing the schooner to a stop as the gentle lapping water brushed its hull. Clara looked about her. It seemed that tens of Vietnamese warriors were standing at attention on each side of the schooner. Daniel excitedly motioned everyone to follow him to the rail on the port side. As Clara came upon his left with Yuka behind her, still holding onto the jar, she saw that Daniel's gaze fix upon one of the warriors.

She looked up and gasped. The young Vietnamese teenager was adorned in vintage battle armor and holding a staff. But it was his face that most surprised Clara. It bore a striking resemblance to Daniel. She, Sung, and Yuka looked at Daniel.

Daniel must have felt all eyes upon him, and he smiled. He reached backwards and pulled out the Horn of *Kting voar* and held it humbly in front of him. He looked down at the red jade and then back up at the statue.

"He was the first," said Daniel. "When the Guardian Buffalo first took me here to show me the Vietnamese warriors of the past, I couldn't help but feel this respect that I never knew I had for all these Vietnamese warriors who came before me. Not only were they protectors of the Buffalo Kingdom, but I'm sure they protected Vietnam back in the day as well. I knew then that I was to follow in their footsteps, as a Vietnamese warrior of the Buffalo Kingdom. This is Emperor Warrior Tran An Dung, the first Buffalo Warrior."

"Dude, he could be your brother," said Sung.

Daniel nodded as he smiled, "I want to believe that. And in some way, he is."

A smile crept over Clara's face as she saw the pride Daniel felt in the special connection to his fellow Vietnamese warrior past. It was the same pride she felt at the unexplained connection with the Panda Warriors, especially Hua Mulan.

Daniel soon turned away and waved everyone over to the starboard side. As they passed the silent buffalo captain and the Guardian Buffalo, the warriors pressed themselves against the rail as the Guardian Tiger, who was lying comfortably on his belly, turned his head toward the curious warriors.

Daniel looked at his friends as he pointed up and said, "And she's the first Buffalo Empress."

Clara looked up and saw a young Vietnamese teenaged girl, also in vintage battle armor. Her eyes were strong and proud. But her pose was more dynamic, with her left foot out in front of her right and her staff in her right hand. Her pose was slightly shifted, readying her to leap off her pedestal. Her left hand was slightly raised as she was sensing the situation before her.

"This is Empress Warrior Trung Nhi," said Daniel respectfully. "Can you imagine her heading into battle?"

"Totally," said Sung as he admired her pose. "How come her pose is different?"

Daniel smiled as he replied, "I'm so glad you asked that. It looks like she knew a statue of her would be created, so she asked if she could pose for it. From there on, each warrior was asked if they wanted to pose for their statue before they returned to Earth."

From behind, the Guardian Buffalo cast a furtive glance at the Guardian Tiger, who also met his glance. The Guardian Tiger flapped his tail and looked back at the warriors.

The Guardian Buffalo then politely grunted as the warriors turned to him. "Emperor Warrior Nguyen, I don't mean to cut short your admiration of our Buffalo Warriors, but we need to head out as the tide is rising."

Daniel nodded as he looked at his friends, "Watch this guys, this is going to be very cool!"

Clara looked confused, but the buffalo captain hit the deck with his hoof. The sea buffalos quickly started to row toward the end of the tunnel. As Clara looked back at the first empress warrior for the Buffalo Kingdom, she realized that the schooner's deck seemed almost level with the ledge. Her eyes traveled upward, and she could see that the mast was precariously close to the roof of the rocky tunnel.

"Is the tunnel getting smaller?" asked Clara as her hands clung to the starboard rail.

Daniel looked at her with a smile. "Kind of. But what's really happening, as high tide rolls in, this entire tunnel gets submerged in water every single night. So we're floating higher up now. Isn't that cool?"

Clara's eyes widened as she looked down the entrance and heard water rushing in. She looked at the exit, which was close by, but they were about three quarters of the way through as she could also hear water rushing in. She looked down at the sea buffalos, who were rowing furiously, trying to escape the tunnel before it was submerged. She could feel her heart race. "No! Not cool! Are we going to make it?"

The Guardian Buffalo looked at her calmly and then back at the buffalo captain.

Sensing her concern, the captain buffalo simply snorted, "It's going to be close."

The Guardian Buffalo looked casually at Yuka and asked, "Empress Warrior Satoh, may we have a gust of wind?"

Yuka, still floating an inch off the wooden deck and holding onto the jar, nodded as she floated to his side. He looked at the captain buffalo and asked him to unfurl the main sail. The captain buffalo grunted out an order, and the flaccid sail dropped from the topmost cross rigging. The top of the mast scraped against the top of the tunnel as the schooner bobbed upward.

"Any time you are ready, Empress Warrior Satoh," said the Guardian Buffalo.

Yuka smiled and nodded as she brushed into the air and invoked the gust Qi element, "*Toppū!*"

The bluish glowing Japanese Qi element for gust dangled from her fingertips as she cast it out. A gust of wind appeared from out of nowhere and filled the sail as the schooner lurched forward. Everyone clung to the rail as the wind raced through everyone's hair. And just when it seemed the top of the mast would hit the top of the tunnel once more, the schooner burst out of The Cave of Horns. White sea foam trailed the schooner's wooden hull as it escaped the rising tide rushing into The Cave of Horns, submerging it for the night.

"That was so cool!" said Sung as Daniel looked on with pride as he reveled in his Azen warrior brother's sense of amazement.

Clara and Yuka turned around and saw that water was rushing into the cave as high tide rolled in. They also saw two more battle vessels anchored on each side of the submerged cave exit.

"They do this every night?" asked Clara.

Daniel nodded. "Every night. It's a like a ritual. Cool, right?"

"Very," said Clara.

"Well done, Empress Warrior Satoh," said the Guardian Buffalo.

"It was fun, Guardian Buffalo!" said Yuka cheerily.

A squawk was heard from above as everyone looked up. Several cranes started to circle them from above.

"Emperor and empress warriors," the Guardian Buffalo exclaimed. "Your ride to Bamboo City is here."

The sea buffalos pulled in their oars and as they dropped anchor. The Guardian Crane gently swooped in and landed on the decking. She nodded at everyone and beckoned Yuka over.

Yuka, who was still floating above the deck, looked at everyone with a smile. "I'll see you guys at Bamboo City! I'm so excited."

Yuka gently floated toward the Guardian Crane and landed on her back. After harnessing herself in and securing her precious jar of *origami* cranes in front of her, she and the Guardian Crane flew away as Shiori beckoned for Clara.

"I'll see you at Bamboo City!" said Clara as she clamored down the steps toward Shiori, who lowered herself for Clara to climb aboard.

Once everyone was aloft on their crane and the Guardian Buffalo on his massive eagle, the Guardian Crane flew southeast toward Bamboo City followed by the other feathered warriors in a standard V formation.

THIRTEEN

Clara glanced behind her and could see the sun starting to set. It was starting to glow orange, like a duck yolk. Clara glanced at her friends and the guardians before she turned her gaze back to the Guardian Crane with Yuka on top of her.

Though Clara could only see the backside of Yuka's flowing white robe as her black hair flowed in the wind, she knew she was happy when Daniel presented her with the thousand cranes. With Daniel earning Yuka's forgiveness, there would be no more estrangement between them. Clara turned to her right to see Daniel trailing Sung. He looked at ease and hoped that being forgiven would be enough to distract him from a second bout of airsickness. Clara was glad that he was embracing the ways of the different Asian cultures. She smiled when she realized why Daniel seemed to be massaging his hands endlessly over the last few days: He had been frantically folding his thousand cranes in secret, even though it was her idea. She would have gladly helped, but she knew he felt he had to do it all by himself.

Clara turned when the Guardian Crane let out a squawk. Below, she could see the outlines of Bamboo City, and a smile crept across her face. Guardian Panda was right: No matter how many times she flew to Bamboo City, it was a beautiful sight to see. Nestled into the rocky bamboo forest was this green circular gem that glistened from above. She could see the hundreds of bamboo stalks reaching into the air. The watery reservoirs were no longer visible, since they were covered by a bamboo flap that prevent the water from evaporating. Bamboo Tower stood out as the largest bamboo stalk among them all. The city exuded serenity.

Shiori straightened her wings to slow for the final descent. Clara gripped her harness tighter and took in a breath as her crane uttered, "Empress Warrior Wu, we are now on final approach. Please hold on."

Clara nodded. "Got it."

She grinned as the cranes swooped in high over The Ring, then flew toward the hangar of Bamboo Tower. She saw a panda attendant on each side guiding in the cranes with illumination jade batons in each hand. Before she knew it, the whoosh of open air stilled in the enclosed space of the hangar. Shiori flew about fifty feet into the hangar before touching the floor with her talons and coming to a full stop.

Clara looked up. She could see the Guardian Panda, who had been waiting patiently for their arrival, standing at the very front.

"*Xie xie*," said Clara in Mandarin for *thank you* as she carefully climbed off her crane. Shiori nodded in acknowledgement as Clara excitedly walked toward the Guardian Panda. Yuka gently floated off the Guardian Crane and looked at Clara with a grin as she held the glass jar in its red pouch. Clara quickly nodded to the Guardian Crane, then briskly walked toward the Guardian Panda.

The Guardian Panda was holding his paws behind him and looking very stately. He beamed down at Clara with his calm brown eyes.

"Empress Warrior Wu," said the Guardian Panda. "Smooth flight?"

Clara stopped in front of him and quickly nodded. "Yes, Guardian Panda, it was a smooth flight from the Buffalo Kingdom."

"Hello, Guardian Panda," said Yuka as she came up alongside Clara. Sung and Daniel soon fell in behind them and nodded to the Guardian Panda as well.

"Hello empress and emperor warriors," said the Guardian Panda who gave a quick nod to his fellow guardians, who fell in behind the warriors. "Welcome back to Bamboo City. I am delighted to host the last stop on your day trip. I'm sure everyone's hungry. I have arranged a wonderful dinner for everyone."

"I'm starving," said Daniel under his breath as he leaned into Sung. Sung gave Daniel a smirk and faced the Guardian Panda.

"Empress and emperor warriors and fellow guardians, please follow me to the dining hall."

* * *

Clara and the Guardian Panda were sitting on the eastern side of the large bamboo table centered in the dining hall. This was one of many within Bamboo Tower, and Clara had not been in this particular one before. She looked to her left and saw Yuka, who had placed her jar of cranes on the table to her right as the Guardian Crane blinked her beady eyes every now and then. Daniel and the Guardian Buffalo were to her right, and Sung and the Guardian Tiger were in front of her.

They were silent, entranced by the melodious music emanating from the corner from a quartet of four panda musicians playing musical instruments that were similar to Chinese instruments back home. Clara wasn't sure if it was the music itself or that four pandas playing that captivated her attention.

But their awestruck fascination with the music was interrupted when scores of panda attendants entered the room from all sides with trays of food. Clara suddenly perked up as her appetite sharpened. Soon small circular bamboo containers were placed in front of her and as they were opened, Clara saw the bamboo *baos*, tofu *siu mais*, bamboo-mushroom dumplings, bamboo sticky rice, and her favorite, spicy bamboo wontons.

With a surprised expression, she turned to the Guardian Panda and exclaimed, "*Dim sum*?"

The Guardian Panda turned toward Clara with a nod and said, "Yes, Empress Warrior Wu, to mark the end of your day trip here on Azen, we thought giving you a varied selection of what Bamboo City had to offer would be the best way to feed your appetites."

"So cool!" said Clara excitedly as she picked up her chopsticks.

"Everyone," stated the Guardian Panda. "Please enjoy your dinner."

Clara smiled as she thrust her chopsticks into the spicy bamboo wantons. She plucked one out and eagerly placed it into her mouth as the warm spicy flavors coated her tongue. She bit into the silky wonton wrapper as its warm sweet bamboo filling oozed out. *Bamboo never tasted so good back on Earth*, she thought as she looked down at all the other delectable choices. She quickly looked up and saw that everyone was busily enjoying the food as well. Even the Guardian Crane, who could not use chopsticks, was easily picking up each piece with her beak. Clara's chopsticks then dove toward the tofu-mushroom *siu mai*.

After their *dim sum* dinner, Clara leaned back in her seat, feeling every piece of *dim sum* happily resting in her stomach. There wasn't much talk during dinner as everyone ate voraciously. She took that as a sign that the amazing *dim sum* was too delicious to be distracted by conversation. She looked at Daniel, who placed his chopsticks down, leaned back into his chair and rested happily.

"Empress and emperor warriors and fellow guardians," bellowed out the Guardian Panda. "I will assume everyone enjoyed their dim sum?"

Just then, the Guardian Buffalo let out a burp as his usually calm eyes widened. He brought a hoof to his mouth as everyone let out a laugh.

"Some of us a little too much," said the Guardian Panda slyly to the Guardian Buffalo as everyone let out another laugh.

The Guardian Panda looked over at Clara and asked, "Empress Warrior Wu, have you decided where you'd like to take your fellow warriors tonight?"

Clara looked down for a moment in thought as her friends looked curiously at her. They wondered what amazing sights they would see in Bamboo City.

Clara looked up and simply asked, "Can we simply walk around Bamboo City and visit the shops?"

The Guardian Panda looked surprised, and he casually looked at his fellow guardians, who also looked bewildered. He looked back down at Clara.

"If this is your wish, Empress Warrior Wu," said the Guardian Panda calmly. "Then so be it. Simply stay within the walls of Bamboo City and be back to get a full night's rest."

Clara's demeanor changed when she asked curiously, "You won't be coming with us?"

"No, empress and emperor warriors," said the Guardian Panda. "You'll be fine within Bamboo City, just be sure to take your weapons with you."

Clara nodded and got up from her chair as the others did the same.

"Guardian Panda," asked Yuka while pointing to the red cloth bag as he turned to her. "Where may I place this?"

"You can put it in my room, Yuka," interjected Clara.

Yuka clasped both of hands together in happiness and nodded.

"I'll take her to my room first and we'll meet you guys back on the ground floor of Bamboo Tower," said Clara as a panda attendant helped her into her robe. Clara nodded as she was handed her bow and quiver, which she slung across her chest.

Clara walked toward Yuka but then turned away. She nodded to the Guardian Panda, then to the Guardian Buffalo, Tiger and lastly the Crane. "Thank you for a delicious dinner, Guardian Panda. *Xie xie*."

Yuka nodded and said *thank you* in Japanese to the Guardian Panda, "*Domo arigato*."

Sung said the same in Korean, "*Gam-sa-ham-ni-da,*" and Daniel said the same in Vietnamese, "*Cảm ơn bạn.*"

The Guardian Panda stood up on his feet as his full belly hung a little lower and nodded. As the warriors briskly walked away, he said, "Please be back before the height of night."

"We will!" said Clara as she exited through the dining doors followed by Yuka, Sung and Daniel.

At the lifts, Sung and Daniel took one down as Clara and Yuka took one going up.

Yuka looked about the lift as it was only the second time she had taken one. She admired the craftsmanship of the cylindrical lift, with its smooth bamboo pole in the center, the opposing curved benches and the placement of the illumination jades. They got off onto the floor for Clara's room as a panda attendant pulled open the door. With a nod, Clara and Yuka entered her room and Yuka let out a surprised gasp.

"It's beautiful!" said Yuka. "Wow, look at your view."

Clara turned to look out her opened windows and saw the swirling navy-blue sky as night descended upon Azen.

"I'm going to miss this place," said Clara wistfully. "Let me take that for you."

Yuka extended the cloth-bagged jar to Clara, who took it gently. She walked to the end table and smiled. She placed it in front of the small bamboo stalk that was given to her by the panda toddler, Ping Ping.

"Come on," said Clara as she brushed past Yuka as she pulled on her hand. "The boys are waiting!"

Clara and Yuka quickly made their way to the bamboo lift and took it down. As they exited into the open air of Bamboo City, Yuka could hear the bustling noise of the night life. Her eyes squinted at the number of pandas, of all sizes, simply strolling about.

"This is so cool," said Sung as he turned back to Clara and Yuka. He and Daniel soon walked toward them.

"So where are we going first tonight?" said Daniel curiously.

"10-1-10," said Clara mischievously.

Daniel looked at her and then at Sung who shrugged as Yuka looked bewildered.

Clara laughed as she explained how the addressing system worked in Bamboo City. Sung's eyes lit up as he intuitively understood the elegant geometric numbering system. He could see all the bamboo stalks laid out on a radial concentric circular grid with Bamboo Tower at its center.

"Let me try to figure this out," said Daniel eagerly. "So the first number, 10, is the tenth ring from Bamboo Tower. The second number, 1, is the first bamboo stalk on the right side of The Meridian. And the last number is the tenth floor?"

"Yes!" said Clara excitedly.

"What's in there?" asked Yuka curiously.

"It's the sentry stalk on the right," said Clara as she started to walk down the path. "Most of the bamboo stalks on the outer ring belong to the panda soldiers. But from there, we can see beyond The Ring."

"Oh cool," said Yuka as she quickened her pace, admiring all the large bamboo stalks that reached into the air. "The bamboo here is so big!"

"You know," said Clara slyly. "All of Bamboo City rests inside what was once a large bamboo stalk."

Yuka, Sung, and Daniel stopped in their tracks, causing Clara to turn to see the look on their faces. She knew they'd be surprised.

"Yep," said Clara proudly. "All of Bamboo City rests inside one massive hollow bamboo section. It's the remains of a large bamboo that grew a long time ago. Isn't that amazing?"

"I can't even imagine that Clara," said Sung as he looked around.

"All the pandas are smiling at us," said Yuka with a grin.

Clara looked around as she saw several pandas passing them with a smile. It was probably one of the few times that any panda had seen all four emperor and empress warriors at one time.

"Just nod and smile to them," said Clara as she urged her friends to follow.

They soon reached the sentry stalk. Clara bowed to the sentry, who gave her his attention. When she asked if they could view The Ring from the top section of the sentry stalk, he nodded and directed her to the stairs. Clara beckoned her friends to follow her up the curved staircase carved into the hull of the bamboo stalk itself. As they wound up the steps, Yuka, Sung, and Daniel looked on with wonderment as the illumination jades reflected in their eyes. Each time they came upon a floor, they looked curiously into each section and could see a number of panda soldiers relaxing, though many straightened up when they realized the empress and emperor warriors were winding up the spiral staircase.

Finally, they emerged onto the open top section of the sentry stalk, to the surprise of a couple of panda sentries. They straightened up upon seeing Clara and nodded to her. Clara and the warriors nodded in return, and Clara explained she only wanted to show her fellow warriors The Ring. They nodded and directed her to the front with their open paws as they withdrew to the back.

Sung couldn't helped admiring the large bamboo crossbow fastened on a swivel mount, giving it a full 360-degree view. In the crossbow, he saw green jade-tipped arrows stacked inside a magazine. *A repeating crossbow,* he thought. Daniel noticed the many loaded arrow magazines that stood along the wall, which reminded him of the jade-tipped harpoons he had seen in the last battle. Yuka's eyes fell onto the compact repeating crossbows that the two panda sentries were holding instead of the usual bows.

"Over here," said Clara as she pressed herself against the bamboo wall. Yuka pressed up against her left, and Daniel stood next to Yuka as Sung pressed up on her right. Clara saw how a few strands of his hair fell playfully against his forehead. As she looked up at him, he glanced down at her, and his soft brown eyes made her heart skip a beat. Suddenly feeling flustered, she looked beyond the wall of The Ring. She pointed outward and said, "See, you think this wall is high, the outer wall is even taller."

"Wow," said Yuka as she saw the large bamboo stalks tightly bound together, forming a protective circle around all of Bamboo City.

"Pretty cool, right?" asked Clara of Yuka.

"It is!" said Yuka.

"Look at the stars," said Sung as his fingers pointed upward.

Clara looked in the direction of his hand and could suddenly feel her herself blushing and her heart racing a bit. She nodded quickly, exhaled, and stepped back.

"Yah," said Clara, flustered. "I've seen them a lot. Let's head down."

Before her friends could say anything, Clara was already walking away. She nodded quickly to the two panda sentries and looked back at Yuka.

"Come on, Yuka," said Clara with a grimace.

Yuka, feeling a sense of urgency, rushed after Clara as she ducked into the doorway. Sung and Daniel followed suit. As they found themselves on the bottom of the sentry stalk, Clara blurted out with a smile, "2-3-1."

"Oh! Let me figure this one out," said Sung excitedly. "So second ring, third bamboo stalk, first floor?"

"Ding ding!" said Clara as she chuckled. "You got that right, let's go!"

Clara briskly walked down The Meridian, and when they came upon the second ring, they turned left. As she walked through the ground floor of the first bamboo stalk, her friends were wowed by first floor of the stalk that was brightly lit by illumination jades. They walked through what appeared to be an apparel shop. As they followed Clara, the looming bamboo stalks seemed to reach deeper into the city, filled with the sounds of pandas talking in Mandarin and Cantonese. But each time they entered the ground level of a bamboo stalk, the pandas within had quieted down.

As Clara hurried along, followed by her curious and excited friends, she bolted into the brightly lit entrance of the second bamboo stalk. Clara's expression became muted, as Sung, Yuka and Daniel almost bumped into her. They looked up suddenly when all chatter in the room suddenly ceased. With curious eyes and mouths agape, the warriors stared back at the dozens of confused red pandas looking back at them. They seemed frozen in place, some at their tables while others were standing, their tiny black eyes nestled in white eye patches staring back at them. They had entered a restaurant full of red pandas, and after a moment of awkward silence, Clara excused herself with a mix of Cantonese and English, "*Dun ji*, we're just passing through."

Clara and her friends quickly bowed in apology for their abrupt intrusion when suddenly numerous red pandas turned from their chairs or places and bowed. A cacophony of greetings suddenly went up from "Welcome!" and "Have a pleasant night!"

After passing through the red panda bamboo stalk, Yuka noticed that each section cornered by four bamboo stalks was either a park or other open space hosting some sort of activity. Panda life was abundantly social.

Sung was incessantly nodding to all the pandas, who were respectfully nodding to them.

"Is your neck starting to get tired?" asked Daniel, who was also respectfully bowing.

"Come on man, you're a warrior," teased Sung. "Bowing is nothing when we have a battle coming up."

Daniel nodded, "You're right, but man, these pandas are so nice to us."

"We're here," said Clara gleefully as she entered the third bamboo stalk at 2-3-1.

Yuka, Sung, and Daniel entered a well-lit shop as the jolly panda shop owner excitedly stood up, his brown eyes wide open.

"Empress Warrior Wu," he said. "And the other emperor and empress warriors, all here in my store? Welcome!"

Clara smiled and nodded respectfully to the owner of the crafts store. "How are you tonight?"

"I'm doing well," said the happy panda shop owner. "Can I help you with anything, Empress Warrior Wu?"

"I'm just showing them around," said Clara graciously.

"Just let me know if you need anything," said the panda shop owner as he nodded and backed away.

"*Do jeh,*" said Clara for *thank you* in Cantonese.

Clara then turned back to her friends, who had already started to admire the trinkets in bamboo buckets placed within circular bamboo sections that acted as product bins.

"How much do these cute things cost?" asked Yuka.

"No cost at all!" blurted out the happy panda shop owner before Clara could answer. "Please, take what you like."

Clara laughed because despite him standing silently in the back, he was still paying attention to them like any proud shop owner.

"Hey guys," said Clara excitedly. "Follow me."

They followed Clara as she maneuvered between the product bins until she came upon several bamboo buckets. Her eyes fell upon one and she fumbled through the medallions. She picked out the warrior medallion for Hua Mulan and smiled before letting it fall back into the bucket unnoticed. Her hands picked up another one as she held up the bright polished bamboo medallion with the beautifully carved Chinese characters "Yee Wun Xing."

Everyone's eyes glazed over for a moment before Yuka innocently asked, "Who's that?"

"He was the eighth Panda Warrior," said Clara. "This bucket contains all the names of the past Panda Warriors. But if you look for the right bucket, you'll find the bucket for your past warriors."

"What?" asked Sung as he started to peer down into the buckets. "One of these buckets is for the Korean warriors?"

"Yes!" shouted the eavesdropping shop owner, now excited.

"No way!" exclaimed Daniel as he started to look through the buckets. "There are Vietnamese ones here?"

"I found the Japanese one!" said Yuka as she excitedly started to dig through the loose medallions. "Oh, these are so cool!"

Soon Sung and Daniel found their buckets and started anxiously digging through the medallions to find the names of every single warrior that they could remember. Clara could see that they were as engrossed as she once was. She had already collected all the panda warrior medallions and was determined to bring them home from her last visit to Azen. While everyone else was digging into the buckets, she walked to the shop owner.

"Is there anything I can help you find, Empress Warrior Wu?" the jovial shop owner asked.

Clara looked around when several bamboo cases on a shelf behind the shop owner caught her attention.

"What's in those?" Clara asked.

The rotund panda shop owner turned around and smiled. With his black paws, he pulled one out and laid it out on the counter. It was a beautifully polished bamboo case. *Whatever was inside had to be beautiful as well,* Clara thought. There were two matte grayish fasteners on the front, which Clara knew were probably made of Clawdium. As if he was teasing her, he slowly unsnapped the fasteners and opened the bamboo case as Clara's jaw dropped.

"*Mah jong?*" exclaimed Clara as she looked down at the beautiful bamboo tiles. The polish on the bamboo *mah jong* tiles glistened as she admired the intricate etchings of the bamboo, coins, and numbers carved into the bamboo tiles.

"Yes," said the shop owner gleefully. "Do you know how to play?"

"I do," said Clara. "But it's a been a long time. Do you know how to play?"

The shop owner laughed. "Of course I do. I'm a Chinese panda!"

He bared his teeth as he laughed, and Clara laughed with him. He closed the bamboo box and placed his paw on top of it. He gently slid the box toward Clara.

"Oh, I can't take this!" said Clara with a surprised look on her face. "It's too beautiful."

"Empress Warrior Wu," said the panda shop owner reassuringly. "How often would I be able to give a bamboo *mah jong* set to the Panda Empress Warrior?"

Clara smiled as she placed her hands on the sides of the smooth bamboo box. She nodded and said, "*Do jeh sai.*"

The panda shop owner nodded and said, "Besides, there are four of you. You can teach your fellow warriors."

Clara's eyes lit up as she called out, "Hey guys!"

Yuka, Sung, and Daniel walked over, each holding several bamboo medallions awkwardly in their hands.

"I think I found most of mine," said Daniel eagerly.

"Me too!" said Sung. "I'm so glad I wrote them all down before."

"What's in the box?" asked Yuka.

"A *mah-jong* set!" exclaimed Clara.

Her response drew blank faces when Sung asked, "The tile game?"

Clara's eyes widened as she said, "Yes! And I'm going to teach you how to play. Now we just need a *mah jong* table."

"Oh, there are *mah jong* tables set up outside through the western door," said the shop owner.

With even more eagerness, Clara blurted out, "Let's go!"

* * *

After several practice rounds and a lot of explaining, the four warriors were able to play a decent game of *mah jong*. The panda shop owner was right: There was an entire outdoor area devoted to playing *mah jong*. After they had seated themselves at an empty *mah jong* table, throngs of curious pandas silently watched them. No other pandas were playing anymore as they'd all stopped to watch the warriors' game curiously and silently. For the pandas in the back that couldn't see, each move was sensationally whispered back to them from the pandas in the front.

Clara looked at her near-complete set of bamboo-etched tiles, called *jook*. They were down to the last tiles, and someone was hogging the one *jook* tile that she needed. Clara gave Sung a careful look, since he had gotten the hang of the game after the third practice round. Her eyes then glanced over to Yuka, who was cautious in what tiles she tossed out. Clara had never seen her so serious before. Daniel was flip-flopping the most, picking up one tile to toss only to toss out another. *It was if he was using poker tactics*, she thought. It was Sung's turn, and she could tell that he was holding onto a tile he didn't want to give up.

"Come on, Sung," pleaded Yuka. "You've been thinking for too long."

Sung looked defeated. "Fine! I know someone must have it, as no one has thrown this out yet."

Sung tossed out a white-board tile as it bounced around the jumble of discarded tiles. The pandas closest to the warriors started to murmur as Sung's play cascaded outward like a rippled whisper before falling silent again.

Yuka was about to reach for a new tile when Daniel yelled out, "*Pong*!"

This meant her turn would be skipped, so Yuka reluctantly pulled her hand back. Daniel happily picked up the tile as Sung said, "I knew it."

Daniel placed it down in front of his rack of tiles and folded down three additional white-board tiles.

"That's not *pong*, that's *gong*," teased Clara.

The murmurings amongst the pandas rippled again before their brown eyes nervously settled back onto the *mah jong* game.

"*Gong*?" said Daniel. "Ugh, I need to keep this straight. *Pong* is for three? Right. Okay, I'll remember. Okay, now I need to throw something out."

Clara looked at him anxiously as his right fingers passed over his tiles. They settled on one, which he lifted out. He held it for a moment before he tossed it out into the discard pile.

Clara's eyes lit up as she shouted out gleefully, "*Seurng*!"

Her hand reached into the pile as she picked up the 8-*jook* tile. She split apart her set of tiles, slotted that tile into place, and flipped down all her tiles, showing a glorious full set of sequential bamboo tiles.

The other three warriors looked on in awe as the murmuring from the pandas turned into excited yips and grunts.

Clara could hear the pandas' quips, from "The Empress Warrior Wu won with a *seurng*, how fortunate," to "The Panda Warrior is all about the *jook*."

"Hey look," said Sung as he pointed to Clara's winning tiles. "She is the Panda Empress Warrior. Look at her tiles!"

"Huh?" asked Clara as her attention was brought back to her winning hand. She then realized her winning hand was made up entirely of the bamboo tiles. "Oh! It is."

Yuka clapped her hands as Daniel nodded to her as he said in a snarky tone, "Panda Warrior, you are one with the bamboo."

The warriors laughed as the pandas around them nodded and started to disperse. That was when the Guardian Panda appeared, his paws behind him.

Clara looked up and smiled, "Guardian Panda."

"Emperor and empress warriors," the Guardian Panda greeted. "It looks like you four had a fun night."

"We did," said Clara.

"I'm glad you did," said the Guardian Panda. "Well, it's getting late, so may I recommend turning in for the night?"

Clara looked at her friends and though disappointed they couldn't continue, they nodded to each other.

"Yes, Guardian Panda," said Clara as she picked up the *mah jong* box and laid it open on the *mah jong* table.

"Empress Warrior Satoh and Emperor Warrior Kim and Nguyen," said the Guardian Panda. "We have set up guest quarters for you in Bamboo Tower. Your guardians will also be spending the night here."

"Thank you," said Sung as he nodded along with Yuka and Daniel.

"No, you have to put all the like tiles with each other," said Clara as she observed how her friends were randomly putting the tiles into their boxes. "That's the right way to do it."

The Guardian Panda then quipped, "When you don't put them back right, we call that the Panda express way."

The warriors looked at each other and burst out laughing.

FOURTEEN

After a light breakfast the next morning, the warriors and guardians flew off from Bamboo Tower westward toward the Portal Circle. As usual, Yuka was in the lead, with Clara in the second position on the left. It wasn't long before the cranes and the Guardian Buffalo's eagle landed by the Portal Circle and dismounted.

Clara thanked Shiori and proceeded to walk toward the Portal Circle. A smile crept across her face as she watched Yuka hugging her jar of cranes as she crossed the circle to her Portal Book. She gently placed it on the ground beneath the stone pedestal, protected in its red cloth bag with its big, white braided tassels. The attendants from each kingdom came forth and took their robes as Clara, Sung, and Daniel disarmed and placed their weapons by the pedestal. The guardians took up their positions in front of the stone pedestal.

The Guardian Panda nodded at Clara as he walked past her and into the Portal Circle. Everyone turned to him as he circled about the center as a gentle wind rippled across his fur.

"Empress and emperor warriors," the Guardian Panda said as one of his black ears fluttered. "You have trained well, your skills are honed, and you have been battle-tested for this last battle. We have already deployed most of our armies to the Sky Pillars. Once we have witnessed the lunar eclipse, it will take almost a full day for the Warlock's army to reach the battle ground. We will depart in the morning and plan for a noon battle tomorrow. Yes, Empress Warrior Wu?"

Clara put her hand down and asked, "Guardian Panda, when is the next lunar eclipse?"

The Guardian Panda stepped out of the Portal Circle as the Guardian Crane stepped in.

She fluttered her wings slightly and folded them neatly against her sleek feathery body as the red feathery tuft on her crown glinted in the sunlight. She turned to Clara.

"It will occur early this evening, Empress Warrior Wu," she said gravely.

The Guardian Crane extended her left wing, and fiery streams floated up from Yuka's Portal Book. She pulled in her wing as multiple dazzling fiery streams wove through the air and created the terrain of the Sky Pillars.

It was a large peninsula, extending outward from the southern cliffs of Azen. At the very far tip of the peninsula was a flattened but rocky terrain as seemingly thousands of stone pillars ascended into the sky and stood in between it and the cliffs.

The Guardian Crane walked around the fiery terrain and pointed with her wing.

"The Warlock's army will appear here, at the southernmost point," said the Guardian Crane. "But before they can even reach our armies, they will need to navigate through these large stone pillars, the first of which are very narrow. It will take time for the bulk of their forces to squeeze through. Once through, they will begin to stream through the next set of stone pillars that are lined up along these paths. As you can see, they are still close together, but they will start to widen out here and converge on these four pillars near the end. These four pillars, forming the corners of a square, are where we will devote most of our battle effort. Whatever happens, we cannot let the Warlock's army cross into the southland from the peninsula. Yes, Emperor Warrior Kim?"

"What happens if they pass?" asked Sung as he put his hand down.

As the Guardian Crane left the Portal Circle to allow the Guardian Tiger to enter, she glanced at Sung and simply said, "We cannot let them pass."

A moment of silence descended upon the Portal Circle as the Guardian Tiger silently circled. He reared onto his hind legs and crossed his arms.

"We have been successful holding off the Warlock's forces in the past," said the Guardian Tiger. "We have no reason to believe that we cannot hold them off this time."

He walked toward the four tallest pillars and pointed to them. "This is the trap. This is where we must defeat the Warlock's demon creatures."

Daniel muttered underneath his breath, "Kill box."

"For this battle, we will be deploying our resources differently," said the Guardian Tiger. "Emperor and empress warriors, you will not be deployed on the ground. Each one of you will be placed atop one of these pillars and will invoke your Qi powers from there. Except for you, Empress Warrior Wu."

Clara looked up confused and asked, "Why?"

"This entire peninsula is entirely mountainous terrain," said the Guardian Tiger. "There is no earth for you to wield."

Clara frowned and looked around at her friends as she asked, "So I won't be helpful?"

"That is not so," said the Guardian Tiger reassuringly. "Your jade will still power the green jades of the of the panda army and their weapons. Along with your fellow warriors, you'll be helping to launch the *Nian* piercers, which you saw back at Claw Mountain."

The Guardian Tiger extended his paw towards Sung's Portal Book and pulled out fiery streams that swirled on top of each pillar. A circular platform appeared as four beams, at right angles to each other, appeared from the center. Each beam extended over the pillar's edge. A smaller circular platform formed over the center, where the beams met. He spread his arms, and the fiery streams expanded, showing just the beam. Mechanical gears, pegs, straps, and levers appeared along the beam. Protruding from beneath the structure were the menacing tips of the *Nian* piercers.

"This is one beam that houses the *Nian* piercers. It is simply called the launcher. There are four of them on each platform," said the Guardian Tiger. "This mechanized weapon is possible through ingenious panda construction, tiger Clawdium forging, and buffalo strength. Each launcher holds fifty of our *Nian* piercers guided by a green jade. Once fully loaded, this strap is pulled back, pushing out the *Nian* piercers through the end of the launcher and toward the trap below."

"Whoa," said Sung as his eyes glazed over at the image of the piercers being dropped.

"How is the next launcher set in place?" asked Daniel with his hand halfway up.

The Guardian Tiger turned to the Guardian Buffalo, who nodded and began to walk in as the Guardian Tiger exited.

"Brute force, Emperor Warrior Nguyen," said the Guardian Buffalo as he entered the center of the Portal Circle. "The *Nian* piercers, dangerous as they may be, are too light to fall with any force, so their cores are filled with sand. That's what the battle soldiers have been doing for the last few days in preparation for this battle. Once one of the launchers is loaded, the battle buffalos will pull back on this strap, which pushes out the piercers. Once the launcher is emptied of its piercers, the entire platform will be rotated ninety degrees. This will position the next loaded launcher while we reload the empty one. Each of the four pillars has about five hundred piercers. We have never used them all, but it's better to be prepared than not."

"Wow," Daniel said as he imagined the entire contraption rotating atop the pillar.

"Emperor and empress warriors," said the Guardian Buffalo in a firm voice. "This will be the last battle. We have our fullest faith in you, and our armies will stand with you. Please use this time to manifest the Qi elements that you feel best, as time will judge our actions."

Clara looked back at her fellow warriors who looked about nervously but nodded to the Guardian Buffalo. In silence and knowing what was ahead, they began to diligently manifest powerful Qi elements in their Portal Books.

FIFTEEN

By evening, the guardians had slowly sauntered up toward the Portal Circle, ending the warriors' silent diligence. They put down their brushes and looked into their guardians' eyes, then toward a moon that was just cresting the horizon.

The moon's reflection shone in the Guardian Buffalo's reddish right eye. He grunted. "Emperor and empress warriors, the next lunar eclipse is about to begin," he announced. "This one we call *pāru*."

Yuka looked up and realized the Guardian Buffalo had uttered the word pearl in Japanese. She grinned at the thought of the Guardian Buffalo speaking Japanese. But the pleasant thought faded as she watched the moon start to rise.

Everyone fell silent as they watched the pearly moon with its purplish halo rise over the horizon. In a matter of minutes, it had arced upward to its zenith in all its bluster when a shadow started to creep in. All of Azen dimmed for a few minutes until the fourth moon escaped from the shadow.

When it was over, Clara's shoulders drooped, and she sighed.

"It is done," the Guardian Buffalo said. "The fourth of the Warlock's army has landed."

The guardians trudged off, and the warriors quickly returned to manifesting in their Portal Books. But Clara was frustrated. With the lack of earth at the Sky Pillars, her Qi elemental powers would be useless, just as it was in the second and third battle. She watched Sung, Yuka, and Daniel all busily manifesting. They had a purpose for the upcoming battle, but she felt helpless, similar to her feeling not being as capable, as she was not able to fly. Still, she found solace that her presence, along with the Bamboo Jade, gave to the panda army the protection and aim they needed. It then occurred to her that each *Nian* piercer would be guided by a green jade, and this would help tremendously in the battle effort. She turned back to her repetitious brushing of the Chinese character for sinkhole, *tei-hum*.

She placed her brush back onto the pedestal to the side of the Portal Book and massaged her right hand. As she did, her jade bracelet slid down her wrist a bit and glistened. A smile crept across her face as she remembered its mysterious power. She accepted the possibility that she may never know the secrets of its origin.

Her shoulders drooped as she exhaled and reached for her brush, with her left hand. The pages on the Portal Book went blank and a new grid appeared. It just knew, and Clara felt the book could always read her mind. She scrunched her face as she attempted to write out the character for sinkhole, *tei-hum*, with her left hand.

Only after she brushed out the character twenty times did it finally manifest. *One*, she thought. After almost another hour and inevitably in the last box, she managed to get a second one to manifest.

She looked down at the page and chuckled under her breath. The Chinese characters looked as if she'd written them when she was in the fourth grade. She felt embarrassed and thought that her Portal Book took pity on her as her mother would not have approved her childish calligraphy. She leaned into the Portal Book to begin a new page when she heard someone creep up behind her.

"Left hand, huh?" asked Sung, who was standing to her right.

Clara smiled as she pushed back from the stone pedestal. Without averting her eyes, she said under her breath, "Yah, it's not easy. I've got wall down and was able to manifest about ten more before our day off yesterday."

"I remember," said Sung. "You were twinning it."

Clara looked up and asked, "Twinning?"

"Yah, you were able to invoke twin Qi elements," said Sung. "That's why you got through the Gauntlet so fast. That was so cool!"

Clara blushed at the compliment before she replied sheepishly, "Really? Twinning. But you thought I was cool?"

"Uh-huh," said Sung. "I've been trying to write with my left hand, but it's not easy. And for Daniel, it can't be easy either with all those accents."

Clara nodded as a strand of hair fell from behind her left ear and before she could think about it, she felt Sung's hand gently brushing it back behind her ear. A sudden sensation of warmth rose from her chest through her neck. As he pulled back his hand, her left hand firmly tucked the stray strand away.

"Thanks," she muttered while looking up coyly.

But Sung only answered nonchalantly, "No problem. You know, each time I think I'm about to portal back to Azen, I don't cut my hair."

Clara looked up quizzically and asked, "Why?"

"Well, think about it," said Sung playfully as his eyes lit up. "If I leave home and come to Azen when my hair is short and then go back home and my hair is long, my parents are going to think something is up."

Clara laughed. She never thought about it. As both her and Yuka's hair were longer, it growing an extra inch would not be noticeable. But she realized it was different for the guys, and she wondered if Daniel did something similar, though his hair was a little longer than Sung's.

"What's so funny?" asked Yuka as she sauntered over as she massaged her hands.

"I was just telling Clara that I don't cut my hair before coming to Azen because my parents would notice it when I portal back home," said Sung.

Yuka looked up at Sung's hair and smiled at the realization that longer hair may give away his time on Azen. She imagined his parents' confusion seeing him with short hair in the afternoon and longer hair later that same day. "That is so funny, Sung!"

"I wonder what's for lunch," said Daniel as he also walked up. "Time for a break; my hands are killing me."

"Do you not cut your hair before coming to Azen, Daniel?" asked Yuka.

"Huh?" asked Daniel.

"Yo, the guardians are coming back," said Sung as everyone straightened up.

"They're probably going to confirm that the *Nian* have landed at the Sky Pillars," said Clara as she watched the Guardian Panda and the rest of the guardians trudging up the path toward the Portal Circle.

Upon reaching the Portal Circle, the other guardians fanned out behind the Guardian Panda.

"Empress and emperor warriors," said the Guardian Panda. "The crane scouts have returned. It is as we suspected. The *Nians* have arrived."

The warriors were silent. With downcast eyes, Clara nodded at the sudden heaviness she felt. She exhaled, glancing at her friends before looking back at the Guardian Panda.

"What's next?" she asked.

The Guardian Panda looked back at Clara. With a nod, he began to explain the final battle as he summoned streams of fire from her Portal Book. As the streams of fire formed, he walked back toward the center of the circle as the other guardians and warriors returned to their books.

"The *Nian* will need to make their way through the large number of Sky Pillars. The first group of Sky Pillars do not offer much space for them to move quickly, so it will be a natural obstacle. The terrain is also uneven, going uphill before it levels out. They will try to stay close together, but the pillars will force them to split up at this point. The narrow paths start to widen out here. This is where the battle tigers will spring into action. They will spring from the sides, leaping atop the *Nian* and wrapping clamps around their necks. The eagles will then fly in and cinch the clamps from above, which will strangle and kill the *Nians*. They will then fly them over the water and drop them in. Yes, Emperor Warrior Kim?"

"What is the clamp?" asked Sung as he lowered his hand.

The Guardian Tiger stepped forward a bit. He reached out with his paw and wove from Sung's Portal Book a slender mechanical device made up of two opposing S-shaped pieces connected in the middle. The bottom part of the clamp had serrated edges while the top had large handles.

"This is the clamp," said the Guardian Tiger. The bottom half will wrap around the *Nian's* neck. Once placed around its neck, it will lock in place. The battle tiger will then leap off. An eagle will fly in and grasp the top by these handles. As it lifts the *Nian* from the herd, the weight of the *Nian* will close the clamp tighter around its neck, killing it."

"Whoa," said Sung as everyone else looked on in awe upon hearing the clamping technique.

"It's not as simple as it sounds though," admonished the Guardian Tiger. "The *Nian* is much too large for us to fight one-on-one, and its hide is very thick. Our battle tigers, for all their agility, will struggle to attach the clamps. Once a clamp is attached, a tiger will need to jump off while in the stampede of *Nians* without getting hurt. The eagle will then fly in low and grasp the clamp with its talons. So thinning out the first wave of *Nians* will require complicated coordination between tigers and eagles."

"That sounds crazy," said Daniel.

The furry face of the Guardian Tiger nodded at Daniel in agreement. "It will be, Emperor Warrior Nguyen. It will be."

"Are they heavy?" asked Yuka with worry.

"They are, Empress Warrior Satoh," said the Guardian Crane as she ruffled her wings a bit. "Much too heavy for our cranes, but the eagles' larger wings will do the job."

"What will the cranes be doing?" asked Yuka as she looked up at the Guardian Crane.

The Guardian Crane looked at Yuka and in an unexpected low voice said, "Slicing the *Nians* that try to climb the four Sky Pillars."

"What?" asked Yuka.

"The *Nians* are aware of the trap," said the Guardian Crane. "Despite their weight, they have very powerful claws, and many of them will try to climb the four pillars. There are claw marks in the Sky Pillars from previous battles to show this, but no demon creature has ever reached more than halfway up. The cranes will guard the pillars and slice through any *Nians* that attempt the climb. But several passes of the *katana* wings will be needed to slice through their thick hide to kill them."

Heavy silence fell onto the warriors. The battle plan was larger and more precarious than any battle they had yet encountered.

The Guardian Panda continued, "As the *Nians* rush through the trap, hundreds of piercers will be dropped onto them. It is the only area of the Sky Pillars that opens up, so we must stop as many of them here as we can. During this time, working together, the pandas, tigers, and buffalos will work the launchers. Empress Warrior Satoh and Emperor Kim and Nguyen, use your Qi powers to keep them in the trap."

"What happens to the ones that do make it through?" asked Clara.

The Guardian Panda flicked his paw and the terrain directly after the trap was suddenly pricked with thousands of spikes jutting out of the ground and angled toward the trap.

"Those *Nians* who are able to get past the trap," said the Guardian Panda, "will be met with a wide and long formation of Clawdium spikes. They will not be able to get through without impaling themselves."

"Will they try?" asked Clara.

The Guardian Panda looked at her for a moment before he responded, "They will. They are relentless."

"And if they get through the spikes…?" asked Clara as her imagination envisioned a seemingly unstoppable force.

The Guardian Panda nodded. With a wave of his paw, the fiery illuminations of the Sky Pillars and the Clawdium Spikes moved past as the land connecting the peninsula to the southland came into view. It sloped upward and ended at the cliffs of the southland, known as The Sheers. But despite the sheer cliffs, it wasn't entirely insurmountable. At the base of The Sheers was a three-tiered stone ledge, and before that was a wide trench that stretched from one side of the peninsula to the other. Each ledge had several large repeating crossbows.

The Guardian Panda exhaled before speaking. "This tiered battle formation is the Last Stand. Our regular arrows are no match for the thick hides of the *Nians,* so the battle pandas will be launching heavy arrows from the crossbows. But the *Nians* that make it past the halfway point will be close enough for our panda archers to use their heavy bows."

"And that is where the buffalos come in," bellowed the Guardian Buffalo as he stepped in. "Any *Nians* that make it past, though their numbers should have been winnowed down by this time, will be confronted by a thousand mighty battle buffalos, who will meet them head on, horn to horn. It is here that we will make our last stand to prevent their incursion into Azen."

A thick silence fell over the warriors. Daniel looked up and asked, "But Guardian Buffalo, what happens if they do?"

The Guardian Buffalo looked directly at the warriors. "They shall not pass."

SIXTEEN

The Ascendant flew gracefully and silently through The Ascending from beneath Crane Castle. The soft glow of illumination jades provided enough light for navigation as she flew by each of the past Crane Warriors. Their young Japanese faces stared silently into the air as they seemed to float through it. Some of them were looking downward, others upward, and others forward. At each beat of the Ascendant's wings, the figures swayed, seemingly coming to airy life. As she spiraled upward, she marveled at the numerous pearl-shaped illumination jades bunched together like grapes hanging from the very top of the magma pocket. She then looked toward the topmost Crane Warrior, the very first, making eye contact with her before whispering, "Protect our Crane Warrior, may she fight well."

* * *

The Horned Protectoress was alone at the bow. She was a majestic buffalo with a regal stature. Accompanied only by a skeleton crew, who silently steered and rowed the schooner, she looked up at each imposing but familiar figure of the past Vietnamese warriors of the Buffalo Kingdom. She may not have been old enough to know each one personally, but she remembered their stories as told to her by the previous Horned Protectors. As the boat approached the last Buffalo Warrior, she looked to her right at the empty stone pedestal, where Daniel would be immortalized with his own statue. As it slowly faded from view, she looked straight ahead and tensed her massive frame as she uttered, "Protect our Buffalo Warrior, may he fight well."

* * *

The crackling of the fire was the only sound in the Warrior's Soul as the flames cast large shadows of warriors in dramatic poses along the curved walls. The Tigeress walked around the Clawdium statues of the Tiger Warriors past, starting from the outside and working her way inward. She stopped and gazed at each with her steely blue eyes. Each time she looked up at one of them, the white-and-black fur on her head softly swayed as her whiskers twitched. She looked soulfully into the faces of the many Korean emperor and empress warriors past who had fought valiantly alongside her brave battle tigers. Then she came to the first Tiger Warrior and looked up. She stared a bit longer into his eyes before saying, "Protect our Tiger Warrior, may he fight well."

* * *

The Panderess was alone in the Warrior's Circle. She had walked toward the eternal flame, where she lit three incense sticks. After bowing, she gently stuck the incense into the sand inside the fire pit with her black paws. She walked out of the inner circle to the outer circle and rested her eyes on the empty space where Clara's carved bamboo statue would be placed. Slowly, she paid her respects to each of the Panda Warriors past, admiring their young Chinese faces. As she neared the center, she finally came upon the first Panda Warrior, Yi Wu-Fei. She looked soulfully into his face and wondered to herself how many more warriors would need to come after Clara to keep the Warlock at bay. She exhaled as the black fur along her snout rippled gently. She turned around to face the Warrior's Circle before looking back at the first Panda Warrior as she whispered, "Protect our Panda Warrior, may she fight well."

The Panderess brought her paws together and was about to walk out when she paused. She looked to her right and stared at one of the past warriors and slowly walked over. She stopped in front of her and admired her young features. She was bold, striking, and powerful and had inspired Clara on her first trip to Azen.

The Panderess nodded and whispered, "*Xie Xie Hua Mulan.*"

SEVENTEEN

Early the next morning, Clara, in her gray-and-green jade-dusted battle gear, walked toward the Portal Circle. She couldn't describe it, but she felt something was different. She felt tight, and her muscles seemed heavier than usual. Yet she felt hollow at the same time. As the Portal Circle came into view, she saw her friends and perked up.

Yuka and Daniel were quietly chatting, and she was glad that they had made up. She looked over at Sung and admired how his battle armor accentuated his tall, sleek figure. He was checking his gauntlet as his longer-than-usual hair dangled gently over his brow. He had not yet noticed Clara when Yuka hollered out *good morning* to her, "*Ohayo gozaimasu,* Clara!"

Clara's eyes perked up as she regripped the Bow of Destiny in her left hand and briskly walked into the center of the Portal Circle.

Clara closed the warrior's circle and nodded to Yuka as she said, "*Ohayo gozaimasu,* Yuka. Did I say that all right?"

Yuka smiled. "Yes! Your Japanese is getting so good!"

Clara blushed as Daniel smiled at her with a nod as Sung said in Korean for *good morning*, "*Joh-eun achim.*"

Clara responded to the challenge. "*Joh-eun achim!*"

"Your Korean is pretty good, too!" said Sung with a smile.

"Aw, thanks Sung," said Clara before she turned to everyone. "How do guys feel this morning?"

"Oh, I don't know," said Daniel. "The sun is up, it's warm, and we're going to be fighting some gnarly creatures."

There was a halfhearted collective chuckle among the warriors, who nodded silently.

"It's the last battle," said Clara. "I don't know about you, but something feels different about this one. Do you guys feel it?"

Sung glanced at Daniel, who then glanced at Yuka as she looked at him with trepidation.

"Yah," said Sung. "Something does feel… heavier about this battle."

"Maybe we're letting it get to our heads," Daniel suggested. "Come on, we've been through three battles. We're ready for this one."

Yuka nodded a few times and looked up at everyone, "Let's do our best!"

Sung nodded. "I know we will!"

Clara felt a new bit of confidence as she slung her bow across her chest. She brought her feet closer, bent down to place her helmet in front of her, and as she straightened up, everyone else did the same. Clara looked at everyone and said, "I'm really glad to be fighting with all of you."

Everyone glanced at each other with a smile. Clara then brought her fists to her chest, elbows at the side and everyone else did the same. With a nod, they all said, "For Azen!"

Clara picked up her helmet and turned to her left as Yuka followed, with Sung and Daniel in tow. They walked toward the southern path and saw their guardians, a small squadron of cranes, and an eagle.

As the four warriors appeared, the winged squadron came to attention, and the guardians all looked up. They were at the launch point. The warriors split up and walked to their winged escorts.

"Empress Warrior Wu," said the Guardian Panda in his bamboo battle gear.

Clara smiled at him as she admired his bamboo chest armor, whose embedded green jade glowed softly. A green bamboo helmet was fitted atop his head, and his black furry ears poked through the top. The helmet's bamboo strap dangled unclasped.

"Good morning, Guardian Panda," said Clara.

"Are we ready for our flight to the Sky Pillars?"

"Yes," said Clara. "I'm ready."

"Very well. Please climb aboard your crane and we'll fly out once we are all harnessed in," said the Guardian Panda as he turned around to climb aboard his crane.

Clara moved toward her crane, as Shiori greeted her. "Good morning, Empress Warrior Wu."

Clara smiled and responded jovially, "Good morning, Shiori."

Shiori lowered herself as Clara climbed aboard and harnessed herself in. She looked up and saw that Yuka had easily invoked her float Qi element and gently settled onto the Guardian Crane.

She looked at Sung and Daniel, who were both checking their weapons before fastening into their harnesses. She gripped her harness. "Ready."

The Guardian Crane looked back and blinked her beady eyes before letting out a squawk. This was followed by a cacophony of squawks from the squadron, and soon, large feathery wings unfurled and flapped upward, and they were off, flying toward the Sky Pillars.

* * *

The winged squadron flew with urgency, and Clara could feel their anticipation as they raced through the air. She also noticed that as her squadron formed the standard V formation, their *katana* wings glistening in the rays of morning light, they were flanked by two additional squadron of cranes.

Within an hour, Clara could see The Sheers coming into view. The peninsula, with the Sky Pillars soaring into the sky, became visible in the distance. The entire peninsula looked like a hairbrush covered with bristles. As they started to swoop low and over the peninsula, Clara could see the sheer cliff below them behind the three-tiered ledge defense system. Several large bamboo crossbows sat atop them, each with a heavy jade- tipped arrow aimed south. Hundreds of pandas were busily working below. In front of the ledges was the wide trench they were shown the day before. Along its length were several bamboo ramps, and between the ramps, Clara could see the fleeting glints of hundreds of Clawdium spikes at the bottom of the trench.

Clara saw the regiments of the massive buffalos clad in armor. The sheer number of them in formation made them look like an impenetrable barrier. Beyond them was the open expanse of rocky land, and as they flew past the mid-way point, she saw the fearsome Clawdium spikes.

The flap of Shiori's wings caught her attention as they started to slow and soar upward. And that's when she saw them: the seemingly endless stretch of tall slender, rocky pillars soaring into the sky. They were a beautiful reddish sandstone color. Along their height, Clara could see distinct horizontal creases at irregular intervals. They were scattered about randomly, but the four that formed the trap were distinct. They were the largest of the stone pillars and offered the only way out of the Sky Pillars toward The Sheers.

Soon the cranes were approaching the four stone pillars, and Clara saw the large *Nian* piercer launcher system above each one. She could see the four launchers extending from the circular platform. There was a team of pandas, tigers, and buffalos atop each one. Her eyes quickly caught hundreds of cranes resting atop the surrounding pillars. She could only imagine that the tigers were lying in wait within the forest of pillars with the eagles resting atop of them. *The number of resources deployed for the battle was staggering*, she thought.

The Guardian Crane let out a squawk. The two escort squadrons peeled off and headed toward the adjacent pillars to take up positions. From Clara's perspective, Daniel's crane, along with the Guardian Buffalo atop the eagle, flew toward the top left pillar. Sung's crane, with the Guardian Tiger along his side, took him to the bottom left pillar. The Guardian Crane with Yuka flew to the top right pillar. Clara and Shiori, along with the Guardian Panda, flew toward the bottom right pillar.

Clara gripped her harness as Shiori spread her wings and gracefully landed on the bamboo platform. Clara unfastened herself and climbed off, looked at Shiori, and said, "*Xie xie.*"

Shiori's beady eye blinked and nodded. She soon found the Guardian Panda's crane and took up position on the massive bamboo circular deck.

Clara looked around. Being on top of the rocky pillar, she suddenly felt tiny. She could feel the vastness of the surrounding air as she stood atop the tall pillar. She looked south, and all she could see was blue water beyond the vastness of the stone pillars. To her left, she could make out the faint outline of the chain of volcanic islands that was home to the Red-Crowned Crane Kingdom. Beyond that, she could imagine the smaller island that was home to the Longevity Pool.

She drew her eyes closer and looked down the peninsula, where she could make out thousands of slender, irregularly but beautifully shaped reddish-yellowish rocky pillars. She could imagine hundreds of menacing *Nians* winding their way through and toward the peninsula's stone sentinels that provided a natural obstacle.

"Impressive, is it not, Empress Warrior Wu?" asked the Guardian Panda as he walked silently toward her.

Clara nodded as she felt the wind flowing around her. That's when she heard the creaking of a *Nian* piercer launcher, and her heart skipped a beat. She looked around nervously as she felt herself high up in the air. But she steadied herself as she gripped her bow and nodded at the Guardian Panda.

The Guardian Panda stood by her as he planted one end of his bamboo staff on the bamboo deck. It was topped off with a Clawdium spear tip.

"Will that spear tip penetrate the hide of a *Nian,* Guardian Panda?" asked Clara.

There was a moment of silence as he looked down at Clara and answered, "No, it won't."

Clara nodded as she looked around. Sung, Daniel, and Yuka were taking position with their guardians. She looked up at the Guardian Panda and asked, "Now what?"

The Guardian Panda simply said, "The stampede will be upon us soon."

EIGHTEEN

Hanro, the Head of the Prowlers, the Tiger Kingdom's army's elite battle team, lay in wait among the rocky formations at the base of a Sky Pillar. His breathing was steady, with each breath from his white-fanged mouth lightly ruffling his long whiskers. He stared straight ahead, bracing his paws against the rocky ground that his claws dug into. He was resting lightly on his belly, enveloped in a mesh battle suit that showed how powerfully sleek he was. His half-raised striped tail swayed. Magnetically attached to his back was a Clawdium clamp in open position.

Hanro looked back at the pack of white tigers behind him. All were ready to pounce onto the first *Nian* they encountered. He made eye contact with a few of them, who nodded in return. He turned, faced forward, and looked across the rocky path, making eye contact with another pack of Prowlers ready to pounce.

It was only a fleeting moment, but a dark green creature whizzed by. Hanro's eyes opened wide. A squawk overhead caught his attention as an eagle passed by, and soon he felt it: the rumble on the ground.

Another large green creature whizzed by, and Hanro could better see his enemy. It was large, shaped much like the mighty buffalos of Azen with broad shoulders, but it had the face of a lion. Its horns were long and slender with a deadly tip, but not as massive as those of the Buffalo Kingdom, more suitable for goring than ramming. But they were muscular, their paws heavy, and their green hide looked impenetrable.

A chorus of squawks rained down on the hundreds of battle tigers, led by the Prowlers, causing their ears to perk up at the dozens of *Nians* rushing by. Hanro's claws shot out, and his furry brow furrowed as he arched his back and let out a battle roar. In a second, he jolted forward, followed instantly by his pack of Prowler tigers, who launched themselves atop the stampede of *Nians.*

The *Nians'* heavy paws pounded the rocky terrain, sending up plumes of dust. Hanro flew over the racing *Nians* and snagged the first one he could with his claws, bouncing up and down along its back. The beast either didn't feel him or didn't care.

Hanro frantically spread his four limbs across the *Nian's* back as it rumbled through and around the rock formations. He roared to give himself the strength to dig his claws into the massive moving *Nian*'s thick hide as the roars of his fellow tigers echoed throughout the canyon. His eyes focused on the scene before him as he saw the hump of the *Nian's* broad shoulders heaving up and down. Atop many of them were battle tigers struggling to hold on with their tails curled firmly against the backsides of the *Nians*. Hanro looked to the side, and several *Nians* thundered by with tigers holding on, growling in frustration. He pulled himself forward and looked down. He could barely see the menacing, stone-cold face of the *Nian*. Its large yellow eyes were unfazed as it rumbled forward undeterred.

Hanro's heart beat mightily as he refocused, watching pillar after pillar zoom by on either side. He pulled himself steady over the *Nian's* broad shoulders. Peering down, could see the *Nian's* thick green neck, covered in part by a mangled yellowish-brownish mane. He pushed his hind legs forward and plunged his back claws into the *Nian's* thick hide as he raised himself upward. The claws of his left paw dug into the thick hide as the muscles along it tensed up. With his right paw, he reached over his back and pulled out the clamp.

His blue eyes focused on the clamp, and with all the might that his rear limbs could muster, he pushed his body forward. His left paw pulled away and grabbed the other handle of the clamp and opened it as far as it could go, exposing its serrated teeth. As he looked up, he roared and shoved the clamp downward around the *Nian's* neck.

The *Nian's* eyes bulged as the clamp squeezed around its neck. Its eyes rolled upward to see the faint underside of Hanro's furry chin. It hadn't even noticed the intruder upon its back and with annoyance, began to buck, trying to fling off the stowaway.

The *Nian*'s buck jolted Hanro, but his left claw dug into the hide as his right arm flailed wildly. He desperately grasped the right stem of the clamp and pulled it up with all his might, causing the lower portion of the clamp to lock in place around the *Nian's* neck. But the *Nian* still raced forward, dismissing Hanro and the clamp as mere nuisances.

Hanro continued to dig his front claws back into the *Nian*'s upper back. He could feel it angrily heaving in all directions. Hanro looked around and could see that many of his tiger brethren had successfully locked their clamps. Now there was a new but different roar echoing through the canyon. It was the *Nians*, finally angry.

Hanro let out a roar as he took in the tens of hulking *Nians* in front of and behind him. The sides of the canyon were racing by along with plumes of dust and stray rocks kicked up by marauding *Nians*. A fellow tiger in front of him leapt off to his left and barrel rolled onto a rocky ledge. Another tried the same but wasn't as lucky. His tail got snagged by the horn of an oncoming *Nian*, pulling him under the stampede.

Hanro tried to see where he had fallen, but it was no use. From behind, he could see hundreds of tigers all looking for their chance to leap off the *Nians*. Hanro then saw his opportunity: a rocky ledge coming up on his left. Without any fear or doubt, he eyed the empty back of another *Nian* on his left and leaped onto it. He dug in his claws as he panted, and focusing on the ledge, he lunged toward it. His body barreled into the wall of the ledge as his belly flopped with a thud onto its dusty surface. He raised himself up and moved away as another tiger hurled himself at the same ledge. Hanro opened his arms and awkwardly caught the flying tiger as both of their bodies fell onto the rocky ledge. In a daze, Hanro looked up. The blue sky soon filled with dark birds.

The other tiger pulled himself off Hanro and shrank back from the edge as the horde of *Nians* passed by. Other tigers were still clinging on, trying to find the opportunity to leap off. Hanro watched in despair as another tiger made a bad leap and was pulled under as his anguished roar was stamped out by the stampede. Hanro lowered onto all four paws and roared at the loss of another one of his fellow tigers. He looked up and roared as he saw the powerful eagles lining up for their assault.

* * *

Takeo's eagle eyes flickered as he scanned the chaos beneath him. Plumes of dust were rising from the rocky ground, kicked up by the paws of the *Nians* rumbling relentlessly down the canyon path. Takeo watched in earnest as the tigers leapt precariously off their *Nians*, leaving their clamps attached to their necks. Now it was time for Takeo and his fleet of hefty eagles to do their heavy lifting.

Takeo sensed the other two eagles on either side of him, just beyond his tail. He turned and saw the eagles lining up in a tight three-eagle formation to traverse the narrow canyon path. He glanced left and right and in between the Sky Pillars, spying the other eagle squadrons doing the same on the other winding parallel paths throughout the peninsula.

He peered ahead into the horde of *Nians* and focused on a clamp attached to a *Nian* at the front of the pack. Passing the Sky Pillars left and right, he waited until the landscape finally opened up to a straight path. He tucked in his wings and let out a squawk to begin the attack.

His streamlined feathery body seemed to fold into a dart as he shot through the air with determination. His eyes focused on the clamp attached to the *Nian* up front. Dust raced upward, and the thunderous rumbling of paws roared around him, along with several roars from the *Nians*, who'd spotted Takeo and his eagles as he lowered his talons.

Takeo swooped in and grasped the clamp with his talons. The *Nian* was heavy, but as Takeo unfurled his mighty wings and flapped upward, he cinched the clamp tightly around the *Nian's* neck.

The *Nian's* eyes popped in shock as the clamp cinched shut with a loud click. As the *Nian* struggled, it felt itself being hoisted upward, and soon it was flying through the air to the bellowing sound of the mighty flaps of the eagle's wings.

The *Nian* struggled, but it was no use. Its front legs couldn't reach the clamp. It could feel its life draining away. As it looked up with bulging eyes, it could only see the outline of the mighty eagle above him. The eagle quickly jerked upward, and the clamp made an ominous click, and everything went black for the doomed *Nian.*

Takeo looked down and could see that the *Nian* was no longer struggling and was hanging limp within the clamp's grasp. He opened his talons as the *Nian* fell away and splashed into its watery grave.

He circled and could see hundreds of eagles releasing the listless bodies of the *Nians* into the water. But there was no time to dwell on the kill. There were only about two hundred eagles and hundreds of *Nians*. They had many more to pull out before they reached the trap. With a rallying squawk, Takeo and his eagles flew back as quickly as their wings would allow.

Takeo flew above the canyon path, lining up his eagles behind him in a stream of three eagle formations. Looking ahead, he could see the *Nians* were approaching the halfway mark to the trap. Focusing on another clamp, he dove down with a squawk as his dark wings pressed against his body. With deadly grace, he grasped the clamp's handles and snapped it shut with an upward jolt of his talons, killing the *Nian* instantly. Takeo flew out and dropped the *Nian* into the water.

But time was running out. Takeo and his eagles lined up for another attack run. As he lined up his eagles over the *Nians*, he believed that the *Nians* had covered two-thirds of the canyon's path. There was only time for only one more attack run. Takeo squawked loudly, and the air was suddenly filled with squawks. All the eagles knew that this was their final chance, and they lined up in formation as Takeo prepared to strike.

Takeo dove in. Focusing on the clamp below him as the air raced over his smooth feathers, he inhaled deeply and grasped it with his talons. As he unfurled his wings to hoist the *Nian* upwards, he felt a sudden downward pull. He looked down in dismay to see that another *Nian* had jumped onto the back of the *Nian* he was trying to pluck from the horde. The extra weight was pulling him down, but with fierce determination, Takeo flapped harder. He let out a shriek when he felt a jab on his talon. The *Nian* had rammed his horns into his left talon, shooting pain up his left leg. But Takeo held steadfast and flew to the left, trying to knock the second *Nian* off balance. The second *Nian* sprawled out along the back of the first *Nian*, who was still running at full throttle. His strength and tolerance to pain seemed unstoppable. The second *Nian* tried again to gore Takeo's talons, but as soon as he tried, Takeo shifted right, and the second *Nian* tumbled off. Takeo mightily flapped his wings to lift the thrashing *Nian* out of the pack.

Blood trailed from Takeo's leg as he flew toward the water. He felt his left talon losing its grip and winced as he tightened his right talon. Without the strength of both of his talons, he couldn't cinch the clamp. But as an eagle, he did what he did best: fly. Soon he was above the water and released his grunting prey. The splashes of water echoed throughout as other eagles did the same. Takeo banked right and he circled around, nodding to his brave eagles. He looked back at the Sky Pillars and wondered how many *Nians* were still left: They were about to come upon the trap.

NINETEEN

"Release now! Release now!" yelled the battle pandas at the end of each launcher overlooking the trap. All the paths coursing through the canyon converged below. From atop her stone pillar, Clara could feel the frantic tension. She looked around at the *Nian* piercer team composed of pandas, tigers, and buffalos. She peered over to Yuka, whose face revealed the same sense of urgency. As she looked across the ways, she could see Sung walking along the length of the launcher via the skywalk.

With a look of shock, she looked at the Guardian Panda. "What is Sung doing?"

The Guardian Panda glanced at her and then Sung as he reached the end of the skywalk alongside the launcher commander panda. "Empress Warrior Wu, there is nothing to fear. He and the other warriors are merely getting into place to cast out their Qi elemental powers."

Clara nodded and saw that Yuka and Daniel had also flown to the end of their launchers. A rhythmic rumble started to vibrate throughout the entire launcher structure. A strap wound around the last of the *Nian* piercers along the inside of the launcher. It exited at the front, then doubled back along the outside of the launcher toward the center. That end was pulled by a team of four buffalos. As they pulled the strap, the *Nian* piercers fell through an opening at the end of the launcher. As they exited, their wing flaps opened, sending them whistling through the air toward their intended targets.

Clara couldn't see what was happening in the canyon before, but she could hear it. It started as a flurry of faraway whispers, then amplified into orchestrated squawks from the eagles. Finally, she was able to see the last of the attack run as the mighty eagles carried the *Nians* over the water and dropped them into their watery graves.

A low, steady stream of thunderous pounding bellowed from the canyon, and Clara could only imagine the horde of *Nians* rushing through the rocky paths as they converged into the trap.

Clara looked at the Guardian Panda and asked, "Can I go out onto the launcher?"

The Guardian Panda looked at her. "You won't be able to invoke any of your powers, Empress Warrior Wu."

"I just want to see."

The Guardian Panda nodded and pointed behind her. Clara turned around to see the launcher commander panda running down the skywalk as the Guardian Panda said, "Follow the launcher commander before the turn."

Clara looked back and asked, "The turn?"

"Just go, Empress Warrior Wu," said an exasperated Guardian Panda.

Clara nodded and ran to follow the launcher commander panda. He glanced behind him upon hearing her footsteps, nodded, and turned back toward the end of the launcher.

Side rails ran down the length of the skywalk, which ended at a small circular bamboo platform, which extended beyond the edge of the stone pillar, exposing the depths below. Clara suddenly realized how insignificantly small she was in the open vastness of the expanse around her. But she swallowed her momentary fear of heights and kept her eye on the backside of the launcher commander panda with his green bamboo helmet.

When Clara reached the end, the launcher commander panda looked down and said, "Empress Warrior Wu, please hold on tightly."

Clara nodded, gripping the bamboo rail of the skywalk facing away from the peninsula. She saw before her the wide swath of Clawdium spikes embedded into the ground, intended to impale any creature unfortunate enough to fall upon them. They cast sinister glints in the sunlight.

"Turn! Turn!" bellowed out the launcher commander panda.

Suddenly, Clara heard a loud creak as the launcher beam jolted beneath her. She widened her stance to stay balanced as the launcher beneath her started turning. Stresses along the bamboo moaned, gears ground against each other, and the wind buffeted the turning launcher. It continued to spin away until the next launcher locked into place beneath her. Clara looked down and could see what was happening in the trap below.

Green-hided creatures lay unmoving on the ground, felled by the first volley of *Nian* piercers. Blood oozed from their wounds and slid over their thick green hides. But the piles of dead *Nians* didn't deter the seemingly endless number of new *Nians* from barreling out from the canyon. Their agility was uncanny for creatures so large.

"Release! Now!" the launcher commander panda called out.

Clara saw the buffalos pulling the strap as a volley of *Nian* piercers dropped from the end of the second launcher. Clara saw them drop and could also see Sung's, Yuka's, and Daniel's launchers and their menacing *Nian* piercers streaming out as they whistled down toward their targets.

"You may go back, Empress Warrior Wu," the launcher commander panda said urgently.

Clara nodded and rushed back toward the middle of the platform without any hesitation.

"How many *Nian* piercers are there again?" asked Clara.

"About five hundred," said the Guardian Panda.

Clara did some quick math in her head. *Two thousand. Will it be enough?*

"It should be enough, Empress Warrior Wu," answered the Guardian Panda as if anticipating her concern. "Feel free to watch the next drop before the next turn."

Clara nodded and rushed down the skywalk as the launcher commander panda ordered, "Turn!"

The launcher platform turned. Soon, the third launcher was over its target area, and the piercers were released into the trap. But this third wave was different. She saw Sung throwing down ice walls ahead of the *Nians*, trying to keep them in the trap. It was a momentary nuisance, but the powerful *Nians* rammed the ice walls and broke through. The *Nians* that managed to escape the deathly piercers trampled over and past their dead brethren with abandon. Death meant nothing to them.

Daniel threw down fireballs, which exploded on the backs of the *Nians* but didn't stop them from powering through. Yuka threw down air walls, which confused them, but didn't stop the nimble creatures from feeling their way around and slipping by. She threw down gusts of wind to push them back towards the torrent of falling piercers.

Clara soon found herself gripping the rail as the platform turned once more. As she relaxed her grip on the rail, her attention was drawn to the number of *Nians* that had made it through the trap.

"They're escaping!" exclaimed Clara as she pointed to the *Nians*.

"The Clawdium spikes will slow them down, Empress Warrior Wu," said the launcher commander panda. "If that doesn't, then those will!"

Clara looked up to where he pointed, and she saw hundreds of heavy arrows flying through the air. They had just completed their apex, and rained down on the *Nians* who were attempting to use their horns to tear through the Clawdium spikes. The heavy arrows found their marks as they sunk into the *Nians*.

The launcher platform started to turn, and Clara's ears perked up at the shrieks of the cranes. Some of the *Nians* were actually clawing their way up the pillar across from her, and she realized they were probably attempting to climb her pillar as well. But as their claws dug into the stone, the cranes flew into action. With their *katana* wings, they began an assault on the climbing *Nians*. As each crane flew in, its *katana* wing sliced at the *Nian's* hide. But one slice wasn't enough to stop their deadly ascent—the fourth or fifth slice finally caused the *Nians* to release their grip and fall dead to the ground.

Once the next launcher beam was in place, another volley of piercers began. This could be the last drop despite having hundreds of *Nian* piercers remaining, as the plumes of dust from the rear of the horde was settling down. *So much senseless death*, thought Clara. She looked down from the launcher and could see massive lifeless green creatures below, their hides crisscrossed with crimson streams. She looked toward the Clawdium spikes, which stopped the *Nians* that had gotten through, allowing them to be felled by the heavy arrows. *This was a suicide mission*, Clara thought. There was no way that the *Nians* could even have gotten to The Sheers. The armies of Azen had planned for success for this final battle.

Soon, the whistling of the piercers was no more. The *Nians* impaled by the Clawdium spikes were lifeless. The stampede was over.

Clara let out a sigh of relief. The launcher commander panda did the same as his shoulders drooped. She heard footsteps behind her and saw that the Guardian Panda had walked onto the end of the skywalk.

"Is it over?" asked Clara.

"It is, Empress Warrior Wu," said the Guardian Panda calmly.

"What's that?" said the launcher commander panda as he pointed to the heap of bloodied *Nians.*

Clara looked down as the Guardian Panda's brown eyes blinked to see what was below.

From under the hulking masses of dead *Nians*, a single *Nian* emerged. It grunted a few times as it crawled out, clawing over the bodies of its kin. There were no more piercers to rain down on it as he exited beyond the trap. He continued to bobble forward and climbed over the *Nians* that had gored their way through the Clawdium spikes before being felled by multiple heavy arrows. It carefully and nimbly made its way through, using the fallen *Nian* as steppingstones over the deadly Clawdium spikes. It then leapt into the air to clear the last row of Clawdium spikes before landing onto all fours, hitting the ground with a thud.

One lone *Nian* emerged to confront an entire army of buffalos and panda archers. It rose, its broad shoulders at full height, the muscles in its powerful legs tensed up as its claws extended, ready to attack. Its tail swayed as its lion-like head turned before facing down its enemy.

"Just one *Nian,* Guardian Panda?" asked Clara curiously from the rail.

The Guardian Panda moved toward the rail; his brown eyes set in his black eye patches focused on the lone *Nian.* "It would seem so, Empress Warrior Wu."

Clara was focusing on the back of the *Nian's* head when a bright white light suddenly appeared. For a moment, the *Nian* was engulfed in the light, but when the light was gone, Clara gasped.

TWENTY

Vo, the Head of the Rammers, fixed his gaze on the *Nian*. It stood tall, its face calm even with nearly a thousand armor-clad buffalos staring it down. Then it closed its eyes, and in an instant was engulfed in a bright white light, which momentarily blinded Vo and his buffalo warriors.

But when the light faded, their eyes widened. Instead of one, there were two *Nians*. Before they could react, another flash of light and yet another *Nian* appeared, for a total of three. Before they could grasp what they were seeing, a sequence of bright flashes turned two *Nians* into four, four into eight, and eight into sixteen. Soon, over five hundred *Nians* were staring down the buffalos.

Vo could hear the grunts of disbelief from his buffalos, but he grunted loudly to keep them focused. With urgency in his low voice, he bellowed out, *horns* in Vietnamese: "*sừng!*"

And with that, the buffalos bore down, their massive horns swiveled forward. With his own horns locked into place, he yelled out the command for *charge*, "*sạc điện!*"

The buffalos' hooves rumbled down the rocky terrain as the *Nians* raced ahead on their muscular and clawed feet. The buffalos lowered their massive horns to meet the *Nians'* slender pointy horns. Heavy breaths and pounding heartbeats could be heard on both sides. Then, in a cataclysmic collision, they met, buffalo horns smashing into *Nians* as *Nians* gored at the buffalos' armor. Guttural grunts emanated from the entanglement of muscular bodies as roars of determination thundered through the scene.

Nians were battered back onto their hinds as buffalos were gored, toppling to the ground protected only by their armor. This made the *Nian* switch tactics to use their horns to rip the armor away.

* * *

"We have to do something!" screamed Clara as she looked desperately at the Guardian Panda.

"This cannot be!" the Guardian Panda exclaimed, staring ahead paralyzed.

"Guardian Panda!" screamed Clara to wake him from his trance. "What can we do?"

The Guardian Panda broke from his trance. He knew that the trajectory of the heavy bows of the pandas were configured for only the Clawdium spikes and beyond. He looked back into the canyon and figured the tigers were still there. That's when he saw the Guardian Tiger mount a crane and fly into the canyon along with the Guardian Crane. Soon, he saw Sung mount a crane and fly toward the new battlefront followed by Daniel and Yuka.

"To the battlefront, Empress Warrior Wu!" said the Guardian Panda as he ambled down the skywalk toward the cranes.

"But what can we do?" exclaimed Clara as she desperately followed him.

"Whatever we can," said the Guardian Panda as he climbed aboard his crane.

Clara frantically climbed aboard Shiori and as she fastened herself in, out of the corner of her eye, she caught another series of flashes and uttered, "Oh no."

"The *Nian*s have somehow acquired the power to replicate," said the Guardian Panda with dismay.

Clara looked at him and uttered, "Like the way Yuka can replicate her moon stars?"

The Guardian Panda looked at Clara gravely as he responded, "Yes."

"But how…" said Clara as her mind raced back to when Yuka was captured and the Moon Star was in the possession of the Warlock. "Oh no."

Their cranes lifted off, then immediately dove and leveled out as they passed through the trap. Clara pulled out an arrow and looked out. She saw Sung on his crane, Yuka and Daniel hovering as they threw down walls of ice, air, and fire. But with no earth, Clara only had her bow. She felt useless. She looked at the gory clash of buffalos and *Nians* below. The armored buffalos had the battlefield advantage, but each time a line of *Nians* were battered back, a new wave of fresh *Nians* would appear in a sequence of white flashes.

"There's too many of them!" screamed Yuka as she threw down air walls and gusts of wind.

"We gotta keep trying!" as Daniel screamed out desperately as he watched in horror as buffalos fell to the *Nians*. "Yuka, whip up a tornado! Suck up as many as you can!"

Yuka nodded as she whipped out both of hands as she screamed out the Japanese word for *tornado*, "*tatsumaki!*"

In a first for Yuka on the battlefield, she simultaneously invoked two tornados along the flanks of the *Nian*s. The *Nians* closest to the forming tornados reared their heads up before being sucked into them.

Daniel invoked a stream of fire and launched it into the closest tornado, burning the *Nians* spiraling hopelessly within. Daniel flew toward the second tornado and repeated the fiery act.

Sung flew behind the clashing of the massive buffalos and *Nians* and saw that some were getting through. His crane turned around to allow him to see the battlefield. His eyes widened. The hundreds of buffalos and *Nians* crashing into each other was ferocious and the sound deafening. He looked down at the few *Nians* that were racing toward the ledge and invoked ice walls: "*Dahm!*"

The ice walls would at least slow them down, but a few *Nians* rammed against them with abandon. That's when Sung looked up and screamed in elation, "Yes!"

Emerging from the Sky Pillars were squadrons of cranes, and he could make out the tigers on top of them. Sung commanded his crane to race ahead as he kept his eyes on the squadrons. In an instant, the cranes flew in low and the tigers leapt off, landing in the middle of the fracas. But using their previous tactic, many of the tigers landed on the *Nians* and quickly attached clamps. If they were not bucked off the *Nians*, they raised their paws for the cranes to swoop in to pull them off the *Nians'* backs. Hundreds of eagles then dove in to grasp the clamps and lift the struggling *Nians* away. If an eagle was lucky, one jolt of its talons would snap the *Nian's* neck.

Another sequence of flashes occurred, and Clara had to close her eyes. When she reopened them, her heart sank to see a hundred new *Nians* appear and make a fresh charge toward the beleaguered buffalos, whose numbers were being decimated. She saw Yuka and Daniel pairing their Qi elemental powers as Sung raced by throwing down icicles and ice walls. Her eyes were then drawn to the ledge at the base of The Sheers, where she saw that her panda spearmen were racing out to form a line of bamboo shields. But they would be overrun if enough of the beastly powerful *Nians* made their way to them.

Out of the corner of her eye, she saw another blistering sequence of flashes and looked to her right. Her expression changed to one of realization. She saw it: the first *Nian*. It had not moved at all, but was surrounded by two circles of *Nians*, which were not moving either. They were protecting the first *Nian*.

She tapped Shiori's neck and pointed to the *Nian*. Shiori nodded and flew directly toward it. Clara pulled back on her bow and aimed for the *Nian's* forehead when she saw his horns suddenly turn a bright white before they blindingly flashed, forcing Shiori to pull up and Clara to brace herself. Shiori pulled out of the ascent and circled back to make another run, but Clara realized something. "The horns!"

"Quick!" Clara hollered out as her heart thumped. She pulled out another arrow and loaded it in tandem with the first. "Before it can flash again!"

Clara's heart pounded, the air racing through her hair from behind her helmet as her arm drew back on the bow. Shiori bore down and pulled in her wings to gain speed. The *Nian* glared at them with its glowing yellow eyes as Clara let loose two arrows. Her two green jade-tipped arrows smashed into the two white horns, shattering them as the *Nian* reared its head back in shock.

Shiori pulled up, and Clara directed her toward Yuka. She kept her eyes on the *Nian* as it violently shook its head in confusion as all that remained atop its head were the two stumps of its once-white horns.

"Yuka!" hollered out Clara. "Push them back over the Clawdium spikes!

Yuka quickly surveyed the battlefield and saw that several buffalos and *Nians* were still engaged in a clash of horns. But several *Nians* were in the rear, and she began to invoke the Japanese Qi element for *gust* as she yelled out, "*Toppū!*"

Clara directed Shiori towards Sung, and as she approached him, she hollered, "Can you lay down ice walls in the back to block off their escape?"

Sung looked toward the back as she saw Yuka blowing the *Nians* over the Clawdium spikes and nodded. He flew away and laid down ice to seal off the escape route.

"Empress Warrior Wu," hollered out the Guardian Panda. "What are you planning?"

"To trap the *Nians* over there," Clara replied as she then pointed to the crossbows. "Get the pandas to fire at will!"

The Guardian Panda's eyes lit up in understanding as he flew toward the battle pandas manning the massive crossbows.

Clara frantically looked for Daniel. It wasn't hard to find him as he was sending fireballs into the *Nians'* hide as anger welled up within him at the sight of his buffalos being gored. He looked up when he heard his name to see Clara rushing toward him.

"Push them back over the Clawdium spikes!" Clara hollered out as she then flew past him.

Daniel looked down at the breaking line of the remaining *Nians* and with vengeance coursing through him, he launched powerful fireballs that pushed the *Nians* back on impact, sending them rolling backwards despite their defiant ferocious roars.

Pushing through the heavy cross traffic of cranes and eagles, Clara found the Guardian Crane and hollered out, "Guardian Crane! Clear the air! Clear the air! Panda arrows!"

The Guardian Crane and Shiori whizzed by each other. The Guardian Crane's saw the *Nians* being pushed back over the Clawdium spikes on her right and the crossbows on her left. In an instant, she started to squawk loudly, ordering her cranes and eagles to clear out.

The cranes and eagles echoed the command until the air was filled with an urgent cacophony of squawks. Eagles frantically pulled tigers out before flying off. Yuka and Daniel saw the aerial fighters leave the air space and they looked at each other as they raced toward The Sheers. That's when they saw the first volley of heavy arrows arc over them, followed by another and another.

The *Nians* clamored reluctantly over the Clawdium spikes as heavy jade-tipped arrows pierced their thick hides. Howls of pain erupted from the remaining *Nians* as the weight of their bodies sent up clouds of dust as they collapsed.

The first *Nian* was also the last. It cowered as the *Nians* protecting it fell. It looked up with trembling eyes one last time as a green jade-tipped heavy arrow buried itself between the two stumps where its horns used to be.

* * *

Clara hovered just above the line of bamboo shields the battle pandas had formed. Her face trembled with worry, but hope sprung anew as she saw Yuka and Daniel fly toward her.

"Is it over?" she asked in a cautious tone.

Yuka and Daniel slowed and hovered on either side of Clara as she blurted out, "Where's Sung?"

"I see him, Empress Warrior Wu," said Shiori, training her eyes in the distance.

"Are you sure?" asked Clara. "How can you be sure?"

"My eyes are much better than yours," said Shiori. "I see the Guardian Tiger alongside him. They are approaching."

"The guardians?" exclaimed Clara as she frantically looked about her when a familiar voice appeared from behind.

"I'm right here, Empress Warrior Wu," said the Guardian Panda atop of his crane as he hovered behind her.

Clara let out a sigh of relief when the Guardian Crane flew in behind Yuka.

"Guardian Crane!" Yuka said with relief and excitement.

"Emperor and empress warriors," bellowed out the Guardian Buffalo as his eagle flew in behind Daniel.

"Guardian Buffalo!" said Daniel with relief.

"Is it over?" asked Clara as her voice wavered.

"I think it is, Empress Warrior Wu," said the Guardian Panda. "The final battle is over."

The warriors' shoulders drooped as the weight of battle fell away from them. Clara still gripped the Bow of Destiny in her left hand while her right hand relaxed against the harness.

"Empress and emperor warriors," said the Guardian Panda. "Let's get you to a safe place, beyond The Sheers. Emperor Warrior Kim will be there shortly."

Without a sound, Shiori flew Clara gently turned toward The Sheers, and Yuka and Daniel followed. The crane carrying Sung was directed to fly by to join his friends. The crane with the Guardian Tiger flew in and joined his fellow guardians.

"It's over," said the Guardian Tiger with exasperated relief.

"Are you certain?" asked the Guardian Panda.

"Yes," said the Guardian Tiger gravely. "I saw the last *Nian* fall."

The Guardian Panda nodded and looked toward the warriors' direction.

"Gao Gao," said the Guardian Tiger to the Guardian Panda.

The Guardian Panda looked up, almost knowing what was on the mind of the Guardian Tiger and the other two guardians.

"There are four of them," said the perplexed Guardian Tiger.

The Guardian Panda nodded as he muttered back, "So there are, Yonggirang."

"How can this be?" asked the Guardian Crane.

The Guardian Panda nodded and replied, "I do not know."

"What changed?" asked the Guardian Buffalo.

There was another pause as the Guardian Panda replied guardedly, "I don't know."

TWENTY - ONE

Clara quickly slid off Shiori and took a few steps away from her when she stopped. She turned around to meet the crane's gaze as she thanked her in Cantonese, "*Do jeh sai!*" Shiori nodded and uttered in a somber tone, "It was an honor to fly with you."

Clara eked out a smile as she saw Yuka and Daniel. She dashed over to them as Sung's crane landed. He quickly slid off and nodded to his crane, then his eyes met Clara's and he smiled. He briskly walked over to complete the circle of Azen warriors. Their weary eyes darted at each other as a delicate silence hung over them.

"Is it really over?" asked Yuka as her voice trembled.

Daniel nodded as he swallowed a breath and muttered, "I think so."

"Azen?" started Sung as his eyes darted to everyone before landing on Clara, "Is safe?"

Clara struggled with a grin as she shook her head nervously before she emotionally blurted out, "I think so."

Yuka was the first to let out an outburst of cautious joy, "Azen is safe!"

Daniel's eyes welled up with joy and relief as he looked towards the battlefield. He tried to hold back his emotions as he wiped away his tears and smiled. But Sung had the biggest grin on his face. "We did it."

A huge smile appeared on Clara, coupled with her tear-filled glistening eyes as she reached out to everyone and exclaimed, "Azen is safe!"

The warriors threw their arms around each other and cried joyously as their helmets clunked each other. Suddenly, all their burdens fell away—all the responsibilities that they were entrusted to by the guardians, the kingdom leaders, and the kingdoms themselves. They held onto each other, their collective breathing became one in their huddle of relief intermixed with grins and the unexpected tears as they rejoiced in just being Asian American teenagers.

Clara looked up at everyone and she could feel that everyone was so relieved. Despite their tear-filled eyes, their grins and innocent chuckles, she knew what they were feeling as she uttered, "We did it."

* * *

After their befuddled huddle, the guardians had flown in, and directed the warriors to one of the many tables that had been set up in the staging area away from The Sheers' edge.

Clara sat with Yuka, facing away from the edge of The Sheers. Sung sat in front of Clara with Daniel beside him. Clara's bow and quiver were laid out in front of her as her helmet rested on top of them. Her hands were gently wrapped over her helmet as she rested her left cheek upon it. Sung, with his Claw Staff leaned up against the table's edge, also used his helmet as a headrest. Yuka laid her helmet beside her on the bench as she placed her right cheek over her hands that rested on the table while Daniel, with his club horn laid across the table, was looking ahead with his palms relaxed on the table.

"It's like a blur," Sung muttered.

"What?" asked Yuka as she halfheartedly turned her face toward Sung.

"The whole battle," said Sung. "It's like a blur."

"Tell me about it," said Daniel as he exhaled loudly. "Thankfully, we had Clara to see clearly."

Clara looked up confused and asked, "What do you mean?"

"In all the craziness, you directed us all to do stuff," said Daniel. "You're the real Azen leader out of all of us."

Clara blushed and could feel her cheeks flush as she dismissed the compliment.

"No, really, you are," said Daniel graciously as he looked at Yuka and Sung. "She is, right?"

Yuka smiled at Clara as Sung gave a thumbs up to her. Then Daniel continued, "I thought it was all over until that last *Nian* climbed over all the dead *Nians*. And then it multiplied."

"Replicated," muttered Yuka from her resting position.

"Huh?" replied Daniel as his gaze fell onto Yuka.

Yuka raised her head off her hands and with her eyes somewhat downcast. She said eerily, "Replicated. The *Nian* replicated itself and then the others."

There was a silence when Daniel asked, "I thought the Warlock's creatures didn't have powers?"

Yuka looked down into her lap. Her hands reached down and carefully detached her Moon Star. She brought it up for all to see as her eyes fell onto the white jade that glinted in the light. Then she said, "It replicated, like my white jade."

Daniel looked startled as he looked about and asked, "But how?"

Clara looked up at him and said calmly, "When Yuka was captured. The Warlock took possession of the Moon Star and the white jade."

Daniel looked away from Clara as his eyes fixated on the white jade of the Moon Star. He abruptly looked up and bolted upright, causing everyone to look at him with startled faces. His heart suddenly collapsed as he uttered, "Oh my god, did I cause this?"

Clara sensing his dismay, reached out toward him and said, "Daniel, what matters is that we won the battle."

Daniel looked at Clara and with a trembling voice, "But, if I hadn't flown out to see the Warlock's Fortress, Yuka wouldn't have been captured. Do you think…"

"I don't know," said Clara.

"For all we know, the Warlock may have already developed this power and launched it in this battle," said Sung reassuringly.

"Clara," said Daniel sternly. "What did you see when you attacked that last *Nian*?"

Clara looked at Sung and Yuka who also turned toward her. She exhaled and looked at Daniel and said, "I saw the last *Nian* and saw its horns light up. That's when the bright flashes occurred, and when they were gone, there were more *Nians*. I thought maybe his horns were giving him the power to replicate, so I flew in and destroyed them."

Daniel turned his head sharply at Yuka and asked, "Does your jade flash when you replicate your moon stars?"

Yuka sensed Daniel's urgent tone and answered, "No, Daniel, it does not."

"It could all be a coincidence," said Sung reassuringly as he gestured to Daniel to sit back down.

Suddenly, large birdlike shadows glided over the entire area, and everyone looked up to see the feathery underbellies and wings of several eagles flying in V-formations. In their talons were large bamboo crates.

Clara rose and with her hand covering her eyes, she blurted out, "What's going on?"

"Empress and emperor warriors," said the Guardian Panda as he came up to them. "It's time to go."

"Guardian Panda, what's going on?" Daniel asked with concern, his eyes meeting the Guardian Panda's.

The Guardian Panda looked to his right, turned back, and responded calmly, "Nothing that should concern you, Emperor Warrior Nguyen; just some cleanup of the battlefield."

"It's a rabbit!" Yuka exclaimed, pointing upward just as a rabbit's head poked out of a box before it pulled its floppy ears back in.

Daniel grabbed his club horn along with his helmet and hopped over the bench. He quickly made his way around Sung and the Guardian Panda and raced toward The Sheers' edge.

"Emperor Warrior Nguyen!" hollered the Guardian Panda as he saw Sung race around him as well. "Emperor Warrior Kim…"

Clara grabbed her bow and quiver along with her helmet and raced after Daniel and Sung with Yuka close behind. The Guardian Panda's plea went unanswered as the warriors raced to the edge.

Daniel and Sung stood at the edge and looked out into the distance. Clara came up upon Daniel's right side as Yuka came up upon hers.

The eagles were descending toward a series of large white tents that were set up in the battlefield, between the first tier of the ledge and the Clawdium spikes. More billowing tents were in the middle and being erected further on down. There was bustling all over with pandas, buffalos, tigers, cranes, eagles, and the rabbits hopping out of the bamboo carriers.

"What's going on?" asked Daniel as he surveyed what befell his eyes.

"Medical tents, Emperor Warrior Nguyen," said the Guardian Panda, who had come up behind the warriors. The Guardian Crane soon floated in as Yuka looked up at her just as she landed. The Guardian Tiger prowled on in as the Guardian Buffalo stepped in on the left of Sung and Daniel.

"Emperor and empress warriors," said the Guardian Buffalo. "We need to be leaving."

Daniel's eyes soon focused on the streams of wheeled bamboo platforms being pushed down the wide path between the two tent formations. Daniel's face crumbled as he saw bloodied buffalos and tigers on the platforms. The rabbits scurried into the tents.

"Did I do that?" asked Daniel as guilt started to fill his heart.

"Emperor Warrior Nguyen," said the Guardian Buffalo reassuringly. "You saved them. They are simply wounded and are being taken care of."

Daniel gripped the club horn and winced. Sung placed a reassuring hand on his shoulder as Daniel smoothly slid the club horn into the holster upon his back and donned his helmet. He brushed into the air the Vietnamese *thrust* Qi element as he suddenly yelled out, "*đẩy!*"

As Daniel impulsively flew off as everyone's eyes followed him, the Guardian Buffalo stared off into his direction as he hollered, "Emperor Warrior Nguyen!"

"Daniel!" yelled Yuka as she suddenly flew off, invoking the Japanese Qi element for *fly*, "*Tobu!*"

Before the Guardian Panda could say anything, the Guardian Crane flapped her wings and said, "I'll go after them."

The Guardian Crane raced forward, quickly gaining on Daniel and Yuka. Clara looked up at Sung. He gazed down at her worried expression. He nodded and looked toward the battlefield, where the Guardian Crane had intercepted Daniel and Yuka. They were descending just as two tents billowed upward.

"I can't invoke a bridge this high up…" said Sung

"Emperor Warrior Kim," said the Guardian Panda as Clara and Sung looked with a weary expression. "There's no need to invoke your powers to join them," said the Guardian Panda as he waved his paw as four cranes and an eagle started to descend. "We'll go to them."

Clara looked up at Sung and saw the same sense of relief she now felt. Once their feathered escorts landed, everyone climbed aboard and with the Guardian Panda in the lead, they flew toward the white tents.

As they flew, Clara could see the Guardian Crane standing tall in front of Daniel and Yuka on the rocky terrain. The six large tents looming behind them bustled with activity. Pandas in white coats were pushing wheeled bamboo platforms down the path that evenly split the six tents. On the platforms were the injured buffalos and tigers, moaning and groaning in pain.

At the far end, with pandas guiding them down in an orderly fashion, eagles carefully lowered thick white sheets gathered at their corners within their strong talons. As they rested the bundled sheets on the ground, their corners fell away, revealing injured buffalos or tigers. Pandas quickly rushed forward and lifted each injured buffalo or tiger by its sheet onto a platform, which was wheeled away. Rabbits in white robes and masks were hopping onto the platforms and directing the pandas.

Clara's heartache swelled at the number of injured buffalos and tigers. As Shiori descended, Clara instinctively gripped the harness tighter so she could see the injured tigers and buffalos more clearly.

When her crane landed, Clara quickly climbed down and thanked her. She could feel her chest tighten as she placed her left hand on the green jade of her bow. She quickened her pace as she came up to Yuka's right. Daniel, who was on Yuka's left, simply stared ahead. Soon Sung approached Daniel's left, but his concerned eyes never strayed from the grim scene ahead of him.

The Guardian Crane blocked their path and was silent as she looked at each of them. She cast an aura of calm. This was not her first battle, and she knew the horrors of war.

As the other guardians closed in, Daniel mumbled, "Did I do this?"

"What exactly do think you did, Emperor Warrior Nguyen?" asked the Guardian Buffalo as he circled around and faced Daniel with a wary expression.

"Did the *Nians* somehow gain the power to replicate because the Warlock got a hold of Yuka's Moon Star?" he asked.

There was silence as the Guardian Buffalo briefly closed his large glassy reddish-brown eyes before gazing upon Daniel once more. He stood tall and firm but spoke reassuringly, "Emperor Warrior Nguyen, in each battle, we always have injured. The rabbits are tending to them; they are being taken care of."

Daniel looked past the Guardian Buffalo as tears started to form on his lower eyelids. But he stifled an emotion welling up in his throat as he said, "But never this many. Right, Guardian Buffalo?"

Despite all the commotion behind the Guardian Buffalo, he was unfazed. He stared back at Daniel and responded. "No, not this many, but their armor protected them. The buffalos and the tigers will heal."

But Daniel couldn't let his guilt go, as a stream of tears flowed from his eyes. From a guttural mix of phlegm and emotions, he uttered the Vietnamese phrase for *I'm sorry*, "*tôi xin lỗi.*"

As Daniel clenched his fists in anguish, Yuka instinctively reached for his right fist, which was hot to the touch, in consolation. She gently held his hand as she looked at him with worry. Sung placed his right hand reassuringly upon Daniel's left shoulder. Daniel sighed as he gently cradled his face in his left hand. Clara placed her left hand on Daniel's right shoulder as she pursed her lips.

The Guardian Buffalo glanced quickly at the Guardian Tiger and Panda as the Guardian Crane looked on. He then spoke to Daniel.

"Emperor Warrior Nguyen," he said calmly. "You are taking too much responsibility upon yourself."

"But I can't help but feel that I may have been responsible for this," mumbled Daniel as guilt hung onto every word as he stared into the large eyes of the Guardian Buffalo.

"What is going on here?" came a voice from below as a large rabbit in a white coat with his white facemask pulled down beneath his chin entered the circle.

Everyone looked at the large rabbit as he raised himself up on his hind legs and looked at the Guardian Panda.

"Juju," said the Guardian Panda. "How are the wounded?"

Juju turned his head as he saw the last of the buffalos and tigers being wheeled in from the end of the medical tents. He turned his head back as his large eyes looked at everyone.

"We have our hands full today, but we'll take care of them," said Juju.

"Hi Juju," said Clara as she gently waved to him.

Juju turned to Clara as his nostrils wiggled gently, "Empress Warrior Wu. Good battle, all of you. You should all feel proud for what you have done here on Azen."

"But how can I feel proud when I may have contributed to their injuries?' asked Daniel.

Juju looked confused, and Clara feeling a sense of awkwardness interjected, "What Daniel is trying to say, with so many injured buffalos, he feels a certain responsibility for them."

"Nonsense!" stammered Juju to everyone's surprise. "You are the Emperor Warrior for the Buffalo Kingdom. Without you, we wouldn't be tending to the injured, but the dead. I'll be right back."

As Juju hopped away, Yuka looked at Clara with a surprised look on her face as Clara chuckled and said, "He can be like that, but he's still so adorable."

Soon Juju hopped back into the circle. Another rabbit joined him. He too was wearing a white coat and had pulled his mask down beneath his chin. He looked up with curious eyes as his nose twitched. He straightened up as well as his ears perked up a bit when he noticed he was around the warriors in addition to the guardians.

"Emperor Warrior Nguyen," stated Juju. "This is Cuong. He is the head medicinist and herbalist serving the Buffalo Kingdom. Cuong, please tell the young emperor warrior what your assessment is."

Daniel, a bit wide eyed as he focused on the tall rabbit standing before him, nodded. Cuong also nodded and took a breath.

"Emperor Warrior Nguyen," Cuong began. "It is an honor to meet you. All the rabbits from across the kingdoms are tending to the injured. Most of the injured are buffalos, but we have a few tigers and small number of cranes as well."

"How are the tigers?" asked Sung as he stepped forward.

"We are tending to them, Emperor Warrior Kim," said Cuong as he nodded. "Mainly broken ribs."

"And the cranes?" asked Yuka as her hands clasped together in front of her chest.

"Mostly dislocated wings," said Cuong as he nodded to her.

Suddenly, Juju interjected, "As you can see, they are being taken care off. I can assure you, that despite the moans and groans, the buffalos will ram again. The tiger kitten whimpers will soon roar again and the cranes, well, they are the stubborn ones, they want to flap their wings all over the place despite their dislocations. No crane likes to be grounded."

Juju saw that Daniel was still looking sorrowful and then said tersely, "Emperor Warrior Nguyen, we mourn the dead, not the injured. Please stop your mournful nonsense!"

Juju's terseness sliced through Daniel's emotional fog. "Can we see them?" he asked.

Juju looked surprised and glanced at Cuong, who also looked equally confused. Juju then looked at all the warriors in their battle gear and retorted, "I'm sorry. You may not. You need to be wearing medical robes, and we simply don't have any that fit you."

The blue eyes of the Guardian Tiger lit up as he pressed his snout into the ear of the Guardian Buffalo, whose red eyes shifted downward as he listened intently. As the Guardian Tiger pulled back, the Guardian Buffalo stepped forward and added, "We have some other garments that may suffice. Guardian Crane, can you have one of your cranes fetch the… robes?"

The Guardian Crane looked down at the Guardian Buffalo dubiously but nodded. She looked up and made eye contact with one of the cranes a short distance away and squawked out some commands. The other crane nodded and soared back to The Sheers.

As the warriors waited, they were instructed to shed their battle armor. With several panda attendants, the warriors slipped off their helmets, body armor, shoulder guards, gauntlets, thigh and shin protection, and were pretty much left standing in their boots and battle bodysuits, each with its embedded glowing jade.

The crane returned, and the Guardian Panda took the package from its beak and pulled out four black robes. As he looked down at the embroidered kingdom logos, he called out each warrior, who came forward to receive the robe. Sung's name was called out first, followed by Daniel, then Yuka, and finally Clara.

Clara reached out for the robe and unfurled it. Like her green robe, it had an embroidered panda head on the left chest area but it was black. She quickly put it on and with a little coaxing, its front black edges magnetically sealed. She quickly adjusted her bamboo ribbon hair accessory and pulled her hair taut. Her bow and quiver were handed back to her by a panda attendant. She quickly slung the bow and quiver across her chest and turned to face her friends.

Despite having just fought a harrowing battle with the most ferocious of all the Warlock's creatures, Clara couldn't help noticing how clean the four of them looked in their robes. Sung was able to magnetically slap his Claw Staff onto his back; Daniel was able to find the slip hole for his club horn, and Yuka didn't need to bother. All eyes were then on Juju, who coughed gently.

"Very well then, emperor and empress warriors," said Juju. "Please follow Cuong and myself."

The rabbits led the way as Clara and the others followed. Close behind were the Guardian Buffalo and Tiger with the Guardian Panda and Crane taking up the rear.

As they got closer, they could hear the moans and groans of pain from the buffalos and tigers. Cuong turned left into the tent, whose white cloth diffused the sunlight. In it were rows of bamboo platforms arranged neatly. Clara saw tens, if not hundreds of buffalos lying flat on their bellies as they were being worked on by several rabbits. The uninjured buffalos, tigers, and pandas helped unfasten the injured buffalos' armor as numerous rabbits hopped about, offering medical treatment to the injured buffalos.

Daniel immediately walked to the closest injured buffalo on his right. His expression of concern showed as he bent down to look at the battle-weary buffalo's face. His eyes drooped and his snout gently flared as his tongue hung out of his mouth. As Daniel's shadow fell over the buffalo's eyes, they suddenly flickered open.

The buffalo came to a start, but Daniel, in a reassuring way, put his hand onto the buffalo's head and looked at his massive horns. The left one was cracked at the tip, and Daniel grimaced.

"Please, don't stand, just relax," said Daniel reassuringly. With the stroke of his hand upon his coarse brownish-grayish fur, the massive buffalo relaxed, allowing his massive shoulders to droop.

The battle buffalo looked up with his beleaguered eyes and said weakly, "It was a good day to ram."

Daniel smiled and uttered from his heart, *thank you* in Vietnamese. "*Cảm ơn bạn.*"

Soon another rabbit came to the front, almost oblivious to Daniel's sentimental well wishes, as it uncorked two glass vials. It then shoved one into each of the buffalo's nostrils. The buffalo inhaled deeply and soon, a peculiar smile came over him as his eyes fell shut and its head plopped onto the platform.

"It's a sedative, Emperor Warrior Nguyen," said Cuong. "Come now, we can see the buffalos in this row and you'll be assured that the buffalos are being well taken care of."

"No," said Daniel firmly as he rose.

Cuong looked startled, and as Daniel realized this, he added, "I'm sorry, I did not mean to be disrespectful. I want to see each of the buffalos and the other animals."

Cuong looked at Juju, who looked at Daniel and said, "Emperor Warrior Nguyen, there are hundreds. You won't be able to speak to each one and not distract the rabbits from administering care."

Daniel looked flustered as he looked about, "But I have to."

"Emperor Warrior Nguyen," said the Guardian Buffalo from behind as Daniel turned to him.

"We can walk down the rows and you may say *cảm ơn bạn* as you pass by them. The buffalos would appreciate that," said the Guardian Buffalo persuasively.

Daniel looked down as he pondered the alternative and nodded. "I'm fine with that Guardian Buffalo, as long as you come with me."

The Guardian Buffalo stepped forward as his hooves thudded upon the rocky terrain. He looked sternly at Daniel. "It'd be my honor, Emperor Warrior Nguyen."

As Daniel smiled, Sung said, "Daniel, you're doing good. I'm going to do the same for my tigers, okay?"

Daniel smiled and replied, "Go for it. I think they would like to see you too."

Yuka turned around and asked, "Guardian Crane, can I see the injured cranes?"

"Certainly, Empress Warrior Satoh," said the Guardian Crane. "Please follow me. They are in the last tent. There aren't that many."

"We'll all meet back here when Daniel is done," exclaimed Yuka as she gently waved. Upon exiting the tent, Yuka stopped. She turned around and with both hands at her side, she bowed respectfully toward the entire tent before following the Guardian Crane.

As Daniel continued down the row, Sung followed the Guardian Tiger down a perpendicular row that led over to the next tent. As her friends went along their way, Clara looked up at the Guardian Panda.

"Are there any pandas that I should thank?" asked Clara.

"There are not, Empress Warrior Wu," he said. "Most of the spear and archer pandas were by the ledge. The *Nians* did not make it that far. The buffalos bore the brunt of this battle."

Clara nodded. While she was grateful that her pandas were mostly unscathed, she felt some guilt setting in as she looked at the hundreds of injured buffalos. She couldn't fathom the sorrow that ate away at Daniel.

"Empress Warrior Wu," said the Guardian Panda waking Clara from her revelry. "When you shot at the last *Nian*, what did you see?"

Clara nodded as she thought about that last moment. "Before another set of *Nians* was replicated, I saw its horns glow white. When it flashed, it blinded me for a moment, and then there were more *Nians*. That's when I guessed that its horns were somehow responsible for the replication. So, I flew in close, and before it could replicate again, I shot at the two horns and shattered them."

The Guardian Buffalo nodded in deep thought.

"Nothing like this has ever happened before, has it Guardian Panda?" asked Clara.

The Guardian Panda looked up and simply said, "No. Nothing like this. We have had surprises, but it's always been physical. Like an unexpected wave of creatures or more agile creatures or augmented creatures. But never a power invoked on the battlefield."

"Do you think somehow the Warlock was able to tap into Yuka's white jade?" asked Clara gravely.

"I do not know, Empress Warrior Wu," said the Guardian Panda. "I will need to discuss this with the other guardians."

In that moment of doubt, Clara nodded and looked down at the new green jade embedded in the Bow of Destiny. It was still glowing gently, embodying all the power it had to power up all the green jade within its reach.

As her eyes traveled down the black robe, she asked, "Guardian Panda, what are these robes for?"

There was a silence behind his brown, black patch eyes as he simply said, "In case it got cold and you needed something warm."

As Clara pondered his answer, he said, "Let's move out of the tent and let the rabbits do their job," as he turned back toward the rocky path. Clara followed as she gazed at the large number of bandaged and sedated buffalos.

As Clara waited on the edge of the medical tent complex, it wasn't long before Yuka returned. She recapped how Juju was right that the cranes were stubborn about being grounded. She recounted how a crane was held down so that its dislocated wing could be set back in place by what seemed to be a violent yank. But after the initial shriek of pain, the crane breathed easily as the pain from the dislocation subsided.

Sung soon joined them. He had a jovial expression as he recounted how he held the paw of a tiger who had a cracked claw pulled from his other paw. He was impressed at how well the tiger bore the pain.

Finally, Daniel rejoined his friends, looking somber. He told them he was able to thank each buffalo and that he helped to hold down and comfort one of them as the rabbits sawed off a cracked horn. When it was done, the buffalo asked Daniel how he looked. He saw that more than half of the buffalo's right horn was sawed off. He feigned a smile and said it looked great, not knowing what else to say. Then he moved onto the next buffalo.

"Emperor and empress warriors," hollered out the Guardian Buffalo as he walked toward them with the other guardians closing in.

"Guardian Buffalo," said Daniel respectfully. "Thank you for letting me see and thank every single injured buffalo."

"It was my honor, Emperor Warrior Nguyen," said the Guardian Buffalo. "It's time to return to your kingdoms."

Everyone nodded and soon, the cranes and a single eagle landed nearby.

"We'll meet up soon, guys," said Clara.

"What's going to happen now?" asked Yuka.

"You'll spend the night back at your kingdoms. Tomorrow you'll spend the day at Zenith Waterfalls, and you'll return to your homes the next day," the Guardian Crane responded.

"What's the Zenith Waterfalls?" asked Yuka.

"One of the most beautiful and majestic places in all of Azen," said the Guardian Crane. "It is there that we will commemorate our victory over the Warlock."

"There are even more beautiful places on Azen?" asked Clara.

"Indeed there are, Empress Warrior Wu," said the Guardian Panda.

"Wow. I wish we could have explored those places too," said a disappointed Clara.

"Unfortunately, that would require more time than you have," said the Guardian Panda. "But tomorrow, you'll all get to see Zenith Waterfalls."

The warriors nodded and said their farewells. They each paired up with their guardian, except for Yuka, who climbed aboard their feathered escorts and soared into the blue skies.

TWENTY - TWO

Yuka turned around to see her fellow warriors flying north atop their cranes looking relieved as she flew south toward Crane Castle. She fixed her gaze on them growing smaller in the distance as they flew past The Sheers and into the southland. Facing forward again, she saw that she and the Guardian Crane were just passing over the billowing tents. She wondered how the wounded were and hoped that they would heal quickly. Her eyes soon passed over the wide and long swarth of Clawdium spikes, where she could make out the gruesome scene of mangled *Nians* being tediously pulled off. Before averting her eyes from the gruesome scene, she saw another large white tent tucked away behind a couple of rocky formations that was not visible when they were on the ground. Yuka tried to get another look at the mysterious tent, but her view became obstructed as the Guardian Crane's wing swooped into view as she veered left.

"Empress Warrior Satoh," said the Guardian Crane. "We'll be at the Crane Castle shortly."

Yuka turned her gaze forward as they veered away from the peninsula of the Sky Pillars. Yuka exhaled as she let out, "*Domo,* Guardian Crane."

It was a short flight as the Guardian Crane flew over the island of the Red Crown Crane Kingdom. Her wings unfurled as she glided over the treetops and *tō* towers peeking through. She soared over the rim of the caldera, glided down into it, and gracefully flew into Crane Castle. Her talons clicked against the deck and she tucked her wings in. "Empress Warrior Satoh, we have arrived," she said.

The Guardian Crane's beady eyes rolled backward when she didn't feel any movement from Yuka. She craned her head to the right and saw Yuka looking down.

"Is everything all right, Empress Warrior Satoh?" asked the Guardian Crane.

"Will this be one of the last times we will get to fly together Guardian Crane?" asked Yuka in a low tone while averting her gaze.

A moment passed, and the Guardian Crane sensed Yuka's sorrow. She dipped her head for a moment before looking back up. She admired the Crane Warrior, who was still draped in her black robe with her battle bodysuit showing through. The black Moon Star was held prominently along her waist, reminding all in Azen of the immense power Yuka wielded. With an honored tone, she said, "Empress Warrior Satoh, I will always remember the times we have flown together. They were beautiful times."

Yuka looked up and saw the beady eye of the Guardian Crane looking at her. Her red tuft of feathers atop her head ruffled slightly. "I will remember them too," replied Yuka wistfully.

With a grin, Yuka invoked the Japanese Qi element for *float* by brushing the word into the air as she said, "*Uku.*"

Yuka gently floated off the Guardian Crane and landed next to her. As her feet touched the ground, she looked up into the face of the Guardian Crane, whose yellow beak and red tuft of feathers gave her a sense of majesty. "Empress Warrior Satoh, you did well. *Domo arigato.*"

Yuka nodded and with that, the Guardian Crane waved her wing to the closest crane attendant. She whispered something to the other crane, who turned and flew gently away.

"What's going on?" asked Yuka.

"I'm having another robe brought down for you," said the Guardian Crane.

Yuka fanned out her arms to her sides as the black robe bellowed out gently, "What's wrong with this one?"

"That is a robe for the battlefield," said the Guardian Crane. "You'll need a more proper robe before we see the Ascendant."

Yuka nodded, despite her confusion. The crane attendant flew back in no time, and in its beak was Yuka's usual white robe with the white edging. Another crane attendant stepped in and with a firm grip of the black robe's nape, smoothly peeled it away from her. Yuka took the white robe and smiled when she saw the black embroidered crane. She put on the white robe and because she was wearing only her battle bodysuit, she magnetically sealed the robe.

With a quick look of approval, the Guardian Crane said, "Now let's go see the Ascendant, Empress Warrior Satoh."

With a nod from Yuka, the Guardian Crane led her through several sliding rice paper partitions. After entering the room in the center, Yuka could see the regal Ascendent beaming at her. They presented themselves to the Ascendent, who also nodded to them.

"Ascendant," said the Guardian Crane. "We have returned."

"Guardian Crane," said the Ascendant. "Empress Warrior Satoh. I heard that we were victorious."

"Yes, we were," said Yuka proudly.

"Excellent," said the Ascendant. "Well then, there is just one more task that needs to be done."

Yuka's eyes perked up as the Guardian Crane turned to her and said, "Empress Warrior Satoh, let's fly."

Yuka's eyes lit up as she floated atop the back of the Guardian Crane. As she fastened herself in, the crane attendants helped the Ascendant in removing her *kimono* like attire.

"Where are we going?" asked Yuka teasingly.

The Guardian Crane rolled her eyes back toward Yuka as the Ascendant turned, flapped her wings, and said, "Down."

The Ascendant flew down into the circular opening in the floor, and the Guardian Crane quickly followed. Yuka gripped her harness tightly as they dove past several floors. Soon they entered the dimly lit void of the collapsed volcano. Yuka heard nothing but silence until the Ascendant tucked in her wings and swiftly dove into one of the lava tubes. The Guardian Crane did the same, pulling in her wings tight as they swooshed into the opening.

With her left cheek pressed up against the feathery nape of the Guardian Crane, Yuka smiled as she could see the feathery backside of the Ascendant, expertly and gracefully flying through the winding lava tube only lit by illumination jades. Soon, they flew into the magma pocket, and Yuka felt as if her ears had popped. The Ascendant and the Guardian Crane landed delicately on the ledge with the carving of the crane etched into the magma wall staring back at them.

Yuka straightened up. She knew was what coming. She relaxed her grip on the harness and stared at the moon-star-shaped recess in the rock and sighed.

"Empress Warrior Satoh," said the Guardian Crane. "You may float off me and land in front of us."

Yuka nodded and floated off the Guardian Crane, gently landing in front of the two majestic cranes before her.

"Empress Warrior Satoh," said the Ascendant with a tone of elegance. "On behalf of the Red Crown Crane Kingdom and all the noble kingdoms throughout Azen, I thank you for your bravery, your courage, and your resilience. Without you and the other emperor and empress warriors, we would not have been victorious against the armies of the Warlock. You will be remembered forever here on Azen. Thank you for honoring your Japanese heritage and bringing it to Azen in our ongoing war with the Warlock. You have made all the Japanese Crane Warriors before you proud. *Domo arigato.*"

The Ascendant and the Guardian Crane bowed deeply toward Yuka and she did the same. The immensity of the Ascendant's words weighed on her, and knowing that they were victorious, she was grateful to be giving the creatures of Azen peace until the next lunar cycle.

"Empress Warrior Satoh," said the Guardian Crane as Yuka looked somberly in her direction. "As your final act as Empress Warrior Satoh, please remove the Moon Star *shuriken* and place it back into the recess of the alcove."

Yuka hesitated as she looked down at her waist. The thumb and index finger of each hand rested gently on each sharp point of the black Moon Star. The small white jade glistened back at her and after a moment, she plucked it from her waist. She raised it to chest level and marveled at it, knowing that it would be the last time she would ever hold it. With a glum expression, she nodded reluctantly and looked at the two cranes.

"Ascendant, Guardian Crane," said Yuka respectfully. "It was my honor."

Yuka turned away from the cranes and walked toward the alcove. She admired one last time the simple carving of the crane in the magma wall and walked toward it. She looked at the Moon Star *shuriken* one last time before she firmly pushed it into the volcanic recess. As she took a step back, the glowing white jade ebbed until the glow faded.

Yuka took a couple of stolid steps back. She brought her fists to her chest, with her elbows out and nodded as she uttered, "For Azen."

* * *

The air was crisp and chilly once more as Sung's crane began to soar. His eyes focused on the casual upturned tail of the Guardian Tiger, which swayed gently on the back of his crane. He had never before seen his tail sway in this way. It was almost hypnotic to watch.

The Guardian Tiger's crane disappeared into a low-hanging cloud, and Sung braced himself. For a moment, nothing but a white mist enveloped him. It was cool as it brushed against his cheeks, and he was grateful for his black robe. *It was convenient that the guardians had the robes for them*, he thought. Soon, the misty cloud faded away as the grand stone terrace of Claw House emerged.

The cranes unfurled their wings, and soon they landed at the top of the grand steps of Claw House. Sung exhaled and quickly climbed down from the crane. He circled about to face the crane and said *thank you* in Korean, "*Gam-sa-ham-ni-da.*"

The crane nodded politely, and Sung turned to meet up with the Guardian Tiger, who was already speaking to a tiger attendant. As Sung walked up next to him, the Guardian Tiger turned to him with his steely blue eyes. For a tiger who had just been in battle, his fur was coiffed beyond reproach.

"I take it the flight was a smooth one, Emperor Warrior Kim?" asked the Guardian Tiger.

Sung's shoulder's drooped as he looked down, causing the Guardian Tiger to raise one of his eyebrows in curiosity.

"Is there something wrong, Emperor Warrior Kim?" asked the Guardian Tiger.

Sung looked up with a glum expression and uttered, "I'm going to miss you calling me that."

The Guardian Tiger nodded and said, "I'm going to miss calling you that as well."

Sung smiled and with a giddy face, he asked, "Guardian Tiger, can you just call me Sung for once?"

The Guardian Tiger scoffed lightly as he said, "That is not the way. Once you are the chosen Tiger Warrior, your proper name will forever be Emperor Warrior Kim."

"Oh, come on," pleaded Sung. "Just once? For me? It'll just be between you and me."

"Nonsense," said the Guardian Tiger firmly. "As the Guardian Tiger, it is my duty to call you by your rightful name."

Sung sighed just as three white tiger attendants came out of Claw House. The middle one had a square pouch in his mouth. As he approached Sung, he bounded upward onto his hind legs, released the pouch and caught it with his two front paws.

"Emperor Warrior Kim," said the Guardian Tiger. "Please switch into this robe instead."

Sung removed the Claw Staff from his back as one of the other tiger attendants gently held it for him. The other tiger came behind Sung and helped him to remove his black robe. With Sung only in his battle bodysuit, the first tiger attendant handed to Sung his blue robe with the embroidered tiger's head on the left chest area. Sung slipped into it, took back the Claw Staff, and slapped it onto his back.

"Come, Emperor Warrior Kim, Sung," said the Guardian Tiger with a snicker.

Sung's eyes brightened and he said with a grin, "Hey, you said 'Sung!'"

A low scoffing grunt came from the Guardian Tiger as his tail wagged playfully. "I did no such thing. I just called you by your full proper name."

Sung smiled and bounded up the stone steps into Claw House to catch up with the Guardian Tiger. Sung smiled down at the Guardian Tiger, who looked up at him with a wink.

They passed through the grand entrance and down the hallway with its grand columns. As Sung walked alongside the Guardian Tiger, many of the tigers milling about nodded in Sung's direction. Sung nodded back. Soon, Sung saw the Tigeress waiting for them in front of The Vault, donned in her usual robe. Sung and the Guardian Tiger, who straightened up on his hind legs, stopped a few feet in front of her.

"Tigeress," said the Guardian Tiger as he nodded. This prompted Sung to also nod and utter, "*Annyeonghaseyo.*"

The Tigeress nodded with a smile, closed her eyes momentarily as she uttered, "*Annyeonghaseyo.*"

"Guardian Tiger," said the Tigeress as she looked back up. "I was sent word of the good news at the battlefront."

"Yes, Tigeress," said the Guardian Tiger as he straightened up further. "We were indeed victorious."

The Tigeress nodded and turned to Sung.

"Emperor Warrior Kim," said the Tigeress proudly. "The White Tiger Kingdom is grateful to you and other warriors for living up to the task of fighting with us to defeat the Warlock. You have fought well as our battle tigers roared into battle with you. With that, and with a grateful tiger's heart, I thank you. *Gam-sa-ham-ni-da.*"

Sung bowed, along with the Guardian Tiger as the Tigeress bowed in return.

"It was my honor to fight for White Tiger Kingdom and all of Azen. But I couldn't have done it without my Guardian Tiger," said Sung as he nodded to him. "*Gam-sa-ham-ni-da.*"

The Guardian Tiger, touched by the mention, nodded to Sung.

The Tigeress' eyes bounced from Sung to the Guardian Tiger and said, "I guess there is only one final task, then. Please follow me."

Sung took a deep breath as he glanced at the Guardian Tiger. Soon he returned his gaze to the Tigeress as she started to descend into the stone spiral staircase. He followed with deliberate steps and soon was at the bottom of the circular stone vault. As he stood next to the Tigeress, the Guardian Tiger came up next to him, along with four tiger guards dressed in battle armor who also silently made their way down the steps. They each took up a location at each cardinal point.

"Emperor Warrior Kim," said the Tigeress with a stoic tone. "Please return the Claw Staff to its case."

Sung looked at the simple bamboo case and saw the open hole socket at the bottom. He nodded and sighed. With reluctance, he removed the Claw Staff from his back and held it horizontally in his hands. He looked down at the dark slender staff as the blue jade glowed.

"I'm going to miss the Claw Staff," said Sung as he looked up at both the Tigeress and the Guardian Tiger.

Sung stepped forward and turned the staff vertically. He carefully inserted the Claw Staff into the socket that held it snugly in place. Sung stepped backward and wanting to acknowledge the Claw Staff and the blue jade, he brought his clenched fists up towards his chest, with his elbows out and with a slight nod, mumbled under his breath, "For Azen."

His hands came back to his sides as he walked backward until he was in line with the Tigeress and the Guardian Tiger. His eyes still fixed on the blue jade as the glowing soon faded.

"The Claw Staff has been returned," said the Tigeress. "Please follow me."

The Tigeress ascended the stone spiral staircase, followed by Sung and the Guardian Tiger. As they moved away from the spiral staircase, the Tigeress nodded to the tiger guard at the western point. With the acknowledgment from the Tigeress, he stomped down on the stone floor with his Clawdium staff. It resonated as the grinding sounds of unseen gears could be heard. Soon enough, one by one, the stone wedges that formed each step of the spiral staircase rose until they were flush with the stone floor. A low sound of unseen metal scraping against stone ended the movement with a final click.

"So cool," said Sung as he mourned the Claw Staff being locked away.

* * *

Daniel looked down at Horned Bay from his crane and saw the beautiful blue water beneath him. There was a schooner moored to the dock, and as much as he wanted to, he was not going to be aboard it. They flew over the rock formation that embraced the bay as the scent of seawater started to waft through his nose. How he was going to miss the sea water of Azen!

His eyes fixed on the array of beautiful limestone outcroppings, which still fascinated him. His crane unfurled its wings as they started to descend into the Crescent Horn, where he could make out the Palace of Divine Horns. Daniel looked up at the massive backside of the Guardian Buffalo being borne by an equally massive eagle, whose tough feathers and powerful wings were ruffled by the wind. A sea breeze came in and buffeted their faces, forcing Daniel to regrip his harness, but the crane instinctively navigated through the minor turbulence. It lowered its talons as it flew over the hoisting platforms until it finally landed on the front steps of the Palace of Divine Horns.

Daniel's crane stumbled forward until regaining its balance. It folded its wings and lowered itself as Daniel climbed off. His feet landed with a thud on the stone slabs, and he circled around to the crane and nodded as he said *thank you* in Vietnamese, "*cảm ơn bạn.*"

The crane nodded, and Daniel turned to see that the Guardian Buffalo was already at the top of the steps to the Grand Hall. Another buffalo had just nodded at the Guardian Buffalo and disappeared into the hall.

"Are we going to meet with the Horn Protectoress?" asked Daniel as he caught up with Guardian Buffalo.

The Guardian Buffalo's strong bull face with its big brown-reddish eyes turned toward Daniel. There was a sense of melancholy in his strong features, but his massive horns swung into full view and Daniel got to admire his Guardian Buffalo all over again.

Daniel looked at the somber face of the Guardian Buffalo and Daniel simply blurted out, "I'm going to return the Horn of *Kting voar*?"

The Guardian Buffalo nodded back in silence as Daniel exhaled. He looked down the grand hall and said, "Well, what are we waiting for?"

But before Daniel could take a step, the Guardian Buffalo blocked his path and uttered, "Patience, Emperor Warrior Nguyen."

Daniel, looking penitent, nodded and uttered, "Sorry, Guardian Buffalo."

The Guardian Buffalo let out a snort as he shook his head.

They waited a couple of minutes in silence as they milled about on the entrance steps when Daniel asked, "Guardian Buffalo, do you have a family?"

The Guardian Buffalo looked up as his ear fluttered and he nodded. "I do. I have a beautiful wife."

Daniel's eyes lit up and he asked, "Any children?"

There was a pause when the Guardian Buffalo answered, "A young bull but…"

"Guardian Buffalo," interrupted the buffalo attendant as she returned with a robe in her arms. "I have the robe that you requested."

The Guardian Buffalo looked distracted but shook his head. "Please help Emperor Warrior Nguyen change into it."

As one buffalo held onto the club horn, the other helped to take off the black robe as the other helped Daniel into the red robe, with the white front edging and the white embroidered buffalo head.

Once Daniel slipped the club horn through the slip hole in the back of his robe, he followed the Guardian Buffalo down the Grand Hall. The Guardian Buffalo's hooves sunk into the red carpet as Daniel could feel its luxurious softness beneath the soles of his feet. Like his first day on Azen, Daniel saw the Horn Protectoress coming into view. He couldn't help but smile in her presence.

They stopped as Daniel admired the resplendent Horn Protectoress in her *ao dai*. The Guardian Buffalo nodded as did Daniel.

The Horn Protectoress smiled and she nodded in kind before she spoke. "We were victorious, I heard."

"We were," said the Guardian Buffalo. "Though we took heavy causalities along with the tiger kingdom."

The Horn Protectoress looked solemn as her large brown eyes looked down. "But they will heal, like we always do."

"Yes, Horn Protectoress," said the Guardian Buffalo firmly. "They shall."

"At least now we can rest," said the Horn Protectoress as she turned to Daniel. "And Emperor Warrior Nguyen, you fought bravely, doing everything you could to protect our soldiers."

Daniel nodded and said, "Yes Horn Protectoress, I did everything within my power."

"Thank you, Emperor Warrior Nguyen," said the Horn Protectoress proudly. "You honored all the Vietnamese warriors of the Buffalo Kingdom before you."

Daniel found himself holding back his emotions as the Horn Protectoress' profound words reverberated through him. He thought about her words and finally felt he belonged to some great line of Vietnamese warriors. With that, he no longer would ever deny or doubt the power of his Vietnamese heritage. Though as much as he fought to protect the Buffalo Kingdom and Azen, the whole experience awoke his Vietnamese spirit that he will forever nurture and protect. He had mighty buffalos to thank for that deep epiphany as he muttered thank you in Vietnamese. "*Cảm ơn bạn.*"

"No, Emperor Warrior Nguyen," said the Horn Protectoress humbly. "It is I who will say to you, *cảm ơn bạn.*"

The Horn Protectoress along with the Guardian Buffalo nodded to Daniel, who nodded back.

"Well, we have one more task then," said the Horn Protectoress. "Please follow me."

As the Horn Protectoress led Daniel to the well, followed by the Guardian Buffalo, she stopped at the beginning of the slope.

Daniel exhaled and could feel the finality of what was to come. He looked at the Horn Protectoress and the Guardian Buffalo as he pulled up along his left. He pulled out the Horn of *Kting voar* and looked down at the glowing red jade. He marveled at its size and wondered if there was more to its hidden power. He nodded a few times and blurted out, "Well, if you can hold the Horn of *Kting voar* for me, Guardian Buffalo, I'll get undressed and put it back into the well."

"That is not necessary, Emperor Nguyen," interjected the Horn Protectoress as Daniel turned to her confused.

"Well, how will it go back into the well?" asked Daniel.

"Gravity," said the Guardian Buffalo matter-of-factly.

Daniel looked at him blankly as his expression turned to one of embarrassment. His eyes smiled as he brushed his hand through his dark brown hair as he exclaimed, "Oh, of course."

"Emperor Warrior Nguyen," said the Horn Protectoress. "Simply stand above the well, hold the Horn of *Kting voar* vertically, and drop it in gently."

Daniel nodded and walked to the other end of the ramp where the well was. He looked at the Horn Protectoress and the Guardian Buffalo as they looked on. He looked down into the clear water and could see the circular opening of the well. Memories of him diving into it and dodging fire bursts flashed back into his mind. He held the Horn of *Kting voar* vertically and looked deeply into the large, glowing red jade. With one final look, he let go as the Horn of *Kting voar* dropped down.

As it pierced the water with its tapered end, Daniel clenched his fists together and brought them to his chest with his elbows out and whispered, "For Azen."

The Horn of *Kting voar* slipped into the well. As the tapered end hit the bottom with a slight thud, it bounced up slightly as an air bubble bobbled upward. The sleek spiral tapered brown horn hit the bottom of the stone well once more and tilted to its side, slicing through the water at an angle until it came to rest. The glow of the red jade then faded.

* * *

With a comfortable tailwind behind them, Shiori glided eastward with her wings stretched outward, showing off her large feathers. When the crane carrying the Guardian Panda started her descent, she angled her body forward as the top of Bamboo City came into view.

Clara pulled herself deeper into Shiori's nape, admiring the magnificent view of her home away from home. Though her life had been put into peril, on Azen she'd become someone who made a difference. She smiled as they passed over the outer bamboo wall and leveled out toward the hangar. Her brown eyes lit up as she saw the plump panda on the left side of the hangar entrance guiding them in with the jade batons.

In an instant, Shiori swooshed into the hangar and opened her wings further to slow herself down. Her talons touched the bamboo deck, and she tucked in her wings as she came to a full stop. She lowered herself and Clara climbed off her. Clara's boots landed on the deck with a slight thud as she circled to the front of the crane.

"*Xie xie*," said Clara.

"It has been a pleasure riding with you, Empress Warrior Wu," Shiori said as she bowed her red crown towards Clara.

Clara smiled and saw that the Guardian Panda had just waved off a panda attendant who waddled away. As she walked toward him, she broke through the magnetic seal of the black robe's front edging and adjusted her robe to accommodate the quiver and bow.

"Empress Warrior Wu," said the Guardian Panda warmly. "Smooth ride, I gather?"

"Yes," said Clara. "It always is. What now?"

"Well, we are going to see the Panderess," said the Guardian Panda. "And then we're… what's wrong, Empress Warrior Wu?"

Clara's left hand was around the glowing green jade of the Bow of Destiny. She looked at her green jade bracelet as well. She rubbed the Bamboo Jade a couple of times and looked back up at the warm brown eyes of the Guardian Panda.

"I have to give it back now, don't I?" she asked.

There was a pause and the Guardian Panda replied, "I'm afraid so."

Clara nodded sadly and replied, "I understand."

"Ah, they have arrived," said the Guardian Panda as three panda attendants came towards them.

As one helped her with her bow and quiver, the other removed Clara's black robe, while the third helped her into the rich green robe with its embroidered panda head. She brushed her hair back and felt that it wasn't as tight as it should be. She had just been in battle and had worn a helmet for most of the time. She pulled off her bamboo ribbon hair accessory and her black hair fell loosely as she shook it.

The panda holding the bow extended it to Clara and with a smile, she took it in her left hand. She was about to take the quiver when the Guardian Panda stopped her by raising his black paw. She nodded as she pursed her lips. As the panda attendants walked away, she asked, "I don't need the quiver?"

"No, Empress Warrior Wu," said the Guardian Panda. "Only the Bow of Destiny. Please follow me."

Clara followed the Guardian Panda and they rose in the bamboo lift. They exited into the large ornate floor and walked down the same path that Clara walked on when she first arrived on Azen. As they approached the center of the floor, Clara could see the calming presence of the Panderess.

They stopped in front of the Panderess as the Guardian Panda and Clara both nodded to her.

"Panderess," said the Guardian Panda. "I have returned with Empress Warrior Wu."

The Panderess smiled and her brown eyes focused on Clara. "Safely, I see. I heard we were victorious."

"Yes, Panderess," said the Guardian Panda. "We have defeated another lunar cycle of the Warlock battles."

"Excellent," responded the Panderess. "And Empress Warrior Wu, how do you feel?"

Clara paused before responding, "I'm fine. I'm just glad that I was able to do my part even though I couldn't summon any of my powers."

"Empress Warrior Wu," said the Panderess reassuringly. "Everyone plays a part. You do not choose the battle, the battle chooses you. As a Panda Warrior, you rose to the occasion. Despite not being able to use your powers, I heard that it was you who destroyed the *Nian's* power with the Bow of Destiny. That act was invaluable. And perhaps, the bow lived up to its destiny."

"Thank you, Panderess," said Clara humbly.

"Very well," said the Panderess as she cast a glance at the Guardian Panda. "Please follow me."

With the Panderess leading the way and the Guardian Panda following her, Clara followed as they made their way to the archway at the other end of the floor. As there was more light this time around, Clara could finally take in the view before her. As they approached the archway, the slender yet beautiful bamboo bridge loomed ahead of her. As they exited onto the ledge, she could finally see the dangling bamboo stalk. She looked up and saw that it was solidly lodged into the underside of a rocky overhang of a sheer cliff that extended on both sides as far as her eye could see. The rear wall of Bamboo Tower was as close as possible to the rocky formation as a deep crevasse separated it from the dangling bamboo stalk. As Clara stepped onto the bamboo planks of the bridge, she looked down and saw that the crevasse extended into a dark abyss. She gulped for a moment as her fear of heights caught up with her, but as she looked up, she saw the Panderess quickly traversing the bamboo bridge.

She regripped the Bow of Destiny and breathed in deeply. With fortitude, she walked forward as the Panda Warrior that she was. She reached the other side and entered the cylindrical room of the dangling bamboo. The Panderess, already beside the empty ornate bamboo rack, nodded to Clara warmly.

Clara stood in front of the rack and looked at it. She brought up the Bow of Destiny and held it in both hands as she looked down at the glowing green jade. She felt deeply connected to the Bamboo Jade, which had been granted to her by the eerie panda monks of the Jade Labyrinth. Her reverie was broken when the Panderess spoke, "When you are ready, Empress Warrior Wu, please return the Bow of Destiny."

Clara nodded and looked down once more into the Bamboo Jade. She smiled as she said, "You are the new Bamboo Jade. Serve the next Panda Warrior well."

Clara moved a step closer and gently laid the Bow of Destiny across the rack. She withdrew her hands and took a step back. She exhaled fondly as she brought her clenched fists together at her chest, with her elbows out as she whispered, "For Azen."

The glow from the Bamboo Jade then faded.

TWENTY - THREE

Clara laid her shirt from home down on the bed in Bamboo Tower. She felt refreshed from a full night's rest after fighting a horrific battle. She was thankful that she'd been allowed to sleep in and quickly devoured the lunch that was brought to her. In her mind, she thought she had the whole day until that night's festivities at the Zenith Waterfalls. But before she knew it, mid-afternoon had come, and she was scurrying to pack all her belongings.

She swept her hair back as she carefully folded her cropped sweater top and placed it upon her pair of jeans. She slipped her hands underneath the bundle of clothes and slipped it into a bamboo pouch she had been given. Her eyes fell onto the flat, green, cloth-covered square box that rested on the bed, hidden before by the bundle of clothes that she had just tucked away. A smile crept across her face as she carefully picked it up. She ran her fingers gently across the textured green cloth before flicking up the latch and opening the box. The Azen green jade bracelet glistened in the light, making her smile. *One day*, Clara said to herself. She gently closed the box and slipped it into the bamboo pouch.

Next, she picked up the bamboo canister. She easily twisted off the cap and halfway emptied the bamboo medallions inscribed with the Chinese names of the Panda Warriors that came before her. Having already brought home bamboo medallions for Hong and Mulan, she was grateful that she could complete the collection. The medallions slipped back into the canister as they rattled against each other. With the cap twisted shut, she tucked it into the bamboo pouch as well.

She ducked into the bathroom and brought out two silken-bamboo washcloths embossed with images of panda heads. *It was the cutest thing*, she thought. She brought each to her cheeks and smiled at how soft they were. Her eyes looked down at each washcloth and suddenly she felt like a thief taking hotel linen to take home. But back home, there was no such thing as silken-bamboo washcloths.

Her eyes flickered open when she heard the door to her room open, and she rushed back to her bed. She quickly tucked the two washcloths into the bamboo pouch just as the Guardian Panda sauntered in. He looked jovial with his black-and-white fur a bit fluffier than before.

"Empress Warrior Wu," said the Guardian Panda with a grin. "Are we ready to go?"

Clara looked around. Her bamboo-framed bed was made, and the open wardrobe held only Azen clothing. Then her eyes caught the bamboo stalk that had grown to about a foot in height. It was stuck in a small segment of bamboo that acted as a vase, filled with pebbles to keep it upright. It had sprouted some new leaves.

She picked it up, thinking of when Ping Ping, the panda toddler, had given it to her as a gift during her second trip to Azen. The adorable memory made Clara chuckle as she turned toward the Guardian Panda.

"I can't take this with me," said Clara as she extended the bamboo shoot to him.

His right eyebrow rose as his large paw wrapped around small bamboo vase. It suddenly looked very tiny in his black paw. He looked up at Clara and said, "*Do Jeh*. This would be a good snack for my youngest."

Clara's eyes blew wide open as she said with shock, "No Guardian Panda! You can't eat it! This is the bamboo shoot that Ping Ping gave to me."

The Guardian Panda, with a mildly startled look on his face looked at Clara and responded, "My apologies. All bamboo shoots are suitable for snacking here on Azen."

Clara let out a laugh and the Guardian Panda followed with a low laugh. Then he said, "I will look after it, Empress Warrior Wu, but I can't guarantee that once it reaches a certain height, it won't be eaten."

Clara smiled and nodded when she realized that what she considered a decorative plant was food for the pandas. She snatched up her bamboo pouch by its strap and slung it across her body.

"Ready to go," said Clara somberly.

The Guardian Panda then turned around to show his white-and-black furry backside as he wobbled out. Clara followed, paused, and turned to the serene view of Bamboo City and its large bamboo stalks, ringed bamboo wall, and the large purplish planet over the horizon. She let out a sigh as she quickly slipped into her shoes and stepped out of her room for the last time.

* * *

The flight, which went in a northwesterly direction, felt long. With their new flight route toward Zenith Waterfalls, Clara saw sights she had not seen before, and despite the higher- than-usual altitude, she was able to see several other structures below. She wished she had more time to explore them.

"Ahead of us, Empress Warrior Wu," said Shiori.

Clara looked up as a beautiful golden cylindrical structure appeared in the distance. It stood atop a tall mountain, perhaps the tallest mountain in all of Azen. From two sides of its base, a waterfall erupted, and Clara wondered where the water was coming from, since there was no visible water source around the mountain. *Another natural wonder of Azen*, she thought. She couldn't tell which Asian culture had inspired its design. The entire structure was made up of several tall circular floors, with each floor a bit smaller than the one beneath it, creating a tapered effect. Golden panels spanned the entire outer wall of each floor. At the very top of the structure was a spire that reached towards the heavens. It too glistened in the sunlight.

As she took in the wonder, Shiori moved directly behind the crane carrying the Guardian Panda. He turned around and waved to Clara, who nodded back. Soon they started their descent and swooped through an open floor in single file, the two cranes landed gracefully. Pandas, tigers, and buffalos were all about, and cranes had perched themselves in the rafters of the spacious floor.

"Come, Empress Warrior Wu," said the Guardian Panda urgently. "We are late and we must get you ready."

Clara climbed off Shiori's back as she adjusted her bamboo pouch. She quickly thanked Shiori and turned to the Guardian Panda. Two other panda attendants were waiting in luxurious-looking robes. One came forward and took the bamboo pouch before Clara could even protest.

"It will be taken care of, Empress Warrior Wu," said the Guardian Panda as a panda attendant gestured for her to follow him.

As Clara followed, caught off guard by the faster-paced-than-usual ambiance, she asked, "Is this the Zenith Waterfalls?"

With the Guardian Panda walking by her side and following the lead panda attendant as the second followed them, he responded. "Yes, this is the Zenith Waterfalls. The tallest point in all of Azen. This is where we have our most auspicious events. Tonight, is meant to honor you."

Clara suddenly felt embarrassed as they followed the panda attendant through a set of sliding partitions. "Really, this is way too much, Guardian Panda. It wasn't just me, it was all of us."

Clara followed through another set of sliding partitions and entered a large room, where there were three doors on the right and the left.

"That may be true," said the Guardian Panda. "But without you and the other warriors, we could not have overcome the Warlock's armies, Empress Warrior Wu."

"The others are already here?" asked Clara.

"Yes, we are last, so we must hurry," said the Guardian Panda as the lead panda attendant stopped in front of one of the doors.

"What's happening now?" asked Clara, still confused as the lead panda attendant opened the door. In the room, Clara could see three other pandas in robes. One was holding a hairbrush, the other towels, and the last a bucket of water so hot, that steam arose from it. In the middle was a large bamboo tub.

"Oh!" exclaimed Clara as the lead panda hurriedly pushed her in before she could protest. The panda attendant that was carrying her bamboo pouch followed and the door closed with a thud.

* * *

When the door opened again, Clara appeared in the doorway in a long silken Chinese dress with a green sheen, which draped the length of her body elegantly. Delicate embroidered bamboo shoots ran along the side slit that ended right above her knee. The dress delicately covered her shoulders, had a Mandarin collar and a knotted button by her right shoulder. An embroidered panda's head appeared where the black knotted buttons met.

Clara stretched her arms out. She didn't know what smooth and fragrant lotion the pandas massaged into them, but they looked healthy and felt great. She brought her right hand to the elegant bun the pandas had meticulously twisted in her hair. They had also adorned her features with makeup that accentuated her natural beauty. She couldn't help feeling grown up and womanly.

"Clara!" Yuka exclaimed.

Clara looked up, captivated. Yuka too had been transformed. Now she was in a colorful *kimono* with her eyes lit up as the two friends approached each other.

"You look beautiful!" they both exclaimed at once, laughing.

Clara admired Yuka's beautiful *kimono* and *obi*, which made her look taller and straighter. The kimono had a pattern of cranes flying upward along its length. Yuka's hair was also styled elegantly with ornaments delicately tucked into it. She had just enough makeup to highlight her delicate features.

"Whoa!"

Clara and Yuka turned to see Sung looking at them. He was dressed in Korean-inspired attire that resembled traditional clothing but had a modern flair. His outfit consisted of layers of blue cloth draped over his shoulders, making them look even broader. They ended at his mid-thigh, where he wore black pants tucked into black boots. The broad black belt gathered in all the layered clothing nicely. Atop his clear face, he wore a black skull cap that bore an emblem of a tiger head in the front.

"You two look so pretty… I mean amazing," said Sung as his cheeks started to flush.

"Wow, don't we clean up nicely," said Daniel as he came out to join the group. He was wearing a long textured black *ao dai*, whose stiff shoulders gave him an imposing presence. Woven into the black fabric was what appeared to be an abstract curvy design that from a further distance revealed itself to be the distinctive shapes of buffalos in different poses. He also wore black pants and an open fabric head piece.

"Bro!" said Sung, impressed. "You're crushing it."

Daniel smiled and straightened up. "You look like you came right out of a K-Drama."

Sung chuckled and splayed his arms to his sides and said, "I do, don't I?"

"Ahem," teased Clara. "And what about us?"

Daniel turned to the two female warriors and smiled. He put his two palms toward them as he turned away and stammered, "I can't take it! Your beauty is too blinding!"

Clara and Yuka laughed as Yuka swayed gently at her hips from side to side. But before they could get another word in, a very serious panda in a Chinese-inspired jacket dress came up to the four of them and cleared her throat loudly. Behind her were a tiger, buffalo, a crane, and another panda. Each wore clothing reflecting their kingdom.

The warriors turned to the newly arrived panda as she spoke firmly. "I am Bai Yung, and I am your High Coordinator for Zenith Waterfalls. We are barely running on time but if we are to keep to the schedule, I need your undivided attention now."

"She's like an *ajumma*," whispered Sung as Clara turned back to him and giggled as he referred to the strict panda as a Korean auntie. Yuka and Daniel exchanged blank looks before turning back.

"We will be entering the Zenith's Halo. Please follow your assigned escort, who will introduce you and show you where to be seated. You will be seated between your kingdom leader and your guardian. Are there any questions? Yes, Empress Warrior Wu?"

"When does this happen?" asked Clara meekly. She may have been the Panda Warrior, but the sternness of the High Coordinator panda intimidated her.

"Right now," said the Zenith Coordinator Bai Yung. "Emperor Warrior Nguyen, you are first; please follow your buffalo escort. Emperor Warrior Kim, you are second; please stand behind your tiger escort. Empress Warrior Satoh, you are third; please stand with your crane escort. And Empress Warrior Wu, you are last; please stand with your panda escort."

Clara nodded silently as her fellow warriors lined up before her with their escorts. Her escort, a stoic-looking panda, approached her and nodded. She turned around and found her view blocked by another large panda wearing a red silken top.

"Clara?"

Clara leaned over and saw Yuka looking back at her. "Why do I feel so nervous?"

Before Clara could answer, the High Coordinator stated, "Empress Warrior Satoh, back in line, please."

Yuka suddenly straightened up and turned forward as Daniel and his buffalo escort disappeared behind a set of sliding partitions.

Clara heard what sounded like muted music, which then subsided. She found her breathing becoming shallow from nervousness. She looked around: The Guardian Panda was nowhere to be seen. *Because he was already in the room*, she remembered. She felt vulnerable without the Bow of Destiny, and it suddenly dawned on her that she may not be able to invoke her Qi elemental powers with the Bamboo Jade dormant.

Soon she could sense that Sung had also disappeared behind the sliding partitions, so she moved up. She heard muffled music, and as she leaned to her right, she saw the High Coordinator nodding, as if in beat to the music. She then turned her gaze toward Clara, causing her to look away.

She heard the partitions slide open and leaning over a bit, she saw Yuka and her crane escort disappear behind them. She moved ahead just behind her panda escort and found herself fidgeting.

As Clara waited, fidgeting with her hands, she heard a low cough. Clara turned to meet the stern eyes of the High Coordinator. Clara froze and had a blank moment before looking down at her fidgeting hands, which she placed by her sides.

She followed her panda escort up to the sliding partitions. They slid open, and they entered a tapered corridor that seemed to grow narrower before ending at another partition. It felt like the longest moment that Clara had ever endured, and she felt an uncomfortable warmth around her neck from her tight Mandarin collar.

The sliding partitions slid open as a blinding light appeared. Clara had to squint as she struggled to keep her escort in her view. For a moment, his entire silhouette was rimmed with light.

The panda escort's baritone voice boomed as he announced, "On behalf of the Panda Kingdom, I present to you Empress Warrior Wu!"

Melodious music suddenly filled the air, and Clara's ears perked up. She couldn't place it but it was distinctive and joyful to the ears, and there was something familiar about it. Her panda escort then took a few steps forward, and Clara followed. As she did, she fell out of the light's glare just as the panda moved to his right.

Before Clara was an expansive round room. The ceiling had to be at least fifty feet high, and at its center was an elaborate dangling glass ornament that captured the sun's rays from the glass windows ringing the top portion of the room. As Clara leveled her gaze, she could see four arch-shaped wooden tables arranged in a circle. Between the tables were four openings leading to the center of the room, which held four draped items in resplendent golden coverings. As Clara followed her panda escort, she saw Daniel with his buffalo kingdom dignitaries at their table further away. At the table next to him was Sung with this tiger dignitaries, and on the other side of Daniel was Yuka with her crane dignitaries.

The mood was celebratory, and Clara saw that behind the four inner tables were additional rows of arch-shaped tables. In each section were additional representatives of each kingdom.

As Clara approached her table, she could see the Panderess in ornate dress, looking at her with pride. The Guardian Panda also beamed at her. His pride and affection were evident. The panda escort led Clara to her seat. All the unnecessary attention on her made her suddenly sheepish. *Serves me right for being last*, she thought.

The panda escort pushed Clara's seat in, and she looked up and whispered, "*Xie xie*."

Soon, everyone sat down except for the Panderess, who walked into the inner circle, standing in front of the mysterious golden drapes. The music soon subsided. She turned to Clara, who looked back with her full attention.

"Empress Warrior Wu Chu Hua," the Panderess said in a grateful tone. "Many months ago, you came to Azen not knowing your true identity. Though you had doubts, you persevered and found the warrior you were meant to be, as did the other warriors of Azen. Together, you fought alongside our armies and defeated the Warlock armies. For that, I and the Panda Kingdom thank you. *Xie xie.*"

The Panderess bowed, and Clara intuitively got up and bowed in return. She waited for the Panderess to return to her seat before sitting down as the Tigeress entered the inner circle.

"Emperor Warrior Kim Sung," she said graciously. "You came to Claw House and paid me much respect for someone from your world who has never met a tiger from Azen. You didn't shy away from your task at hand, which was to defeat the Warlock armies and to save your Earth. That is no easy task. In fact, it takes discipline and courage, which you exemplified throughout your actions here on Azen. Along with your fellow warriors, you embodied everything we have come to expect of an Emperor Warrior of the White Tiger Kingdom. We thank you. *Gam-sa-ham-ni-da.*"

Sung rose and bowed deeply to the Tigeress who made her way to her seat.

The Horn Protectoress walked into the inner circle and faced Daniel.

"Emperor Warrior Nguyen Danh," said the Horn Protectoress. "When you came to Azen, not only were you doubtful about your role, but you were doubtful about your Vietnamese heritage. But with curiosity and what Azen showed you, your Vietnamese blood grew strong. It courses through you but was only fully awakened by the great needs of Azen. In the end, your heart was Vietnamese, and your pride in your heritage powered you and your fellow warriors to lead the kingdom armies to victory over the Warlock's armies. Know that. Know in your heart your Vietnamese pride was the powerful force that defined you and gave you power to protect us. With that, thank you on behalf of Buffalo Kingdom. *Cảm ơn bạn.*"

Daniel stood up but felt his legs shaking as he absorbed the words from the Horn Protectoress. His heart raced with a mixture of happiness, new confidence, and pride. As the Horn Protectoress sat down, Daniel turned to look at her graceful presence as a tear seeped from the corner of his eye. He quickly wiped it away and looked straight ahead as the Ascendant entered the inner circle.

She was draped in a lose robe with a pattern reminiscent of those found on Japanese kimonos. A puffy black obi rested atop her back and swayed as she turned toward Yuka.

"Empress Warrior Satoh Yuka," said the Ascendant. "I am so proud to call you Empress Warrior. You have honored the Red Crown Crane Kingdom with your dedication to your Japanese heritage. You were ready to learn, fight, and defend Azen because you knew you were the warrior of the Crane Kingdom. Your grace was only met by the fierceness of your command of the air Wu element. You and the other warriors fought selflessly and honored all the kingdoms of Azen, and for that, I deeply thank you. *Domo arigato.*"

Yuka got up, bowed respectfully, and was ready to receive the Ascendant. But the Ascendant did not move her from spot as she looked up and spun around. She cast her gaze on Yuka and began to speak once more.

"On this special night," began the Ascendant as her red tuft of feathers flicked for a moment. "We wanted to show you something beautiful and wonderful. So, members of the Top Talon team, you may begin."

The Ascendant walked away, and Yuka sat down as her eyes were drawn upward. Four members of the Top Talon team lifted off from the rafters above and started to fly in a perfectly coordinated circle. The Top Talon lead squawked and they began to spiral down as everyone watched them in awe. With another squawk, the four cranes made their final pass and with a snap of their beaks, whisked away the golden drapes to reveal four statues.

The four warriors' mouths fell open as they saw the statues that would immortalize them on Azen. Daniel's eyes filled with emotion as he saw his large statue stare past him. He was tall, imposing, and in full battle armor. He held the Horn of *Kting voar* with confidence, and for once in his life, he saw his likeness with his Asian features displayed proudly and prominently.

Sung admired his stoic statue, whose finish was unmistakably Clawdium. He stood facing forward, holding the Claw Staff vertically in front of him, with a blue jade replica facing out. It seemed like he would not let anything pass.

Yuka stared at her intricate Clawdium *origami* statue, which captured her soaring into the air, freed from the confines of the earth. She was in full battle armor, and the sculptor even captured her hair flowing behind her.

Clara's statue was the only one not of Clawdium. Instead, her likeness was carved from a single solid piece of bamboo. The details were amazing. She could never have imagined seeing herself as a statue. Her image stared at something far away as she held the Bow of Destiny with her left hand. An arrow was cocked and aimed downward but at the ready. Her statue exuded confidence.

"I hope we captured your spirit, Empress Warrior Wu," said the Panderess who looked down on her with pride.

Clara looked up as joyful tears filled the bottom of her eyes. Her choked emotions left her with no ability to speak as she simply nodded with pride.

"Well, then," said the Panderess. "I hope your happy silent smile is also a measure of your appetite."

Just then, a server came from behind and placed a bowl in front of Clara. She looked down and her mouth watered when she saw the delicate wontons drizzled in hot chili oil sauce.

TWENTY - FOUR

The large pouch was emptied, and the shattered, dull white pieces from the horns of the last *Nian* clattered onto the bamboo table.

The Horn Protectoress nudged the pieces with her hoof with a snort. "White jade. This should convince you now."

The Ascendent's beady eyes looked down at the pieces in disbelief. "But how?"

"Does it matter?" asked the Panderess. "A decision in the past has now come back to haunt us."

The Ascendent bent down for a closer look, saw the shattered white jade staring back at her, and nudged a piece with her beak. The sound it made as it rolled on its side onto the bamboo table was all too familiar. It was indeed white jade, though seemingly inert after the battle.

"Well, Ascendent?" asked the Tigeress. "This may be our only chance."

The Ascendent rose. They had celebrated and honored the emperor and empress warriors the night before. After a night of festivities, the warriors rested within the comfort of the Zenith Waterfalls and were allowed to sleep in before making their way back to the Portal Circle right after lunch. It was then that she and the other kingdom leaders had gathered in the Council Chamber of the Zenith, a room that only kingdom leaders could enter.

The Ascendent closed her beady eyes and thought deeply as the Panderess spoke. "It has to be unanimous."

The Ascendant's beady eyes opened, and she turned around to face her fellow kingdom leaders. She blinked. "I've made my decision," she said.

TWENTY - FIVE

Clara changed out of her training gear and held up her top, which bore an emblem of a panda head and her Chinese name. She looked at it fondly, but her eyes wandered to the closet, where several more training tops bearing panda emblems still hung. She let out a chuckle as she set her top down on the bed in her tent quarters. She folded it neatly and placed it on top of her pants.

She checked her jeans, her cropped sweater top, the comfortable T-shirt she wore underneath, and her socks. She scanned her tent quarters one last time and spotted her bamboo ribbon hair accessory. She walked over to the end table and gently picked it up. She admired the simple bamboo segment and the green ribbon she had used to gather her hair during her training. With a smile, she turned around, opened her bamboo pouch, and slipped it in. She then headed to the entrance, where she slipped into her shoes and paused.

Clara looked up and turned around to look at her comfortable tent quarters—the bed with its silken-bamboo sheets, the end tables and their illumination jade lights, the wardrobe in the corner, the low shelf with the empty bamboo rack for her the Bow of Destiny and its quiver, the entrance to her private bathroom, and the tough bamboo mats along the floor. It didn't have much, yet it held so much.

Clara pursed her lips and whispered, "Bye tent."

She pulled back the flap and left her tent quarters for the last time. As she walked up the path to the Portal Circle, she nodded to the few pandas still in the tent compound. As she walked up a hill, she could see the meal prep area from which came some of the best Asian food she had ever tasted. She turned and kept her eyes on the path, suddenly feeling a looming sense of loss. Being in Azen with its precarious battles was one thing, but knowing she would never see the Guardian Panda again was another. She didn't know how much she'd miss him, but she knew she would. How many people could claim a talking panda as their friend?

Passing the boulder on her left reminded her of when the Guardian Tiger first appeared and leapt upon the Guardian Panda on her first day in Azen.

She heard a chorus of greetings and saw that everyone had already arrived.

Yuka was by her Portal Book along with the Guardian Crane. Sung and Daniel were talking up a storm as their guardians stood off to the side. She looked at her Portal Book as the Guardian Panda smiled back at her.

"Everything all right, Empress Warrior Wu?" he asked.

Clara stopped in front of him. Her shoulders drooped as she clutched the bamboo pouch low with both of her hands. She hesitated a moment before she asked, "There's no way that I can come back is there?"

"No, Empress Warrior Wu," said the Guardian Panda. "Once you give up the Portal Book in your world, it'll find the next Azen warrior for the next lunar cycle war."

"I see. And if I keep it?"

"Then the next Azen warrior will not be found, and Azen will be in peril," said the Guardian Panda gravely.

Clara was silent for a moment. "I guess I can't let that happen."

There was a chuckle before the Guardian Panda spoke. "I have something for you, Empress Warrior Wu."

Clara's eyes lit up as she brushed back her hair in disbelief as she asked, "Really? What is it?"

"Open your hand," asked the Guardian Panda.

Clara extended her right palm, feeling a bit giddy. The Guardian Panda's black paw dropped something into her hand. As he pulled back his paw, Clara's eyes lit up at the sight of a bamboo medallion.

"Is this what I think it is?" asked Clara as she brought it closer to her face where she could read the characters of her Chinese name, "*Wu Chu Hua*."

"Yes," said the Guardian Panda with happiness. "I was able to get my paws on an early run. This one is customized. Turn it over."

Clara's expression perked up again as she flipped over the bamboo warrior's medallion and she could see two Chinese characters. She read them aloud, "*Gao Gao*."

"That's your name, Guardian Panda!" said Clara happily.

"It is indeed," said the Guardian Panda. "Something to remember me by."

Impulsively, Clara threw herself into the warm white-and-black fur of her Guardian Panda. His eyes flew open as Clara pressed herself into him, and he smiled as he wrapped his right paw around her.

As he patted her gently, she uttered, "I'm going to miss you, Guardian Panda."

"I will miss you too, Empress Warrior Wu," he said warmly.

Clara hugged him for a few moments longer before pulling back, and through her tears, she smiled at his furry face and warm brown eyes.

"Hey Clara!" Sung shouted.

Clara looked over and saw that her three warrior friends were gathered in the center of the Portal Circle. They beckoned her over.

"I'll be right back," said a giddy Clara as she left the Guardian Panda as she pocketed the medallion.

"Hey guys," said Clara.

"Just saying your goodbye now?" asked Daniel.

"Yah," said Clara longingly. "Did you guys?"

"I already hugged my Guardian Crane," said Yuka. "I'm going to miss flying with her."

"I'm going to miss my Guardian Buffalo," said Daniel. "You know, I think I'm going to swear off eating beef from now on."

"Dude," said Sung before he asked. "What self-respecting Vietnamese person eats *pho* without beef?"

Daniel looked at him with the reality of those words that were just lobbed at him as he said, "Maybe it'll be okay back home."

Everyone laughed and that soon dissolved into a silence.

"I'm going to miss you all," said Yuka sadly.

"Well, not really," said Clara hopefully. "We can finally connect in the real world!"

"Just without our superpowers," said Daniel resignedly.

"Well, we still got our fighting skills," said Sung confidently. "It has helped me to win over my *abeoji*."

"That's cool, bro," said Daniel. "You're right, we still have our fighting skills. Gotta fight back sometimes you know."

"Okay," said Clara impatiently. "Let's meet up once we're back home."

"We can't," said Sung.

"What? Why not?" asked Clara.

"Because we live in different states and we're all like fifteen and we can't buy airplane tickets by ourselves."

There was a pause as Clara felt a sense of embarrassment. She brushed her hand through her hair as she then suggested, "Okay, let's call each other…"

"I won't be able to do that right away," said Yuka. "I have no phone…"

"Oh yah," said Sung. "You're on that family camping thing. Yah, one time my family went camping in the woods with all of our relatives in northern California, and there was like no reception."

"Yah," said Yuka. "That's my situation, but if you give me your addresses, I can write you."

Clara, Sung, and Daniel stared at Yuka before Daniel asked, "You want to like write us a real letter? Like mailing it through the U.S. mail?"

Yuka smiled and said, "Yes. I like to write, and now that I won't be manifesting anymore, I have lots of time to write."

Everyone laughed as Yuka pulled out a piece of paper and a pencil.

"Where did you get the paper?" asked Daniel.

"It's *origami* paper," answered Yuka. "Guardian Crane said I can take some back. To make more *origami*."

"Can you send each of us a new *origami* with your letter?" asked Daniel.

"Daniel!" said Yuka with giddiness. "That is a wonderful idea! I will!"

Yuka took down everyone's address and put it into her bag. She looked up and said, "Well, I guess that's it."

Everyone looked at each other before Clara said, "I'm going to miss Azen."

"I'm going to miss flying with my Guardian Crane," said Yuka.

"I'm going to miss all of our meals together," said Sung.

"I'm going to miss my Guardian Buffalo," said Daniel. "Without him, I wouldn't have found my true self."

"What about us?" asked Sung. "We're like the best Asian friends you'll ever have!"

Daniel let out a laugh and in a self-deprecating expression, nodded furiously and said, "Yah, that's true. You're the best Asian American friends that I could ever have."

"But you know what I'm not going to miss?" said Clara. "I'm not going to miss the *Huo Dou* demon dogs, the Nue and its snake-like tail, the sea serpents…"

"Oh yeah! Those sea serpents were horrible," exclaimed Daniel.

"Or those ugly *oni*," said Sung.

"Well maybe you won't hate the nine-tailed fox, the *gumiho*," Daniel teased.

Sung glared at him and grinned. "OKAY! I think it's time to go!"

Everyone laughed.

"Hey," said Clara. "I'm really glad I met all of you and fought with you. We were amazing."

Everyone nodded silently, then Clara brought her clenched fists with palms facing out to her chest, and with her elbows out. Everyone looked at each other and brought up their clenched fists, then in unison uttered, "For Azen!"

The warriors nodded and walked back to their Portal Books.

Clara looked down at the open page of the Portal Book and admired its luxurious allure and how it held a mystical power great enough to bring Asian warriors from Earth to fight in Azen.

"Are you ready, Empress Warrior Wu?" asked the Guardian Panda as he took position in front of her.

"Not really," said Clara. "But I don't have a choice."

The Guardian Panda nodded as he said, "It's been an honor, Empress Warrior Wu. Goodbye."

Clara exhaled and picked up the bamboo brush. She turned around one last time to see her fellow warriors, whom she could see were showing the same reluctance. But she turned back to look at the Guardian Panda as his deep brown soulful eyes stared back at her. She admired his big fluffy white-and-black head and black ears. She so wished at that moment that she had her phone so that she could take a selfie with him. Then, she said what she didn't want to say. "Goodbye, Guardian Panda."

The Guardian Panda nodded. But as Clara began to lower her brush onto the silken bamboo page, a piercing squawk from above caught her attention. She spun around along with everyone else and looked up.

Three cranes were headed for them, followed by one eagle. The two cranes behind the solo lead crane carried a panda and a tiger. On the eagle was a buffalo. But behind them were three squadrons of cranes, with their *katana* wings glinting in the sunlight. Each of them carried a panda or a tiger. In the very back was a squadron of eagles, each carrying a buffalo.

The lead crane dove toward the Portal Circle at such a high speed, that Clara wasn't sure if it'd be able to pull itself up. It squawked urgently and the Guardian Crane listened intently.

"It's the Ascendant," blurted out the Guardian Crane. But before she could continue, the Ascendent landed in the Portal Circle, followed by the cranes bearing the panda and the tiger, who turned out to be Panderess and the Tigeress. The eagle made a hard landing, but the Horn Protectoress was able to bound off and rush to Daniel's Portal Book.

Without warning, the Horn Protectoress slammed the fire Wu Portal Book shut with her hoof. Then the water and air Portal Books were slammed shut, and the Panderess rushed up to Clara. With her black paw, she slammed her Portal Book shut to her shocked expression.

The Ascendent turned around and looked at the shocked empress and emperor warriors. She then said, "You may not leave."

THANK YOU

If you have come to the end of "Clara Wu and the Final Battle," which is Book Four of the Clara Wu Books, I hope you enjoyed the sights and sounds of the Azen kingdoms but were also enthralled with the harrowing and dangerous final battle. Were you piqued as more secrets of Azen were slipped out and were you kept on the edge of your seat with the cliff hanger ending?

My goal is to create authentic and fun Asian American stories so that Asian American readers can see themselves as the heroes. We've always been, we just need more writers to put them on paper.

Please tell your friends about this book series and flip to the section where I give some tips on how to promote this book to better Asian Representation!

A big thank you to my illustrator, SantiSann who brought my characters to life with incredible talent. Check out SantiSann's work at:

Instagram: @santisann88

Another thank you goes out to Gloria Tsai for voicing the audio teaser for Book One which you may find on YouTube by searching for "Clara Wu." Check out her work at:

http://www.gloriatsai.com/voiceover.html

I also wanted to take a moment to thank my editor, Felicia Lee of Cambridge Editors, who has been my editor since my first book. Check out her profile at:

https://cambridgeeditors.com/editors/

Please be sure to check out www.clarawubooks.com and www.vincentsstories.com where you can check out my two other books, which are also available on Amazon:

The Purple Heart
The Tamago Stories

There is one more book in this exciting young adult Asian American fantasy series! Flip to the next page to see the title of book five!

Book Five

Clara Wu
and the
Warlock

by Vincent Yee

Expected Debut: November 2022

ABOUT THE AUTHOR

Vincent Yee was born in Boston, Massachusetts. For most of his career, he has worked for several Fortune 100 companies in various managerial roles. At all other times, he has a vision…

"To write for better Asian Representation."

His first novel, "The Purple Heart," is a story about love and courage set during the Japanese American experience in WWII. His second book is a collection of 8 riveting contemporary Asian American short stories. His third book project, the Clara Wu Books, is an epic young adult Asian American fantasy series consisting of five books that will be all launched within one year. So far "Clara Wu and the Portal Book, Jade Labyrinth and Rescue," have been launched with two more in the series to come. Vincent Yee was a former National President for the National Association of Asian American Professionals (NAAAP). He also co-founded the ERG at his last employer and grew it to be one of the largest ERGs with over 450+ members within a few months. He's also been known to create artistic culinary dishes for friends. When he is not writing, he may be binging a K-Drama on Netflix. He now lives in Cambridge, Massachusetts.

HOW TO SUPPORT

Help spread the word on this young adult Asian American fantasy story:

1) **FACEBOOK**
Go to facebook.com/clarawubooks and LIKE the page to stay up to date with updates and be invited to future online events with other fans.
2) **INSTAGRAM and TIK TOK**
Go to Instagram and Tik Tok and like @clarawubooks
3) **SELFIE or PICTURE**
TAKE a selfie picture or a picture with your child, if you are comfortable with that and without exposing any identifying information, with the book or your e-reader.
Please tag the Facebook Page clarawubooks and IG/Tik Tok @clarawubooks and use the hashtags #clarawu #clarawubooks #AsianRepresentation #AsianStories

   TAKE a staged picture of the book with your favorite mug or other fun item, and post it on your social media page and please tag the Facebook Page clarawubooks and IG/Tik Tok @clarawubooks and use the hashtags #clarawu #clarawubooks #AsianRepresentation #AsianStories
4) **WEB**
Go to www.clarawubooks.com and add your email to the distribution list to find out the fun ways on how to engage with these books. You'll find my contact info there.
5) If your child goes to any Asian cultural school (e.g. Chinese, Korean, Japanese, Vietnamese, etc), please tell the other parents and students.
6) Does your child go to any martial arts school? Consider telling the parents and students at those schools. I will attend any event over Zoom with them.
7) If you belong to a book club, please consider recommending this book for your next read. I will attend your book club over Zoom if so desired.
8) **AMAZON/GOODREADS**
If you loved this book, please write a review for each book in the Clara Wu Books on Amazon or Goodreads.
9) **EDUCATORS**
Are you an elementary or high school teacher? This would be great for your students!

10) **LIBRARIES/BOOKSTORES**
Are you a librarian or a bookstore owner? Please consider getting this book into your library collection or store. The "Clara Wu Books" are available on Amazon's Expanded Distribution.

11) If you are part of any Asian American community organization, please consider reaching out to me to do a Meet the Author event, in person or over Zoom. Go to www.clarawubooks.com for more info.

12) If you are part of any Asian American corporate ERG/BRG/Affinity group, please consider reaching out to me to do a Meet the Author event, in person or over Zoom. Go to www.clarawubooks.com for more info.

13) If you know of any Asian American Influencers/Podcasters, please consider recommending this book to them.

14) If you would like to host a Meet the Author event over Zoom for your group of friends, your organization or your work AA group, I'll be there!

Let's **PROVE** that there is a market for positive and authentic Asian American stories especially ones that will give the next generation of Asian American readers, heroes that look like them.

DICTIONARY

Word	Language	Meaning	First Appeared In
abeoji	Korean	father	B1
aigo	Korean	oh my goodness – usually used to express annoyance or surprise	B3
Ajumma	Korean	Korean aunty	B4
Aki	Japanese	Name for a boy that means, bright and clear	B3
Annyeonghaseyo	Korean	Hello	B2
áo dài	Vietnamese	A traditional Vietnamese dress that is a long gown worn with trousers.	B1
appa	Korean	Father informal, affectionate	B2
Arigato gozaimasu	Japanese	Thank you for when someone has done something for you	B4
baba	Cantonese – Chinese	Father informal, affectionate	B1
bakemono	Japanese	A shape shifter that usually comes in the form of a beautiful woman to seduce unsuspecting men	B2
ban chans	Korean	A collection of side dishes like kimchi, radish or cucumber usually served along with meals.	B1
bánh mì	Vietnamese	A Vietnamese sandwich which may contain marinaded meat and fresh picked vegetables served in a soft baguette	B2
baos	Chinese	A Chinese white bun filled a variety of ingredients.	B1

bi bim bap	Korean	Bibimbap is served as a bowl of warm white rice topped with assorted vegetables and sometimes a sunny side up egg	B4
bing	Korean	ice	B4
boba	Chinese	A refreshing milk tea drink with tapioca pearls	B3
budi	Korean	Please	B2
Buổi sáng tốt lành	Vietnamese	Good morning	B3
Bukdaemun	Korean	North Big Gate – One of the eight gates in Korea.	B1
cảm ơn bạn	Vietnamese	thank you	B1
char-siu wonton mein	Cantonese	Roasted pork and wonton egg noodle dish	B3
chigae	Korean	Korean stew made from a variety of ingredients.	B1
chu	Cantonese	pillar	B2
da bin lo	Cantonese	Chinese styled hot pot	B4
dahm	Korean	wall	B1
dali	Korean	bridge	B1
đẩy	Vietnamese	thrust	B1
dim sum	Cantonese - Chinese	An assortment of Chinese dishes usually served in small portions so that many items may be enjoyed	B4
dōitashimashit	Japanese	You're welcome	B3
dojang	Korean	Tae Kwan Do training hall	B3
dò-jeh	Cantonese – Chinese	thank you	B1
dolgyuk	Korean	charge!	B2
domo arigato	Japanese	Thank you very much	B1
domo	Japanese	Saying thank you casually	B4
dōmu	Japanese	dome	B3
Dongdaemun	Korean	East Big Gate – One of the eight gates in Korea.	B1
đốt cháy	Vietnamese	ignite	B4

dun ji	Cantonese	Excuse me	B4
eomma	Korean	Mother informal, affectionate	B1
fai-dee	Cantonese	Quickly or Hurry up	B3
galbi	Korean	grilled ribs (aka kalbi)	B1
gam-sa-ham-ni-da	Korean	thank you	B1
Ganbatte!	Japanese	Good luck to you!	B3
gimbap	Korean	A roll of rice and cooked items wrapped in seaweed	B2
gō	Japanese	Multi-tiered slender towers in Japan with a spire on top though officially known as tō	B1
go	Japanese	game played with black and white stones	B3
gochujang	Korean	A fermented red chili paste	B4
gỏi cuốn	Vietnamese	Spring rolls wrapped with rice paper	B3
gong	Chinese	A command in the game of Mah Jong where a player catch collect a tile from the discard pile to form a combination of 4 tiles that are the same	B4
gong gyuck	Korean	attack	B1
gook	Korean/Mandarin	Country in its respective language however, it is taken out of context in America that has become a slur	B1
gumiho	Korean	A version of the 9 tailed fox creature that is common in east Asian culture (aka kumiho)	B2
Hạ Long Bay	Vietnamese	Famous beautiful bay in Vietnam that is also a UNESCO World Heritage Site	B1
Hangul	Korean	Writing system of the Korean language.	B1
Hirami	Japanese	Name for a girl that means, good flower	B3

Huli jing	Chinese	A version of the 9 tailed fox creature that is common in east Asian culture	B2
Huo Dou	Chinese	A large black dog that can emit flames from its mouth.	B1
Ikuchi	Japanese	Mythical sea serpents	B3
jeung-gi	Korean	steam	B3
jinju	Korean	pearl	B1
jo sun	Cantonese – Chinese	Good morning in Cantonese	B1
joh-eun achim	Korean	Good morning with beautiful sun	B1
Jook	Cantonese	Similar to rice porridge served with slices of meat, preserved duck egg along with Chinese fried dough. May also refer to bamboo.	B2
jōshō suru	Japanese	ascend	B1
jum-doong	Cantonese	tremor	B3
kabe	Japanese	wall	B1
Kalbi	Korean	grilled ribs (aka galbi)	B2
Karate	Japanese	A Japanese martial art that means *empty hand.*	B1
kata	Japanese	In Karate, a set pattern of movements that is practiced as part of training.	B1
katana	Japanese	Usually refers to a long single edged sword usually used by the Samurai.	B1
kimchi	Korean	A spicy fermented cabbage that is a delicacy in Korea.	B1
kimono	Japanese	A beautiful and traditionally wrapped garment for Japanese women that may come in a variety of colors and patterns.	B1
Kintsugi	Japanese	Art of fixing broken pottery with gold	B3
Koko wa doko	Japanese	Where am I?	B3
Konbanwa	Japanese	Good evening	B2

Kting voar	Vietnamese	Mystical horned creature that existed in Vietnam and Cambodia. Its true origin has never been determined though its unusual horns have left researchers puzzled about the creature.	B1
Kung Fu	Chinese	A Chinese martial art with many styles.	B1
mah jong	Chinese	A Chinese tile game played with four people	B4
makimono	Japanese	A Japanese roll of seaweed and sushi rice that may contain vegetables, fish or both.	B1
mẹ	Vietnamese	mother	B1
Michi	Japanese	Name for a girl that means, pathway	B3
Min'na doko ni iru no	Japanese	Where is everyone?	B3
molu	Korean	anvil	B4
moushi wake arimasen deshita	Japanese	No excuses can justify my actions and I apologize	B1
Namdaemun	Korean	South Big Gate – One of the eight gates in Korea.	B1
ngọc trai	Vietnamese	pearl	B1
Ni Hao	Mandarin	Hello	B2
Nian	Chinese	flat faced lion with a dog's body or as large as an elephant with two long horns and sharp teeth	B4
nigiri	Japanese	Usually, a ball of sushi rice that is topped off with raw fish or other seafood.	B1
nue	Chinese	A creature with the face of a monkey, a body of a tiger and a venomous snake as its tail	B2
nun	Korean	snow	B3

obi	Japanese	is a belt of varying size and shape worn with both traditional Japanese clothing	B4
ohayo gozaimasu	Japanese	good morning	B1
oni	Japanese	Ogre like creature that exists in Japanese folklore	B2
origami	Japanese	The art of folding paper.	B1
otosan	Japanese	father formal	B1
pãru	Japanese	pearl	B1
pong	Chinese	A command in the game of Mah Jong where a player catch collect a tile from the discard pile to form a combination of 3 tiles that are the same	B4
pho	Vietnamese	A Vietnamese soup noodle dish usually made from a slow cooked beef bone broth, with rice noodles and beef slices or brisket.	B1
sạc điện	Vietnamese	charge	B1
Seodaemun	Korean	West Big Gate – One of the eight gates in Korea.	B1
seoping	Korean	surf	B1
Seosomun	Korean	West Small Gate - – One of the eight gates in Korea.	B1
Seurng	Chinese	A command in the game of Mah Jong where a player catch collect a tile from the immediate previous player and form a 3-tile combination that are in sequence	B4
shuriken	Japanese	Throwing star made popular in the era of Ninjas.	B1
shí	Mandarin	ten	B3
shí-liù	Mandarin	sixteen	B3

Sho	Japanese	Name for a boy that means, one to soar to great heights	B1
siu mai	Cantonese	An open wonton shrimp and pork dumpling, though it is tofu in Azen	B4
Sonomama de ite	Japanese	Remain true	B3
Soohorang	Korean	Tiger of Protection – *Soohoo* means protection and *rang* comes from Ho-rang-i for tiger. Known to be a sacred guardian animal in Korea.	B1
Soyōnara	Japanese	goodbye	B3
Sungeuni mangeukhaeumnida	Korean	Your grace is immeasurable	B1
sưng	Vietnamese	horn	B2
surujins	Japanese	a length of rope that was weighted at both ends	B3
Tae Kwan Do	Korean	A Korean martial art that is known for its powerful and dynamic kicks.	B1
taegeuk	Korean	In Tae Kwan Do, a set pattern of movements that is practiced as part of training.	B1
taifū	Japanese	typhoon	B4
Takeshi	Japanese	Name for a boy that means, a warrior	B1
tei-cheng	Cantonese	earthquake	B4
tamago	Japanese	Elegant Japanese version of an egg omelette	B2
Tanchō	Japanese	cranes	B3
Tanchō! Washi	Japanese	red crown crane	B3
tatami	Japanese	A type of traditional Japanese flooring.	B1
tei hum	Cantonese – Chinese	sinkhole	B1
teng-bing	Cantonese – Chinese	wall	B1
thit bo voi bo	Vietnamese	well known beef dish	B1
thù lao	Vietnamese	charge!	B2

tō	Japanese	Japanese pagoda like tower structure.	B1
tsukkome	Japanese	dive (into air)	B3
tobu	Japanese	fly	B1
toppū	Japanese	gust	B3
tôi xin lỗi	Vietnamese	I'm sorry	B4
tường	Vietnamese	wall	B4
uku	Japanese	float	B4
utsukushī	Japanese	beautiful	B3
Vovinam	Vietnamese	A Vietnamese martial art	B1
Wakaranai	Japanese	I don't understand	B3
Watashi no inochi wo tasukute kurete arigatō	Japanese	Thank you for saving my life	B3
Watashi wa kowarete imasu ka?	Japanese	I'm broken inside	B3
Watashi wa shinde imasu ka	Japanese	Am I dead?	B3
Wuxia	Mandarin	A style of Chinese movies depicting Chinese martial arts in ancient China with superhuman strength	B3
yaki onigiri	Japanese	Lightly fried rice ball with seaweed on the outside	B3
yakitori	Japanese	skewered grilled meat	B1
yi ge jiu cai san xian jiao zi	Mandarin	One leek and bamboo dumpling	B2
yi ge bai cai san xian jiao zi	Mandarin	One cabbage and bamboo dumpling	B2
yi ge san xian jiao zi	Mandarin	One pea, carrot and bamboo dumpling	B2
Yonggirang	Korean	Tiger of Courage – *Yong-gi* for courage and *rang* comes from Ho-rang-i for tiger. The Guardian Animal from the White Tiger Kingdom.	B1
Xuong Cuong	Vietnamese	howling demon trees	B3
zao shang hao	Mandarin – Chinese	good morning in Mandarin	B1
zhēnzhū	Mandarin – Chinese	pearl	B1

Made in the USA
Columbia, SC
02 October 2022